DOUBLE DANGE

Though Leonora was ...... her country cousin Annabelle, she was infinitely wiser in the ways of the world. Clearly it was her responsibility to watch over the welfare of this girl whose delicate blond beauty and vulnerable innocence were bound to attract the eyes and enticements of society's more dishonorable gentlemen.

Thus when the Marquess of Severne threatened to waltz Annabelle beyond the boundaries of propriety, Leonora stepped in.

The only difficulty was, in seeing that Annabelle kept her distance from the irresistibly seductive Severne, Leonora had to get perilously close to him herself. . . .

False Angel

More Delightful Regency Romances from SIGNET

Edith Layton
False Angel

A SIGNET BOOK

NEW AMERICAN LIBRARY

Copyright © 1985 by Edith Felber

SIGNET TRADEMARK REG. U.S. PAT. OFF. AND FOREIGN COUNTRIES
REGISTERED TRADEMARK—MARCA REGISTRADA
HECHO EN CHICAGO, U.S.A.

SIGNET, SIGNET CLASSIC, MENTOR, PLUME, MERIDIAN AND NAL BOOKS
are published by New American Library,
1633 Broadway, New York, New York 10019

First Printing, October, 1985

1 2 3 4 5 6 7 8 9

PRINTED IN THE UNITED STATES OF AMERICA

For Estelle and Irwin, who defy the laws of relativity.

ONE

It was the evening of a day that few in the city of London wished to see ended. Even free and blameless citizens regretted the onset of evening almost as much as the condemned in their cells at Newgate did, though those wretches might be expected to begrudge any dimming hour that swept them forward to a dimmer dawn. But it had been a pure fragrant spring day such as seldom came to the great city. Such had been its rarity that all who experienced it felt a certain sinking of their spirits even as the sun sank low, knowing that tomorrow, no matter how clement, would never be the same as this pristine day had been, knowing that like all innocents, Spring itself would be changed and sullied by its continued stay in Town.

So the windows in the grand salon of a great house on a fashionable street in the heart of London this April night were thrown open wide and not even the most overbearing dowagers in attendance at the gathering there demanded that they be closed. There was no complaint even when the long sheer curtains bellied out on each puff of the soft breeze that blew through the room, though the ladies' long narrow draped gowns belled out about their ankles and their feathered fans and elaborately dressed hairstyles were gently stirred as well. There was no need for any of the ladies present at the small soiree to take alarm, since Spring, like all artful newly arrived visitors, was on her best behavior and gave no hint of her true nature lest doors and windows be closed to her immediately.

By fashionable London's current standards, it was an intimate group that amused themselves at the Viscount Talwin's townhouse this evening. But then again, by those

7

standards, Wellington's army being feted in the ballroom would have been simply called "a crush," and Napoleon's legions making do with a buffet in the garden would have been deemed "a squeeze." A simple matter of some seventy-odd souls in the salon, sipping punch and ratafia, subsisting on lobster patties and cold collations while not attending to four musicians in a corner sawing away at some composition by Mr. Handel as they chattered, could hardly have been called notable, or even moderately impressive. So it was odd that the viscount himself, emerging from an upper room with four other gentlemen in tow, should pause upon the stairs as he saw the gathering below and whisper, "Oh Gad! I forgot Nell's party completely. Now I'm for it. And so are you lads, so don't snicker."

The gentlemen accompanying the viscount, arrested on the stair by the simple expedient of having their host come to a dead stop in front of them, did not precisely snicker at his distress. Rather it could be said that they wore various expressions of bemusement as they too looked down at the throng that could be seen at the foot of the great stair and across the wide hall. The polished doors to the salon had been thrown open as wide as the windows, and since the parquet floors of that room and the marble squares of the hall were both now completely covered by diverse slippered feet, only the footmen poised at the boundaries knew exactly where the salon left off and the vast entry hall began.

The viscount scowled down at his nominal guests as he placed his hand on the banister and said crossly, "The deuce! I would've taken the back stair if I'd remembered. Even so, you'd think they'd have kept the doors closed so we could have had you fellows slip away unnoticed. There's no hope of that now. But you see," he went on, almost to himself, "they none of them were here when we began."

Since the gentlemen had been sequestered with their host in an upstairs room for upward of three hours, not one of them disputed his observation. Instead, they stood and gazed down at the crowd of people and waited for their host to take the next step. And as they paused for those brief seconds, the company below began to take note of them. It might have begun with one guest glancing upward for an instant and then continuing to stare, but like a field of ripened grain blown in the wind, each head raised in turn, as though in a rippling wave, until all the assembled guests were staring speechlessly back at the wordless quintet upon the stair. For one silent, horrid moment, the viscountess later confided to her husband, it seemed that there might be an enormous social gaffe in the making.

But then the viscount smiled and waved a hand in salute to some unspecified person in the company and, with every evidence of pleasure upon his face, signaled that he was about to go down to greet his guests. However, it might be noted that under the cover of the general conversation as it picked up again, he said *sotto voce* to his companions upon the stair, "Terribly sorry, gentlemen. It was a bad mistake on my part. Accept my apologies. But if you don't at least make some attempt at 'how-do-you-do's,' my lady wife will have my heart on a skewer to serve up to the lot of them."

"I should think," mused one of the gentlemen as they slowly descended the stair, "that she may well have it so anyway . . . but for your introducing us to her guests, rather than for omitting to do so."

As his companions chuckled in agreement, the viscount said softly, "Nonsense, Joss, yon lot may have their tongues wagging for a month after this, but I assure you, she'll be the envy of all her acquaintances for having had you at her little soiree."

"Ah yes," the gentleman answered with a twisted smile, "we certainly do ensure a hostess's social triumph."

"Why, yes, Joss," another gentleman commented in low, fogged tones. "Having us present, is, I should imagine, very much like having someone fall dead at your feet at your dinner party. It may not enliven the proceedings, but it is sure to make them memorable."

As the gentlemen laughed, another of them said with some mock pomposity, "Why, speak for yourself, Jason, now that I'm a married man, I'm the soul of propriety."

"Why so am I, Sinjun," the other answered sweetly. "But it hardly matters if you had married a saint or if I had taken holy orders and gone to live in a cave. I join Joss here in wondering that our host has the temerity to introduce us to his company. It's our names, my dear, that account for our fame. Why, I hear that young ladies can still be sent to bed without dinner for so much as uttering them aloud."

"There is something about our names," another of the gentlemen mused aloud, "that tends to ensure some mention of beds, isn't there?"

"You make too much of it, lads," the viscount said with as much censure as if they had indeed been lads, and he their stern schoolmaster. And although he was only a decade or so senior to the oldest of them, and they none of them could fairly answer to the name "lad," even the youngest of them, they left off their laughter and followed him in respectful silence. He paused before he reached the foot of the stair, then turned to face them with a sober face and said with some urgency, "Please don't forget, lads, the business that we were about discussing upstairs was merely that, *business*. Investments, as we had agreed to say. Obviously, there's no way to conceal the fact that we've met, even if we hadn't been observed by this lot. But it doesn't matter if we're not believed, it only matters that we are consistent. And you don't have to stay if you don't wish to, but please believe that I welcome you to my house, and always shall. I didn't invite you to this affair tonight," he concluded with a frown, "only because it's merely a little 'do,' for my daughter and I believed you would have found such a gathering insipid."

Over the other gentlemen's protests, the one called Joss said, just as seriously as his host had done, "Calm yourself, sir. I know I speak for all of us when I say we don't take affront in the least. It's your reputation and that of your daughter that we were concerned with, not our own."

As the other gentlemen agreed, the viscount said gruffly and with some trace of embarrassment, "Nonsense. I'll introduce you to my family, and then you may stay or leave, as you wish. But there's nothing to be concerned with."

Then, with as much cool presence as he would have shown if he were presenting his maiden aunt to the bishop, the Viscount Talwin crossed the room with the four gentlemen in tow. And then, true to his word, he proceeded calmly to introduce the four gentlemen, who possessed some of the most notorious, shocking, and dangerous reputations in the realm, to his wife, his daughter, and his assembled honored guests.

It did, of course, make the party a sensation. A simple gathering that would have been forgotten in a week—except by those fortunate few who had managed to make an engagement, a wedding, or a liaison from the opportunities presented by the evening—instantly became one of the most talked about social affairs of the Season, for the four gentlemen were almost legendary figures, and an aura of delicious scandal hung about each of them. Although no one of them was so lost to decency as to have been totally unacceptable socially, neither did any of them have a pure enough background to have gained admittance to Almack's this evening. Most disgracefully titillating of all, no one of them seemed to care a jot about whether they would have been or not. They were seldom seen at such strictly correct affairs as this one, but in all fairness, from the way they were goggled at as their host introduced them, even though they were quite correctly and soberly dressed, one could scarcely blame them for their disinclination to grace such gatherings.

They were introduced by order of rank and age, so Jason Thomas, Duke of Torquay, made his bows first. His golden hair and his almost angelic smiling good looks still belied the reputation he had earned in his youth. But then, there was no way he could have earned his outsize rakish fame if he had been any less comely than an angel. Though no word of disrepute had been attached to him for all the years since he had wed and left Town to live in rustic, domestic bliss, his name still caused a stir, and his sidewise knowing smile showed he knew it well, and rather enjoyed the idea of it still.

Cyril Hampton, Duke of Austell, came next, tall and straight. With his serene and youthful face and curiously silver hair, there was only that faint air of reserve to lend credence to his reputation. But then too, one seldom said much when one was being introduced, and he appeared to like his host, so there would have been no need for him to exercise his lethal wit and stiletto-sharp tongue.

The dark gentleman who stood as tall and proud as a Red Indian was the mysterious St. John Basil St. Charles, Marquess of Bessacarr. It was said that he had recently

wed some lady that he had met upon one of his frequent
clandestine trips to the Continent. And it was this that
caused romantic young females in his vicinity to sigh, as
much as the fact that he had always been as elusive and
exciting as quicksilver.

But when the last and most youthful gentleman, Joscelin
Peter Kidd, Fifth Marquess of Severne, was at last announced, ladies of all ages who were watching grew wide-
eyed. It was not only because two of the shocking gentlemen
were already wed and the other remaining bachelor frightened
them too much to even dream upon. It was because if
Severne's fame did not cause heads to turn, then certainly
his appearance would have done so. And that reputation
only seemed to enhance his appeal, for there was nothing
like a disastrous impediment to give a fellow stature, sort of
repelling females while attracting them, as Lord Bigelow
whispered spitefully to a friend even as the marquess took
his hostess's hand. But his friend didn't bother to answer,
for everybody knew that Biggie had been trying to get Jane
Turnbell to notice he was breathing for months now, and
there she stood, breathing as hard herself as if she had run
a foot race, and never taking her eyes off Severne for a
moment.

But no matter how fascinating the gentlemen were in
sum, there was only so long a space that one could forget
one's breeding. By the time all the errant gentlemen had
been presented to the viscount's wife and daughter and
relatives, there was no longer the faintest shred of an
excuse for the rest of the company to press close and linger
on in hopes of catching a wandering eye or a stray word.
And if the assembled guests forgot that, there was always
the stern eye of the master of the house himself to contend
with. For when the viscount perceived how still and enrap-
tured the audience of guests clustered about him had grown,
he fixed those unfortunates nearest to him with such a
speaking gaze that they fell back, glad to remember a
friend across the room they wanted a word with, or suddenly desirous of another cup of that excellent punch.

Thus the Incomparable Miss Merriman cast one last longing look at the Marquess of Severne and then bade one of
her suitors to fetch her something cool and sweet. She
simpered happily as two other suitors claimed at once that

alas, there could be nothing cooler nor sweeter in all the land than she herself, but even as she did so, she moved imperceptibly toward the windows with her entourage, under the prod of her host's unblinking stare.

In fact, if they had no valid excuse to stay now, most of the company began to regretfully edge away. The Viscount Talwin might be a trim, slight, baldish, and bland-appearing middle-aged fellow, but he had an air of command. No one was too surprised to have seen the notorious quartet he had entertained leaving his private quarters, for rumor circulated about him as well. Nothing so shocking as that which attached to his infamous companions, but it was said that Talwin was deep in doings for the foreign office. It was whispered that he might even be a spymaster, but such rumors were common as fears of invasion in the spring of the year of Napoleon's flight from Elba. So a wise man did not refine upon it too much, but then neither did a patriotic one speak it too loudly.

Still, though the crowd around the viscount thinned after he introduced his gentleman guests, it did not disappear completely. There were always those who were impervious to any hint more subtle than a sword's point. As it transpired, there was no gentlemen that cared to risk his host's wrath tonight, but some of the ladies were undeterred. A dowager who wanted to show her daughter-in-law how liberal she was, since they had spent the afternoon wrangling over the older lady's dislike of her granddaughter's latest beau, demonstrated her broad-mindedness by immediately collaring the Duke of Torquay and badgering him as to the health and welfare of numerous relatives of his who had quit the planet decades before.

The Marquess of Bessacarr, for all his famous skill at evasion, was similarly backed to the wall by a pair of spinster sisters who had known his late father and who now demanded to know the lineage of his new bride, as well as the size of her waist. This was either so that they could fashion a morning robe for her or to help them to ascertain whether her marriage had been imperative or not. The marquess could not tell which was their precise intent, since he could not have gotten a word past them edgewise.

The Duke of Austell found the helplessness of these two

worldly, roguish fellows when confronted by elderly and vastly proper females vastly amusing. Or at least he did until he found himself fixed by the rheumy stare of an ancient toothless social lioness who proceeded to question him in loud and quavering tones as to why he was as yet unmarried. Since he was not cad enough to insult a female of such profound years, and since he very much doubted whether she could have heard his insult anyway, he soon discovered once again why it was that he so often shunned such proper entertainments.

And so it happened that at that precise moment, for only the briefest space of time, Lord Severne found himself standing completely alone in the midst of a roomful of company. His hostess had turned from him to say a word to her husband, and his host's daughter and cousin had said good evening and now had been engaged in conversation with some earnest young man.

It might have been because there was no one in his general vicinity that knew his family, such as chanced to know the others'. It may have been that those dowagers who did know his family yet disapproved of him so much that they refused him speech. It may even have only been that as he was not an easy fellow to approach, there were those who wanted a word with him who were presently steeling themselves to do so. But whatever the reason, for that brief time, he stood quite alone.

This neglect did not seem to discompose him much. He stood and surveyed the room, casually taking note of the younger ladies, caught for a moment, as most men might have been, by the beauteous Miss Merriman. For she threw back her long white neck and gave forth her famous long rippling laugh at some sally some lucky fellow had made, and yet managed to cast the most roguish glance in the direction of the marquess at the same time. A most talented young woman, and a brave one as well. For while a great many females covertly noted the marquess as he stood alone, few dared attempt to attract his notice. He was quite good to look upon, but not a comfortable fellow in any fashion.

He would have been noticed in any crowd even if he were not a little taller than most men. His hair was lustrous and thick and dark as night. But that was all that was lavish about him. He was lean, his face so thin that his cheek-bones stood out in bold relief. Yet he was not gaunt. Nature had not been stingy with him, so much as careful. His forehead was high, his skin clear and pale, his nose thin and straight, as were the brows which were etched above his wide, observant eyes. His lips were full and well defined. His features seemed to have been shaped with a fine keen steel blade, they were so cleanly delineated.

In fact, there was that about him that bespoke a cutting edge. There was his taut, muscled figure, and the danger-ous easy grace with which he moved. And then even when he appeared to be at his ease, there was that glint of light that could flash unexpectedly from his fathom's deep blue eyes, sometimes so brilliant that it seemed to be struck from the spark that arises from the clash of steel upon steel. No, not a very comfortable fellow, the Marquess of Severne, but not one easily forgotten either.

But his voice contradicted all that his wolfish face and form implied. If there were some instrument that could erase his countenance and form and leave only his voice remaining, one would think of velvet and deep safe places, it was so low, seductive, and smooth. But now he had no chance to exercise it. For the moments dragged on, and no one greeted him, or sought a word from him, until his host's daughter, whose party it was, broke off from her conversation with the earnest young man and attempted conversation with her newest, most silent guest.

He looked down at her with a slight smile upon his lips as she began to speak, and it may have been more than mere courtesy, for Lady Leonora was a taking creature. No, she was rather more than that, for everyone said that she was as sweet a looker as could stare actually, and it was a constant wonder that she was still unwed. The lady had hair almost as dark as that of her guest, but there all similarities ended, for all that was spare and lupine in his aspect was lush and gentle in hers. They looked so well together, that dark couple the Marquess of Severne and the Lady Leonora, so oddly matched and yet so perfectly at odds in their appearance, that unwittingly the Honorable Miss Merriman began to frown, and Jane Turnbell closed her hand so tightly about her fan that she snapped two of its ribs.

The pair attracted even more attention when Lady Leonora brought her female companion, her cousin Miss Greyling, closer and into their conversation. For that dainty young woman was day to their night, being small and fair and flaxen-haired. Seeing the attractive trio close together, Jane Turnbell looked so ill and near to weeping that Lord Bigelow took alarm and wondered if his dear girl was going to expire before he ever got the chance to declare himself. But he needn't have fretted on any score, for in a trice the Lady Leonora brought the conversation, and the encounter, and the brief visit of Lord Severne to her house to an abrupt ending.

It was a pity, observers were to complain later, that the viscount had done such a superior job of warding off sensation seekers, for no one was close enough to the participants to actually hear what was said. Sir Phillip had been, of course, since he had just left off speaking with Lady Leonora. But he was an earnest, honorable young man and the gossips' despair, for wild horses couldn't drag what he'd overheard from him. But there was no doubt when the thing was said, for everyone was observing the scene closely and it unfolded as clearly as a well acted pantomime might have done.

They were talking, and the marquess was asked a thing by the Lady Leonora, and he answered, with a small smile. And then Miss Greyling breathed a few words, for she was a shy little creature and seldom said a great deal. And that made Severne smile again. A brief silence followed in which Lady Leonora looked uneasy and then she said something. The marquess's smile faded, and he looked at her sharply. She seemed unaware and then slowly aware of something wrong, since Miss Greyling turned a delicate but distinct shade of pink and fell to inspecting her fingertips. Lady Leonora's gloved hand flew to her lips and she looked aghast. She said something else, while shaking her head in denial. And then the marquess forced a smile that nevertheless looked rather grim, said a few more words over the lady's continued protests, and then, bowing, he took his leave of the pair, and then his host, and then the house.

"Not that I'm complaining, my dear," the Duke of Torquay murmured as his coach started up and his passenger sat back in his seat, "for you're something in the way of being our savior tonight, if you'll forgive the heresy. When we saw you reaching for freedom, we other prisoners took heart and made our break as well. The last I saw of Cyril, he was whistling down the avenue like a schoolboy skipping classes, and Sinjun was on his horse and down the street like a streak, for he's newly wed and quite naturally eager to be back in his bride's embrace. The only thing powerful enough to have drawn him forth tonight would have been Gabriel's trump or Talwin's summons."

When his companion gave no answer, the duke went on imperturbably, "I'm glad, actually, that Sinjun hasn't got to do any more havey-cavey business. He's risked his neck enough abroad, it's only right that he should act as advisor now he's settling down. Cyril has no ties so he's happy enough to waltz off to the Continent in his stead. I'm far too old, and far too far under the cat's foot to don my cloak and slip my dagger into my pocket. And my duchess would use that instrument on me if she thought I was about to risk so much as one of my lovely long eyelashes, even in the service of my country."

"Ah," commented the marquess from his corner of the darkened carriage, "you have my sympathies, Jason, you truly do."

"Thank you," the duke said, with the merest hint of laughter in his voice, before he went on laconically, "And so I am happy enough to simply evaluate information as you other retired agents do, and will be pleased to continue to until Bonaparte's fate is sealed. . . . For pity's sake, Joss, what in God's name did the wench say to you?" he appealed suddenly in livelier tones. "I've been sitting here and chatting as though I couldn't care a rap, and all the while restraining myself from leaping up and throttling it out of you! How do you expect me to go home and face Regina without knowing what happened under my very nose tonight? It'll be all over town by tomorrow and though we're rustics, she and I, we do draw breath, you know. Out with it."

"The lady," the marquess answered in thoughtful tones, "has been pursuing me, it seems."

"A novelty for you, no doubt," the duke said dryly.

"Well, yes," the marquess responded musingly, "for she

is a lady, you see. Still, for the past two weeks or so, since
she arrived in Town, I've been running into her and her
shy pretty little companion quite by accident in the oddest
places: bookshops, street corners, and the like. I've begun
to develop a rather outsize caution of the outdoors."

"Poor Joss," the duke sympathized, "I know just what
you mean. What's London coming to these days when a
fellow can't stroll the streets without fear of some exquisite
young female accosting him?"

"Not *some* young female, Jason. Talwin's daughter,"
the marquess answered. And to the thoughtful silence which
followed, he added, "I met her years ago, when she first
came on the Town and was well on her way to ruining
herself. I saved her one night then, I think, from making a
fool of herself, or worse. I can do no less for her, for her
father's sake at least, now."

"And her interest in you is so disastrous?" the duke
asked mildly.

"Why, yes," his passenger replied, "because I fear she
hasn't changed much at all. She must still be wild as
bedamned and dead set on making a sensation. For she
doesn't know me at all really, and that means that there's
only one thing about me that interests her. One large and
pertinent thing."

"Braggart." The duke laughed. "Have you no shame, if
no modesty?"

"And that one thing," the marquess went on in his soft,
rich voice, "is precisely what she let slip tonight when she
sweetly asked me why I seemed so—" and here he raised
his voice a treble note and mimicked in mocking falsetto
tones—" '. . . divorced from the company . . . ah no, d-d-d-
detached, that is to say, my lord . . . Oh lord, forgive me,
for I never meant to say that at all.' "

" 'Oh lord,' indeed," groaned the duke.

"Yes. It's not delightful, you know, to be valued for the
one thing that you least value. The one thing that you can
do nothing about. The one thing that is, like it or no, such
a rarity that it is become your most outstanding characteristic," the marquess said in tones that were not so much
saddened as resigned.

"Do you never cease showing off?" the duke asked
merrily.

"I meant my divorce." The marquess sighed.

"I know," his companion said seriously for once, "I was only attempting to lighten the subject."

"I know," the marquess replied; "consider it lightened."

"And as to the lady . . . ?" the duke asked in an off-hand manner.

"Why, since I refuse to oblige her, I suppose I'll just have to wait it out until she becomes interested in some other chap's outstanding characteristic," the marquess said, his teeth showing white in his smile even in the dim light.

The duke chuckled, and then after a pause in which they were absolutely silent, they both began to chortle, and then they burst into laughter together just like the lads the lady's father had named them. And their relieved laughter hung in the soft night air even after their carriage had rolled off into the April night.

TWO

The fair-haired young woman lowered her hand from the door and let her arm fall to her side in a sad little gesture of defeat. Although she uttered no sound, her whole countenance was so abject that the whisper of her light blue skirts as she backed away from the closed door was as an involuntary sigh. She had just turned and begun to walk away down the long carpeted hall when the door she had approached swung wide and a lowered voice called excitedly,

"Annabelle! Belle! The very one I was hoping to see. Oh Belle, you have no idea how I've wished you would come. Come in, please do. And quickly."

As Annabelle turned and came into the room, the dark-haired young woman who had summoned her made rapid little gestures with her hands, signifying stealth and speed. Once the blond young woman entered the room as she had been bade, the other closed the door quickly behind her and then rested her body against it as though to hold it even more securely shut.

"Good lord! Belle, you can have no idea of how desperate I was," she breathed. "I couldn't send word through the servants, for then the fact that I was up and about would have gotten to my father. I know that I'm to have a peal rung over me, believe me I'm aware I deserve it. I'm not trying to evade that, but I wanted to have some time to myself before I entered the dock. I'm that embarrassed. I pretended I was still asleep when Katie came in with my chocolate, but dressed as soon as she had left. Then I waited and waited for you to appear. I was going to slip out and creep to your rooms on my hands and knees if I had to."

"I was here an hour ago, cousin," Annabelle said in her soft voice, not reproachfully but rather with a sort of sad surprise. "I supposed you were still asleep."

"It's probably because you scratched at the door, didn't you?" her cousin accused. At the smaller girl's weak shrug and downcast eyes, she went on with a note of exasperation, "Good heavens, Belle, how many times must I tell you? You're not some sort of lower servant. Knock upon my door, kick and bang it if you must. But a weak little scratch and a whispery little 'Leonora' won't get you anywhere. And I wasn't sleeping," she said on a gusty sigh, "for I couldn't all the night. Good lord, Belle, how old do I have to grow before I stop making such a clunch of myself?" she asked with such a note of sincere misery that her cousin's pale brows went up in alarm.

"Here I am at three and twenty," railed the dark-haired lady as she left the door and paced across her room, "and still committing social errors so ghastly that I stand apart and watch myself as though I were seeing some other person—at some other person hell-bent on destroying myself at that—take over my body. And now still hiding from Papa as though I were a guilty toddler because of it! Oh, Belle," she cried wildly as she sank to sit on the edge of her bed and stared at her cousin, "shall I never grow up?"

Since it was an unanswerable question, Lady Leonora did not wait for a reply, but only went on to say feelingly, "What a dreadful thing to have done. And to such a man as Severne, as well! I don't see eye to eye with Papa on many things, as you well know, but in this case I shouldn't blame him in the least if he shipped me off home this very day. It would put paid to all our plans, but I don't think I'd blame him in the least. No, and if he shouted the house down over my head before I left as well, I shouldn't blame him either."

As the lady sat and hung her dark head as though the thoughts it contained made it too heavy for her to hold erect, her cousin said in puzzled tones, "But cousin, it's nothing like that, I assure you. I went down to breakfast this morning. And your papa came in when I was halfway done. He asked after you, and your mama said you were still abed. She did say that she thought you might be avoiding him," Annabelle added consideringly, "but he said nothing further until your mama asked if he knew what you had said to Lord Severne, and if he was very angry at you for it."

"And . . . ?" Lady Leonora prodded, some life and animation coming into her eyes.

"And," Annabelle said calmly, "he said he hadn't the slightest idea, nor did it matter. 'For it's only more of the same,' he said, 'and only what I've come to expect from her. And Severne is a grown man,' he said, 'and well used to slings and arrows.' Then he left for the day, for his club, he said."

"Ah," Lady Leonora breathed, as all energy and color fled from her face, "but that is even worse."

She sat with her eyes closed a moment and then opened them and met her cousin's wide blue and uncomprehending stare. "It would have been better to have been scolded," she explained softly. "Even a sound thrashing would feel better, I think, than that cold disappointed resignation of his does. But you don't understand, do you Belle? I suppose it's because you lost your father so young. And I, on the other hand, lost mine so late. No, don't look so shocked. I know he still lives, silly, and a long life I wish to him, too. But I lost him long ago, you see. No, you don't." The lady sighed. "Well, no matter."

She rose and seemed to give herself a little shake, and then turned a singularly gentle smile upon her cousin.

"The light blue frock," she commented in a brighter tone, and with evident approval as she inspected the other girl as she too stood up. "Now if you go and get your figured rose wrap, the new one we picked out at the Pantheon Bazaar last week, and your biscuit-colored bonnet with the rosebuds on it, you'll do very nicely. Then we'll go off to the booksellers, and have a long stroll while we're about it, so that we may meet up with some of the young gentlemen you were too unsure to say boo to last night. We shall make a social success of you yet, my fair and timid lady. And then," she added with a wry grin, as much to her cousin as to her herself, "I can go home and live content, with no one to scandalize but the geese."

"But you haven't had your breakfast," Annabelle protested as her relative ordered her to the door.

"No," Lady Leonora said as she shooed her cousin off

down the hall to her own room, "but then, I don't deserve one."

As she watched Annabelle obediently leave to fetch her wrap and bonnet from her room, which Mama had insisted on being located in that netherland somewhere between the servants' quarters and the best guest rooms, Lady Leonora sighed again. It had been useless to argue that Annabelle ought to have accommodations as fine as her own, for Mama had steadfastly insisted that impoverished distant cousins do not belong in, or feel comfortable when being accommodated in, lavishly appointed bedchambers. But then, Leonora thought as she turned to go back to her own bedchamber to await Annabelle, Mama did not understand that the only reason her daughter had agreed to return to London after all this while was so that she might see to that same impoverished distant relative's future.

She had been happy enough, she thought, as she went to her wardrobe to get out her own wrap, to live quietly in the peace of the countryside and watch the seasons turn and listen to her birthdays tick away. Not "happy" precisely, she frowned now to herself, for she was a stickler for honesty, even when only arguing with herself, but content. No, not that either exactly, she thought, but living on all those acres in the North, so far from London and society and past shame, had numbed her nicely.

There was society in the countryside, of course, but not precisely suitable for young, wealthy, nubile noblewomen. And so of course, rather than going to London again, she was resigned—yes, she smiled to herself, there was the exact word, "resigned"—to stay at home and wait until she was old enough to properly sink into the local whirl of matrons' teas, church bazaars, and charity work without a ripple.

There were gentlemen in the North too, of course. But if she'd refused to have any of the most eligible partis from the cream of ton society when she'd had the chance, the best of a few remaining bachelors of the proper age that her small district had to offer weren't likely to make her long for wedded bliss. Especially since she spent a great deal of time avoiding them, as well. No, attracting the gentlemen, wherever she happened to be, had never been the problem. Or rather, it had always been a problem in itself.

The fact was that she always had difficulty with the way she interested gentlemen since she'd come of age. Although she knew it wasn't fair, it always annoyed her when a male immediately responded to her looks. Then too, she knew, to her sorrow, that her physical appearance often dissuaded other females from befriending her, even if her reputation did not. But just as she often felt that she stepped outside herself to watch in horror whenever she committed some social suicide, as she had last night, she always felt as though her physical person belonged to some other female. And one, moreover, that she did not care for at all. It wasn't surprising that she was not the greatest admirer of her own style.

Her hair was dark, and that was the fashion this season. But it wasn't black as a daw's wing such as the Incomparable Miss Merriman boasted. It was only very dark brown, so dark as to appear to be made of smoke when she brushed it out at night. It didn't curl riotously as Caro Lamb's did, though, but rather it lay smoothly until it came to the end of its length, and then it tended to spring up in frothy waves, as though it regretted its earlier sobriety.

Her skin was pale, but there were no shy pinks to tint it such as she admired in other fair ladies' cheeks, rather it was the crimson damask rose that lay beneath her skin. Her eyes were not the blue of lakes and pools that poets found so entrancing in their mistresses' regard. Hers were large and generously lashed, to be sure, but they were dark brown to echo her hair and not the summer sky. Her nose was straight, but it too tended to give way to levity at its end, for it turned up just at the tip. Her lips were rosy and full. Too full, she thought. As a besotted and sottish fellow during that disastrous last year in London had whined as he attempted to excuse his advances after she'd boxed his ears, it seemed as though she had already just been soundly kissed, her lips had looked so swollen and ripe for him.

That was only part of the difficulty, Leonora thought as she drew her wrap about her. For if her lips gave men strange fancies, why then, no matter how she draped it, and the fashion of the day did not permit too much coverage, her form gave them even stranger ones. She was high and full-bosomed, and her small waist drew in only to flare out again in rounded hips that gave way to long and rounded limbs. Not as a lady's figure should be, she thought, like Mama's small trim form or even her elder sister's tall, thin elegance. Rather she wore the blatant body of a gypsy or a sultan's favorite. She couldn't blame the gentlemen for what they thought her since that last Season, even if it had not been for her actions. They might admire such looks, but she never could.

When Annabelle had arrived that windy night three months ago, with her poor bedraggled traveling cases at her side and the family bible in her hand to prove that she was at least related to them, Leonora had only needed to take one look at her. It only took that long for her to decide that there stood the beauty in the family. For apart from her clothes and bewildered expression, of course, Annabelle perfectly suited her idea of precisely how a lady should look.

Annabelle was small and delicately made, just as ladies were classically supposed to be. The first gowns that Leonora gave her that first morning after she had come to stay with them, so that she might have something fitting to wear immediately, hung so loosely about her slender body as to make it appear that she were a child dressing up in antique clothes taken in play from some attic trunk. Leonora had begun to feel clumsy and cumbersome even as she watched her maid pin a very recently favored frock closer about Annabelle's insubstantial frame.

And though Leonora was only of average height, Annabelle was so diminutive that her relative felt like a great gawk when she had to look down in order to converse with her. And Annabelle had eyes as blue and round as robins' eggs, with lashes and brows so light as to make her countenance as open and perpetually surprised as a wondering child's, and skin so white that each moment of embarrassment or confusion was plainly, pinkly written upon it, and her hair was as fine and light as milkweed pods blown out upon the wind.

A great many young women would have detested Annabelle on sight. There were also a number of otherwise good-natured ones, who at the very least would have shunned her company in public. It was not that they feared being judged against her beauty, for she was not an exquisite by any measure. It was simply because the cannier females would intuitively realize that they must always suffer by comparison with her sort of artless female. Her simplicity made even prettier blond ladies seem overblown, her coloring made more vividly styled young females appear to be dark as moors, even as her fragility made most other young ladies, no matter how petite, seem coarse. Her shy silence would make magpies out of the wittiest of them, while her humility would make any decisive female appear to be overbearing. In fact, even the other women in the viscount's own family, his wife and elder married daughter, disliked the new arrival amazingly.

But Leonora championed her, and it was her plea that the girl be given a home that had secured her one. Though Lady Leonora and her father seldom spoke to each other even when that gentleman was making one of his rare visits home, he had been home the day Annabelle arrived. He was a generous man and her timorousness, such an uncommon trait in his family, had touched him. He hadn't seen any reason why the chit shouldn't be given a roof over her head, nor why that roof shouldn't be his, despite his wife's disapproval. Then too, that lady's objections had been the very sort of vague, formless things filled with innuendo and foreboding that females often express and that the gentlemen always detest. His elder daughter was married and living in Town and not present to give support to her mother's opinions. The viscount had been looking for a reason to say yes and put an end to the bothersome matter, so when Leonora had quite surprisingly spoken up and actually addressed words to him, and those in the wretched chit's behalf, he had been only too happy to end the discussion in an affirmative manner.

Leonora had been delighted, for from the moment she clapped eyes upon Annabelle, she had decided that the poor child's fate had been placed in her hands.

It was not only because of Annabelle's tale, told in a bleak monotone, of the loss of her widowed mother after years of living in grinding poverty when her ne'er-do-well father had deserted them, though that had sent shudders through her. Nor was it only guilt because that father had been her own distant relative. Neither was it solely because she hung on every sorrowful word of Annabelle's harrowing narrative about the other distant relatives in Ireland who had first succored her, then misused her and thrown her out when she had refused the advances of their boorish son.

Nor was it even that everything about Annabelle so very strongly recalled to mind the legions of imperiled heroines whose adventures had been related to Leonora during those unguarded, impressionable hours as she lay at the brink of sleep through all her childhood years. For hadn't her favorite, Cinderella, a similar history of deprivation and abuse? This might have worked against Annabelle's best interests, for most young women would have resented sharing their lives with a bonified heroine, and one, moreover, who was classically fated to snabble up Prince Charming the moment he showed his nose. But here Annabelle's luck at last surfaced, for since Leonora had given up all expectations for herself, it made no matter to her, it only made Annabelle's tale more poignant.

It was true that all these factors weighed upon Leonora. But although she had a strongly developed conscience and was a very good sort of young woman, she was leagues away from being a saint and would have been the first to admit it. But then saints are in notoriously short supply, so it is as well that their work upon the planet is carried out by those with other, more worldly ambitions. In fact, as in the case of most lesser mortals who will never have shrines built to them, Leonora's true reason for assisting Annabelle was not only very distanced from anything remotely heavenly, it was also one which she did not fully understand or admit to herself. Which was as well, since it was really quite a selfish one. It was because in Annabelle she at last found a cause, a reason to be, and some surcease from her own life of desperate, unending tedium.

Because with all she had, the Lady Leonora had nothing of her own. Oh, she had her horses, and her dogs, and the run of the countryside, but the house was her mama's to run, and even it would in time belong to her younger brother. It was that younger brother, her dearest Bertie, at home on sick leave from school, who'd been the closest thing to her own in the lonely years since her aborted Season. But his constitution improved and he'd been sent back to be properly educated. And though she had awaited his return by carefully counted hours, when he at last came home for vacations it soon became clear to her that he had matured enough to become completely his own creature. She could not regret his growing up. She may have been selfish, but she was never a monster. But he left a great vacancy in her life.

Her sister had two children, but they had been reared in London, so she hardly knew them. Even so, she could not care for them, poor things, because they reminded her so forcibly of her brother-in-law. And that she could not like, even if they had been the first living things she spied after dwelling in solitary state in a hole in the ground for the past five years. So serving Annabelle's interests served her well.

She was honest enough to admit this to herself, but human enough to believe it had all been some fortuitous accident. She certainly couldn't have known how well things would work out, nor could she have guessed, Leonora thought, as she smoothed down her hair and prepared to go out upon the streets of the town that she had vowed never to grace again, that she would be so glad to be where she was, thrilled to be back in London again, and so very grateful to Annabelle for putting her precisely where she now stood.

She never would have had the courage or the excuse to return alone, she'd made such a thoroughgoing botch of it, just as she'd intended to, when she last had been in Town. But if she hadn't done it up to the nines then, she thought now, facing her own level, accusing stare in the glass, she'd have had to stay on in Town that entire Season with her parents, and that, she could never have borne. But here she was in London, only five years after the debacle she'd made of her first Season, in the same house with both of her parents, and yet having the best time she'd had in years.

Life was so comfortable now not only because she had no schemes or dreams or plans for herself, she realized. It was also because she had no reason to chat with her father, and he had no expectations for her either. So neither of them could fail the other this time. Mama might be ecstatic, thinking that her prickly, wayward daughter had finally seen the light and bowed to all those years of nagging, hinting, and downright threatening, and had condescended to come to London at last to seek a husband.

So much as she disliked deceiving her mama, there was not a grain of truth in that lady's happy fancies. This visit, Leonora knew, was all for poor Annabelle, so that the child could secure a husband and a respectable future for herself, even without a dowry or a family to give her countenance. Unfortunately, however, this visit would have been impossible if she hadn't allowed her mama to indulge in those glad fantasies.

But it would all be worth it, for in one way or another, Leonora did plan to heed some of her mama's cautions. She would, she decided, finally make provisions for her future. Perhaps when it was all over and she had danced at Annabelle's wedding, she would stay on in London, stay on where there was all the art and music and conversation that she had been starved for, for all this time. Because very much like the self-made fellow who can sit back full and contented after a feast and happily regale all his company with tales of how wretched and hungry he had been in his youth, now that Leonora was out of her self-induced seclusion and back in Town, and surprised to be enjoying every moment of it, she could at last afford to remember how wonderful it had been. Or at least how wonderful it had been up until that moment when it had all come crashing down about her ears.

It had been those keen ears, perhaps sharpened by years growing up in the relative quietude of the countryside, that had been the instruments of her enlightenment and the destruction of her innocent pleasure. It was entirely possible that some London-bred miss might not have heard that voice above all the others, or have been able to pick it out and identify it above the music and babble and laughter that night in the Vauxhall Gardens.

And at the thought, and at the remembrance, Leonora, sitting at her dressing table as she awaited the girl she was hoping to marry off this Season, forgot the girl and the present, as she always did when she revisited that night in that other vanished Season. That last Season, when she had made her decision and vowed to never wed.

She oughtn't to have been where she was at all that night, and she'd known it, Leonora thought, frowning now as she had then, at the uncomfortable thought that she had strayed far from the paths a proper young female ought to tread.

But then, she had never been a sheep and a wee bit of wildness, a very little taste of wickedness, was expected of a spirited young female, and that, yes that, she had always been. So it hadn't been too unthinkable to go to Vauxhall that night five years ago, even though it wasn't the night she'd planned to grace that pleasure garden. And then, too, Charles Dearborne was a rackety young dog, and everyone knew it, so perhaps that's why she'd been willing to accompany him.

But she wasn't lost to reason. She wasn't even alone in her folly, since two of her other young friends were there with their young gentlemen to squire them. And that is probably what her chaperone, Miss Thicke, had whispered to the other young ladies' chaperones as they sat and fanned themselves and kept a sharp eye on their young charges in the warm torchlit evening. Because the young people were supposed to be at Lady Clayton's musical evening, and it was that charming young rogue Dearborne's earnest entreaty that dissuaded them, and his less earnest but merrier cajolery that persuaded them to listen to the music of Mr. Handel at Vauxhall Gardens instead.

But then it was a small naughtiness, Miss Thicke had thought complacently, the sort of foolish escapade that her charge could smile back upon when she was safely wed. At the most, there might be a stolen cuddle and a sweetly furtive kiss achieved before a chaperone could locate a truant couple in the crush of pleasure-seeking patrons of the fabulous gardens. Still, it was the sort of liberty that perfectly suited a knowing chaperone to grant, since it gave the illusion of forbidden pleasures, while in actuality it was safe as houses. But Miss Thicke would have lost both her smile and her position if she had been able to foresee the events engendered by this night's work. For though she may have been an excellent companion, she was a disastrously poor oracle.

She was a fatally bad judge of just what might transpire at night at the gardens as well. But that was a fault that she couldn't, in all fairness, be blamed for. Being a maiden lady of very good ton, she could hardly have been expected to understand the workings of the other, darker world of London, the one she had never seen or acknowledged. Yet then again, had she known of the doings of the demi-monde that made up that underside of social life, she could scarcely have been a proper sort of companion for a noble young woman in the first place.

But she was very proper, and she had excellent commendations from previous employers, and though they all of them were up in years, yet she was still the senior of the three chaperones present that night. So if she did not know that this particular night her charge would have been better off at Ranelagh Gardens, or even the Pantheon in Oxford Street, since there were certain infamous areas at Vauxhall solely for the use of gentlemen entertaining their Cyprians or seeking new ones, then none of the other chaperones could have been expected to know that truth either. Thus the three elderly females sat placidly in a notorious section of the Gardens, as oblivious to what was going on about them as the trio they so curiously resembled might have been, since those three legendary monkeys also had some difficulty in recognizing evil. Lord Dearborne knew the whole of it, of course, as did his friends, but they were all such high-born, hell-bent, care-for-nothings that they thought it all a lark.

It might have been no more than that if Lady Leonora hadn't possessed such sharp ears. She and her friends had been discreetly seated at tables in a remote section, a bit apart from the center of the attractions. They sat in the moving shadows of the torchlit, gaslit darkness beneath the flowering trees and spooned ices and watched fireworks and listened to the music and the increasingly florid compliments of the young gentlemen, even as the three chaperones at their separate table were slowly becoming aware of just what sort of creatures the majority of the other females present were. In fact, had Leonora coughed at that precise moment, or had Charles given out one of his infectious laughs at one of his own naughty sallies, as he so often did, the moment might have passed and her future might have shaped itself in an entirely different fashion.

For Miss Thicke and her counterparts were already in huddled, agitated conversation, and within a few moments they were fated to rise and order the young people to leave at once. They had finally noted the general level of communication between the sexes that was going on all about them as well as the fact that an increasing amount of it was being held in what appeared to be mime, since so little of it was verbal. They had also discovered both the wealth of cosmetics covering the faces and the dearth of material covering the forms of the other females present.

But at that exact moment, Charles turned around to see how his friend Georgie was faring in his attempts to get Lady Ann up and away from the others. The moment Georgie and his Ann arose, Charles intended to ask Nell to go for a stroll with him to some darker place, so he at last could have a taste of those promisingly plushy lips, and with luck, some more intimate knowledge of some other soft and yielding parts of her as well.

So at that precise moment, Leonora, all unaware of Charles's plans for her future entertainment, was left alone to entertain herself by watching a young female that she spied a few feet away from her. The young woman stood beneath the direct light of a Japanese lantern that swung from a willow tree, and such was her colorful aspect that she caught Leonora's astonished eye. She stood in front of one of the many decorative pavilions, those curtained recesses euphemistically termed "supper booths" that the proprietors of the garden had erected for patrons who required more privacy. And in her red and gold and black finery, she looked as though she had stepped off a stage where she had been enacting "Vice" in some strange morality play.

Her hair was gold as brass doubloons, her skin was as white as a lie in the dark of night, though her cheeks and lips were red as flame. Her figure was even more lavish than Leonora's, but instead of being uneasy with such bounty, as Leonora so often was, the unknown young female had a gown so tight as to be a redundant skin and so low in front as to place her high, firm, pear-shaped breasts almost entirely on display.

It was a gentleman's strong white hand suddenly appearing from behind the young female, encompassing one of those bare mounds so completely as to hide it from view as the frock had not, that caused Leonora to take in her breath and avert her eyes at once. And she would not have looked back, she was so distracted and dismayed with her twin emotions of embarrassment and arousal, had she not heard that one word, spoken by that one voice, in that one moment when there was no other other thing to divert her from it.

For the young woman had wrenched away from the gentleman's encircling hand with a charade of annoyance, when he had pulled her back and said, "Phoebe." And though she knew no one by that name, Leonora looked back toward the young woman, her eyes very wide. Then the gentleman had pulled his Phoebe even closer and taken her in a heated embrace, kissing her most violently as his hands roved about the front of that shameless gown in even more shameless fashion. But now, embarrassed or not, Leonora continued to stare. And then the gentleman pulled back his head and laughed and said clearly, "Phoebe, you little wretch. You want me as much as I want you. Now come with me and let's finish it." And he ended the display by abruptly dragging his chosen young woman with him, even as he continued dragging the meager top of her gown down, and they disappeared into the draped recesses of the little tent beside the great willow tree.

No one else had heard it. And none of her company had seen it, for Georgie had just succeeded in getting Ann to stand with him, and Charles had turned about eagerly to get Leonora to do the same. In that same moment, the chaperones came to a unanimous decision and rose themselves to cluck like goose girls and chivvy their little flock away from the green and wicked meadows of Vauxhall Gardens this night.

And between Charles and his friends imploring the chaperones not to herd their charges into their coaches to take them home, and the chaperones huffing their displeasure, and the other girls tittering softly, no one noticed that Leonora had lost all her color. In the darkened coach they could not see that her deep rose cheek had turned sallow, and with all the accusations and counteraccusations flying, they couldn't notice that the usually ebullient young woman said not a word, but only sat and stared straight ahead as though there were something vital there in the dark that only she could see.

When they got home, and Miss Thicke got her charge safely to her rooms and into her bedclothes, her strange behavior was noticed. But then it was richly commended, for it was taken to be a good thing and was thought to be either a sign of remorse or excessive gentility. And since Lady Leonora immediately if absently agreed that since no harm had come to any of the participants, it would be as well to forget the entire incident, Miss Thicke, who had convinced herself that it was not deception but discretion that prompted her to spare her employers any mention of the matter, breathed a sigh of relief and was happy to leave her charge in peace.

Only it was not quite peace, unless the quiet of a battle-field after a massacre can be called peaceful. And it would never be forgotten.

Lady Leonora had passed that interminable night watching and listening to the same incident again and again as she replayed it in her mind's eye, just as she did now, five years later, as she sat before her looking glass in the same bedchamber in London. For she had known that voice, and had known it instantly. And so she had not needed the gentleman to pass beneath the Japanese lantern to have seen and known the exact contours of his face, although that avid, sharpened expression he wore was alien to her. And she had known his name. And she breathed it now just as she had uttered it then, involuntarily, almost as a plea for help, and almost in the same, sick, shocked tones.

"Father!" Leonora whispered to her looking glass, as she sat alone in her room.

THREE

Leonora blinked. Another face slowly swam into view and came into focus in the looking glass before her. She had been so intent upon her visions of the past, it was as if they had begun to take on reality and actually come into physical being again before her eyes. But now as she relaxed her attention, she eased her hold on them, and they faded as all day and night dreams do and must do. Then the only thing she saw in the glass, and that so unexpectedly as to be completely alien at first sight, was her own face made unfamiliar by its surprising presence where a moment before there had been only phantoms.

It is hard to judge the passage of years upon one's own visage, even in the finest glass, so Leonora could only hope that she could truly read wisdom and knowledge in the great brown eyes that stared steadily back at her now. Although the features had firmed from their puppy softness of five years ago, there was no other hint of the extreme change that had been wrought behind them. But for a certainty, the girl that had occupied this chamber then was vanished forever. And good riddance to her, Leonora thought, with the first lightening of spirits she felt since she had begun her reverie. Because she had been such a chucklehead, such an innocent, and such an utter goose, that it was no wonder that even her own sister had grown all out of patience with her.

How she had moped about this room then, she thought, smiling now at the childishness of that former self, snuffling and wringing her hands and sending back her dinner trays untouched, until her mama had begun to confer with Cook as to how to conceal physics in savories so that they might be ingested undetected. But it was not until Father had knocked upon the door and requested speech with her that she knew she must somehow learn to deal with the problem. As a stopgap measure, she had answered him in monosyllables, and then hung her head and replied, missishly and so cravenly as to make her cringe even now in recollection, that her problem was some female indisposition that would surely pass.

But she had been unable to look at him. Even with her head down, the unavoidable glimpse she got of those strong white hands which once had tossed her in the air until she shrieked with laughter, and had placed her on her first pony, and held the books she loved to hear him read aloud, distressed her. For she remembered their most recent employment and the words stuck in her throat. If she dared look him in the eye, she knew she would tell him all, as she always had, and then all would be lost. And he was a great deal for her to lose.

She had always adored him. And it was not only because he was so infrequently home with her. She was proud of that absence, since she knew it was highly important work with the government or the foreign office that kept him from the family. But when he could come home, wasn't it always their laughter which matched when an amusing thing happened, even though everyone else at the dinner table would look at them in incomprehension? And didn't they come to share the same taste in books and poetry? And as she grew couldn't they talk politics together until everyone else had gone to bed, until the footmen shuffled their shoes in the hall, hinting at the cold late hour?

So she had yearned for her London Season as much to be with her father as to find herself a husband. And that husband, she hoped, would be a friend of his, and like to him in many ways, for she could think of no finer thing than to find a gentleman she could have all to herself, for all time, who would be so much like her father. And now, she could not even look at him, much less go out upon the town to find a fellow like him.

She couldn't speak to Mama. It wasn't a thing she could mention to her, even if they had enjoyed that sort of confidential relationship. Although Mama was a very good sort of parent, and they rubbed along together very well,

Leonora had always been aware that her mama had given her whole heart away to Sybil, her eldest daughter, years before she herself was ever born. Leonora could see nothing wrong in that, for Sybil and Mama were very like in both appearance and preferences. Both had smooth dark hair and smooth white faces, and knew all about fashion and fads and followed them explicitly. Leonora reasoned that if one liked oneself a great deal, why then it only stood to reason that it would be very difficult not to admire someone who so nearly resembled the object of your deepest affections. Sybil was taller, thinner, and colder than Mama, to be sure, but then Sybil had been married to Lord Benjamin since Leonora had left the nursery, and she thought that might account for a great many things.

Leonora could not admire Sybil's taste so thoroughly as Mama did, but Lady Benjamin had been in the thick of the ton for over a decade and was, if not the most understanding sibling, then at least a very worldly one. Besides, Leonora's problem wasn't a thing that she could discuss with the viscount's own heir, and it was unthinkable that little Bertie should ever hear anything but golden tales about his father. No friend ought ever to learn of it, so by default, and by despair, Leonora had decided that she would seek Sybil's counsel, since she felt that if she didn't tell someone soon she would burst, either into tears or literally into pieces.

Sybil had reclined upon her récamier and listened to her sister's hushed retelling of the tale, and her fine-featured, thin-browed face had remained still, her expression hadn't changed at all throughout the narration, except perhaps her chill little smile had grown more marked. Then when Leonora had done, and was mopping up the few foolish tears that had escaped her vigilant self-control, Sybil uttered not one word, but only made a sound of exasperation. Then she rose and rang for her maid and told Leonora to wait until she dressed.

An hour later, when she felt she could be seen by the world, she at last left her chamber and beckoned for her sister to follow. But instead of telling the butler to send for her carriage, she told him instead to call for a hackney. She said nothing to Leonora's quizzical expression until they were within the hired carriage, and then she simply said, in her bored drawling accents, "It would be best if we went unremarked."

Sybil had given the driver an address on Curzon Street, and yet when they arrived there, she only told the fellow to go to the head of the street and wait until she gave him further directions. Then she sat back and gazed at her sister. "It is nearly two in the afternoon," she said in bored fashion. "I expect we shall have to wait here no more than a quarter of an hour; he is very punctual and predictable in all things."

"Who is?" Leonora asked in confusion, for although Sybil enjoyed being oblique, this was, in her sister's opinion, coming it too strong.

"Lord Benjamin," Sybil replied coolly.

And "Oh," Leonora replied, just as though she knew what was going on. But she didn't say a word more, since that gentleman was never her favorite subject. As she waited and gazed out the window at the relatively empty street, Leonora thought that it was typical that after all these years of marriage Sybil still referred to her husband only as "Lord Benjamin," as she had done for so long that no one in the family could readily remember what his Christian name was, if indeed he had been given one.

He wasn't a bad-looking fellow actually, being fair and of middle height and having regular, if undistinguished, features, although Leonora considered him a bit too stout even if Mama termed his physique "robust." But that might have been because Leonora was always looking for fault in him. It wasn't any one thing that she could specify that he was or had done that made her dislike him, it was just that she always found him too pedantic and strait-laced. In fact, she could not remember what his laugh sounded like, since his highest expression of good humor was evinced by a tight, toothy grin and a sound something like a clearing of his throat. Still, he must have suited Sybil perfectly: they were a well known couple in society, and Leonora had never heard Sybil breathe a syllable in his disfavor.

Just about the time that Leonora was about to break the silence within the hackney and ruin Sybil's dramatic gesture, whatever it was, that lady sat up and peered out the back window. "There," she said with smug satisfaction. "Now just watch, simpleton."

And as Leonora looked through the window, she saw Lord Benjamin come strolling up from the foot of the street. He was neatly, if unremarkably, dressed as usual. The only thing that was a trifle unusual about him was his outsize air of casual disinterest. He took out his fob watch, glanced at it, and permitted himself a smile as he tucked it back into his pocket. Then, swinging his walking stick in almost jaunty fashion, he went up the stairs of the third house on the street and employed the door knocker. A moment later, he was admitted, and before the door closed, Leonora could see him doffing his greatcoat.

"There!" Sybil said with infinite satisfaction.

"There what?" Leonora asked.

"And where do you think Lord Benjamin was going?" her sister said with a great air of vindication, as she sat back and rapped upon the ceiling of the carriage with her parasol.

"Good grief, Sybil," Leonora answered with some unhappiness, for she had come for advice and only been treated to another example of her sister's disinterest. "How should I know? To his physician, or to his weekly chess match, or to a visit with his elderly uncle, I suppose. I wish Mama had named you Frances or Mary Jane or something else, for I believe that you take this Delphic oracle pose far too literally," she complained.

"He was going to his mistress," Sybil announced with a certain pride, ignoring her sister's outburst. "Didn't you see the creature?"

"I saw a maid take his coat, I think," Leonora murmured in confusion.

"Then she was most likely waiting for him in her bed. Sometimes he likes the idea of finding her unclothed and waiting for him in her bed in the middle of the day," Sybil replied thoughtfully.

Instead of asking any one of the myriad questions that swarmed in her mind, Leonora was so shocked and appalled by her sister's attitude and revelation that she only said challengingly, "How do you know?"

"Why, she told me so," Sybil answered on a yawn, and then after telling the driver to go around the park a few times, she settled back to tell Leonora everything she knew about Grace Webb, her husband's third mistress.

"That Adele creature didn't last long," she finally commented wisely, "and though he and Mary Small were together so long that they were become almost a settled thing, he threw her over last year. I do think she took him too much for granted, and Lord Benjamin dislikes that enormously. Grace, I believe, is a good choice, and will work out very well, for she is an obliging girl, and very sweet-natured and flexible," Sybil said contentedly.

"And you know of it and have to countenance it? Ah, poor Sybil!" Leonora cried before she could stop herself.

"Now that is precisely why we are here," Sybil said testily. "Please open your ears, Leonora, and mark me well. You must not be such a rustic. Of course I know of the creature, and believe me I do not *have* to countenance it. I do, and gladly. I owe a great deal to the poor chit, indeed, I believe my life, as well as those of so many of my contemporaries, would be far more difficult if such arrangements were not in the common way of the world.

"Yes," Sybil said with some satisfaction as she saw her sister's jaw drop open, "you heard me correctly. Good heavens, Leonora, you are of an age to wed, you must know these things. Gentlemen require certain attentions, Leonora. I am sure Mama told you about that years ago."

At Leonora's nod, her sister sighed and went on, "The thing is unavoidable if we are to bear their heirs. But no matter how it is dressed up, the getting of children is just as unpleasant as the having of them. For a lady, of course," Sybil added thoughtfully.

"That," Leonora blurted, fighting up from her dismay like a swimmer in distress trying to break to the surface of the water to get a good clear gulp of air, "is rot, Sybil."

Her sister arched one impeccable eyebrow, and said smoothly, "Oh yes? Tell me, my dear, has that been your experience?"

"Well no, and well you know it," Leonora said, stung, "but it can't be such a dire thing when poets have sung about it for ages. And it wasn't Mama that told me, she had the headache that day Nurse said, so she told me, for it was the day I first got my courses and Mama felt it was time I knew."

"That explains it," the older lady said complacently. "Poets are all men, my dear, and they write a great deal of rubbish anyway. And Nurse was a great hulking farm woman before she came into service with our family, and that class enjoys the basest diversions. I don't know what she told you, but believe me, Leonora, it is the most uncomfortable, unpleasant, and demeaning activity possible for a lady to be party to. In fact, though I respect Lord Benjamin enormously, and so you must know, still, just between us as sisters, it has always lowered my opinion of him to watch him enjoy that which is so repugnant to me."

"You watch him with Grace Webb!" Leonora gasped.

"I watch him when he is with me, for there is nothing else to do," Sybil said angrily, and then added censoriously, "I don't know what sort of mind you possess, Leonora."

She paused and fixed her sister with a look of great distaste, which showed her enormous displeasure, since she was always careful to avoid strong facial expressions in order to prevent premature wrinkling. Then she recalled herself and went on to say somewhat defensively.

"It is not my wish, of course, but even though we have our heirs, still every now and again, Lord Benjamin feels it necessary. But it would doubtless be far more frequently than every so often if it weren't for Grace Webb, and that is why I am so grateful to her. And that is why so many females of our class are tolerant of these sorts of liaisons. He, of course, does not know that I know of her existence, but unlike many wives, who prefer to remain in ignorance, I believe it is a good thing to know where and how he disports himself. I should not want him in some shocking place displaying unhealthy passions. That would be fodder for blackmail, my dear, or a source of disease to myself. So the more fool I, if I didn't pay well for information and keep abreast of his activities."

After a silence in which Leonora did some rapid thinking, she asked quietly, "And so, you are trying to tell me that is also the case with Mama and Papa? And that what I saw was commonplace?"

"What you saw was unfortunate," Sybil said carefully,. for once seeming a trifle discomposed with the subject herself. "But yes, it was commonplace."

When Leonora did not reply, Sybil added, "Although I do not think Mama is as enlightened as I am as to her husband's doings, for truthfully, Leonora, I do not think she cares. I like Lord Benjamin very well, you see, and have his best interests at heart."

"And you are saying that Mama does not care for her husband?" Leonora asked disbelievingly.

"Yes, of course, my dear, I thought you knew," her sister answered with some trace of sympathy in her voice for the first time in the long interview.

As the hackney circled Greene Park again and again, Sybil explained all the things which Leonora then realized that she ought to have known. For it wasn't only the war office or the foreign office or even the King's offices which kept her father from home. And there was very good reason for the oddly spaced intervals in which the viscount's children had arrived. The viscount and his lady had been wed for decades, and for decades they had tolerated each other, but only just that.

A great many couples in society lived in mutual dislike, Leonora learned, that was, if they did not live in mutual hatred. Marriages were contracted for greed, or gain, or social grace, and then, even when undertaken in the best faith, they often grew stale. But divorce was out of the question, since it cost both a fortune and a reputation. So the parties involved, sometimes the females, but most frequently the gentlemen, led lives of very creative duplicity.

As the carriage at last headed for the Viscount Talwin's house again, Leonora did not know whether to feel ashamed at having been such a thorough fool as to have never guessed at this, or whether she ought to be chagrined because she believed her sister, who might be lying to her for her own devious reasons. So all she could say in a dazed voice was, "But then, you say that *all* marriages in our circle are like that?"

"Ah no," Sybil corrected her, "for some unions are genuinely exclusive and seem quite rewarding to both parties. There is, for example, the Duke and Duchess of Croft, and there's the Mastersons, of course, and the Swansons and the Earl of Skelemore and his Elizabeth, and oh yes, father's crony Jason Thomas, Duke of Torquay, and his lady. And he was used to be the most infamous rakehell," she interrupted herself to muse, an unreadable expression coming over her usually serene countenance, "quite insatiable, I believe. But then again, she is not well-born, so I suppose that explains her preferences. And then too, they do not reside in Town."

"And those are the only exceptions you know?" Leonora asked in disbelief.

"All I can think of at the moment who have been wed more than a year," Sybil said after a pause, "but then, I never thought to compile such a list."

"And you are saying that some of this unfaithfulness is caused by the gentlemen's natural physical demands, but some of it is because the couples simply cannot bear each other even though they reside together?" Leonora mused wonderingly. "But that is to say that every wedded pair you are acquainted with lives in a constant state of hypocrisy," she continued, thinking to catch Sybil off guard so that she would betray her falsehoods.

"Why, yes." Sybil sighed with genuine relief and the merest gratified smile. "At last you understand."

And then Leonora believed her.

Sybil had delivered some more sisterly advice before she let her off in front of the family's townhouse that day, Leonora remembered now, unconsciously grinning at herself in the looking glass. She especially remembered the serious and detailed speech listing "helpful things to think about during the marital act." For when she had snickered, even then, even as she suffered the pain of her first awakening to adult reality, Sybil had said angrily that her rudeness was distressing but understandable. Her lack of ladylike sensibility was unfortunate, Sybil had declared without the least bit of sorrow, but explicable because she had been so close to her father rather than her mother and sister when she was growing up, and because she had such warm associations with Nurse and other low-bred country folk. Why, Sybil had said loftily, in an attempt to frighten her into paying closer attention, it was entirely possible that Leonora might be the sort of debased female who actually enjoyed such sport.

Well, and if she was, Leonora thought now, it was also entirely possible that she would never know. For if she had

learned no other thing that Season, it was that she would
never marry, never be party to such a cold-blooded, cold-
hearted, and mean-spirited life. She wouldn't take a husband to her heart only to watch him go off to visit with his
Grace Webb, or seek and then take to his own breast some
lush, common little tart at Vauxhall Gardens. No, she wouldn't
wed. If those were the stated rules of the game, she simply
wouldn't play. Neither would she be a spectator of such
sport. She decided she couldn't stay in Town to become
like the rest of the great parade of hypocrites she suddenly
perceived marching in locked step all about her.

And when Mama wouldn't hear of her cutting the Season short to go home at once, and since she refused to
have speech with Papa, she had gone and made sure that
she was sent home post-haste. And only by the by, she
had convinced Sybil that her dire prophecy had come true.
But it wasn't so, she hadn't enjoyed anything she'd done
during that painful blur of weeks. But then she hadn't done
anything that she might even learn to enjoy. Fortunately
for the sake of her own soul, they had sent her home
before she could actually discover whether or not Sybil had
indeed lived up to her portentous name, as she so often
pretended that she did.

But, she thought now, grimacing at her own image—that
dark and sultry, sensual stranger whose face always stared
back at her from her looking glass—it was entirely possible
that Sybil did possess some sort of second sight. For she
had sailed very close to the wind those five years ago, and
not a few times had narrowly avoided permanent disgrace,
and once had been fortunate enough to have been rescued from worse. Indeed, she owed the gentleman she'd
so roundly, if inadvertently, embarrassed the previous night
a debt of gratitude for that. And she acknowledged it, and
more, for him. Yet, instead of feeling constantly relieved
that she had always escaped unsullied, as she knew she
should have done if she were a proper lady, there were
times, there were those few and secret times in the heart of
her darkest nights, when she felt not so much grateful as
denied.

"Oh, wicked wench," she whispered to herself, lifting a
dark brow and giving the temptress in the glass a look of
bold invitation. And then she giggled, because she knew

that both the strange wanton that appeared in her looking glass each day, and the stranger yearnings that sometimes visited her in the night, had nothing to do with the reality of the Leonora she knew, and never would. For now, gazing into the glass, she saw mirrored there the dark and pouting sensual face of a passionate pleasure seeker, and right above it, what should have been, if nature had been kind, her true reflection a white, light, innocent countenance, blameless and bland as that of an angel. And then Leonora looked harder into the glass, startled, and spun around.

"Lord, Annabelle!" she sighed, her hand still upon her rapidly beating heart, "you gave me a turn, creeping up like that behind me. I thought that I was seeing things. How long were you standing there?"

When her cousin did not reply, but only kept her head downcast while a slow pink flush appeared on her neck and cheek, Leonora laughed.

"A long while, I'll wager. And you thought I'd run mad, didn't you? Well, my dear," she said, rising and throwing her wrap around her, "you took a while getting your things, as well you know, and when I'm left to myself I tend to wool-gather. And that is what I was doing, no matter what you may have thought," she concluded as she led Annabelle out into the hall, although she was still smiling at what she thought the other girl might have imagined as they left the house.

It was still radiant spring out of doors, although the cynics might be pleased to see that it was not quite so fine as the previous day had been, since the breeze was a bit less freshening. But then no one in London expected to live in Paradise for long, and most were happy enough to find it still warm and fair weather. Or so they must have thought, since it seemed that half of London's society was on the strut this bright and glowing day.

Leonora and her companions walked six long streets, and stopped to converse with several people who were known to them. Although it was only Leonora who conversed, since Katie, her maid, had neither the opportunity nor the place to do so, and Annabelle stood mute as a mummy with her lips sewn together, even when Jeremy Tutton eyed her speculatively. She had even only murmured something mumbled and vague when Lord Greyville addressed a pleasantry to her, and had been totally silent when the dashing Harry Fabian hailed them and passed the time of day with Leonora for a space. It was true that they weren't highly eligible fellows, Leonora thought, but Annabelle's demeanor had done nothing to encourage them and so they soon forgot her, even as she stood before them.

But then, Leonora thought with a little spurt of vexation, the girl did not have much conversation. Oddly enough, in the wilds of the North country, where all was serene, Leonora hadn't noticed her silence so much as she did here in the throbbing heart of London. Perhaps it was because then she had been so happy to find someone near her own age to speak with that she had done all the talking. Now that all her tales had been told and she wished to share the pleasures of Town with a lively companion, her cousin's taciturn nature became more noticeable.

Leonora briefly thought again that it was a pity that all her one-time London friends had been either wedded or warned away from her, and that she had so few peers to befriend in the countryside, for she realized that poor Annabelle thus bore the entire weight of all her expectations. And that, Leonora admitted to herself, was far too great a burden for anyone, much less someone with such narrow shoulders, to carry.

"We're going to Mr. Reynolds's bookshop instead of Hatchard's today," Leonora said pleasantly enough as they turned down Oxford Street.

At her cousin's curious expression, Leonora said hurriedly, "Well, I thought that it was time to try some new bookseller's.

"And," Leonora went on doggedly, continuing her uphill conversation by ignoring Annabelle's silence and the knowing look that came into the eye of Katie, who trudged behind them, "then too, I'll admit it, we're less likely to run into the Marquess of Severne there. He positively haunts Hatchard's, you know. It amazed me how we were forever running into him there."

At a sound that was suspiciously like a stifled laugh coming from Katie's general direction, Leonora added hastily, "But I don't think I can quite face him today. Not after I made such a cake of myself last night. Imagine, saying "divorce" just when I thought it, and then compounding the issue by apologizing all over the lot. He doesn't deserve to be subjected to me again this morning, and I certainly don't think I could carry it off either."

Leonora was still grimacing at her own folly and looking back at her companions as she achieved the doorway of the bookseller's, and so did not pay full attention to the gentleman coming out through the door. She almost collided with him, but her peripheral vision saved her from that embarrassment. She looked up with a great smile upon her lips at her narrow escape, and met the steady gaze of the Marquess of Severne. Even through her own blaze of embarrassment, she noted that he wore a rather strained expression as he began to make his bows to her.

She wanted so very much to right the wrong she had done him the previous night, and to impress upon him her sincerity, and to give him some little hint of how very much she admired him, without causing him to think that she was pursuing him or calling on his friendship with her father to plague him. But she also had very much not wanted, nor expected, to see him so soon, nor to literally fall over him in public so as to seem that she was panting after him.

It had been a long time since Leonora had had any dealings with sophisticated London gentlemen. And longer still since she cared a rap what any of them thought of her. She drew in her breath and sought the exactly right words to say as he straightened from his bow.

"Lady Leonora," he greeted her most correctly, schooling his face to impassivity, but not quickly enough to hide the hunted, beleaguered look in his startled, startling blue eyes.

"Oh no!" thought Lady Leonora, in sympathy and pity for him, and despair and fury at herself. And then her hand went to her lips in horror as she realized that in her distress, she had spoken the words aloud.

From Katie's gasp and the interested stares of not a few patrons of the crowded bookshop, Leonora knew that she had erred again. She could only stand and stare at him mutely, as horrified as if it had been she who had received not only the insult, but a wet fish across the face as well. But the gentleman was not a reputed spymaster's familiar for nothing. He only blinked as he quelled an involuntary start, and then said at once, smoothly and with a world of regret in his rich warm voice.

"Oh, yes." He sighed ruefully. "I'm afraid, my lady, that it does seem as if I've been following you about the Town, and that might well be discomforting for you, no matter how a lovely lady such as yourself may have gotten used to us poor smitten fellows forever tagging after you. But rest easy please, for it wasn't Cupid, it was only that other mischief maker, coincidence, at work.

"I know that we seem to be running into each other everywhere these days. And knowing that Hatchard's is one of your favorite places, I deliberately avoided it today and came here so as not to appear to be hanging on your sleeve. However now, seeing you so radiant this morning, my lady, I begin to wonder if I haven't been wasting my time by *not* following you as closely as your own shadow."

It was a very pretty speech, delivered in front of a growing and appreciative audience, and given, moreover, without the least hint of the insincerity its author felt, or its recipient suspected.

At that point Leonora could have simply simpered, curtsied, and walked away from a social blunder that had been neatly turned into a small social coup for her. But she had never chosen the easy path. And his politic retrieve of a disastrous situation reminded her of another embarrassing time when he had saved her from herself. Even worse, for all his coolness, she detected a flash of humor in his sparkling eyes.

She was tired of amusing him and disgracing herself, and furious with her own clumsiness. She knew she was not a graceless female, yet in all her dealings with him, somehow she always put her foot wrong. And as always, she was impatient with hypocrisy, even her own. She had been the one who had discovered his favorite bookshop, and she had been the one who had found herself patronizing that same shop almost daily from the moment that she had made the discovery. She had run the poor gentleman to earth today, if only by chance, and she had been the one to insult him, however unwittingly. Yet here he stood, apologizing to her amid a crowd of strangers, for all the world as though he were at fault, and even adding the notion that it might be because he admired her so well, which she knew was never true. It was not fair. It was time for her to take some responsibility for her own actions. She was not a child. She decided that her own honor, as well as his, called for her honesty about her part in this meeting.

"Your lordship," she said clearly and with decision, squaring her shoulders and leaving off her apologetic air, "I appreciate your gallantry. But I insist, you are not at fault. It is *I*, and I assure you that this is true, who avoided Hatchard's today, for I was the one who earnestly attempted to avoid *you* today."

A profound silence greeted this statement, for in many ways it appeared to have turned all the surrounding eavesdroppers to stone. Seeing the immediate look of shock in the marquess's wide blue eyes, Leonora belatedly reviewed her speech. As the marquess tightened his lips, nodded, and walked away, she could only say faintly, "Oh, but that is never what I meant to say." Then she could only stand and stare after his retreating back and wait for some kindly providence to take pity on her and come and cause an earthquake to swallow her up completely.

FOUR

A great many gentlemen pride themselves on their utter inability to fathom the feminine mind, as though that were some sort of hallmark of their own masculinity, but Joscelin Kidd, Marquess of Severne, was not among them. It wasn't that he considered himself omniscient, or even a jot more gifted than any of his fellows, it was only that he had always believed and acted upon the notion that except for a few areas of human experience, the minds of males and females were more similar than not. This belief had always served him well. So as he strode away from his disastrous encounter with the Lady Leonora, he wondered just what in the fiend's name he had done wrong.

He could hear the whispers of gossip picking up behind him even as he walked away, but that did not bother him, it had not for years. More disturbing was the thought that somehow he had wounded the lady, and that was why she sought to pay him back. It was inconceivable that she had acted as she had for no reason, few young persons could be that venomous, and the only cause that he could see for such an attitude would be a desire for revenge for some mortal insult that he had given her. But as he walked the streets of London lost in thought, reviewing his past relationship with the young woman, he could not discover a clue to her malice.

Because, he concluded after a few moments, so far as he knew, they had no past relationship that he could dissect.

He had met the lady five years ago, when she had first come out, even though he had not been present at her formal presentation. Her father had invited him, of course, but he had known it was a courtesy, and out of courtesy, he had stayed away. He owed the viscount a great deal, but it would have been wrong, the young marquess had decided, to repay such a gesture of friendship with an action that could only cause unhappiness. For a gentleman who had just come through the divorce courts, and who still bled the ink of scandal from every caricature and broadsheet in Town, could scarcely go unremarked at a young woman's come-out ball.

But like all other incendiary matters, scandal's smoke blows away quickly if there is no fire to feed it. And it was not long before he had been able to attend some affairs, and since his affairs had required that attendance, it hadn't been long until he had met the lovely Lady Leonora.

He would have noted her even if she had not been his patron's younger daughter. She had the sort of dark good looks that especially appealed to him. Of course, he had to admit now that at that time, those five years ago, the blond, brunette, red-haired, and possibly even bald-pated good looks of any young female would have appealed to him equally as well. He had not been half so immune to the scandalmongers as he had pretended to be. And a young man, for he'd been only four and twenty at the time, who had just obtained a shocking divorce on the grounds of his own inability in the marital bed, would be likely, no matter how he kept up the pretext of not caring, to seek to prove his masculinity incessantly for all the whispering world to see and hear about.

So, as much as he might have admired her fashion, he had done no more than to speak a few polite words over Lady Leonora's little white hand at that time. For he couldn't offer her what a proper young lady was obviously looking for in her presentation year, and she could scarcely offer him what an improper young man was seeking in the year of his absolute disgrace. But there was no denying that he always noted her presence, and not just for her father's sake, whenever their paths happened to cross. And that happened far more frequently than might have been expected of two persons traversing such absolutely diverse paths of society.

But then, London was much like a small town for all its size, and since people always tend to travel in the same tight congenial groups, just as some species of fish do even in the widest seas, those paths are well marked. So even as all the goldsmiths in Town knew of or about each other, as did all the poets and printers and pickpockets, so then all the members of the ton could be said to be constantly tripping over each other.

Even so, although the marquess had been born to the same world that Leonora had been, he had been cast out from it by his actions, and might have absented himself from it forever had it not been for the lady's father. The viscount had heard of the young gentleman's disgrace, and had seen him in a house of ill and wide repute as he attempted to ruin what little reputation he had left to himself. As he was upon the premises for his own purposes anyway, the Viscount Talwin had waited until the following morning, when the young marquess was attempting to restore whatever health he had remaining after his roisterous evening. Then the older gentleman had served up a proposition to the younger, along with his fifth cup of strong and steaming coffee. That proposition, the marquess was fond of remembering, had been his salvation and the making of him as a man.

What he had so urgently needed, he had been given. And that was not just a constant supply of sweet young womanflesh, as he had thought. It was, that first time, just one dangerous, responsible, and important task to perform for his country. And when he'd returned from the Continent, having executed that mission creditably, there had been another for him to essay. It was not until fairly recently, when the French authorities had begun to take note of that lean wolfish face and form to the point where he earned the chilling and deserved nickname of "le loup Anglais," that he had been forced to return to England for good. But there was still employment for him, his patron had insisted, and he had passed his time these last weeks in Town learning what he could from English sources. Not all of his countrymen were patriots, as the viscount told him, and so until Nappy had given up every last dream of world conquest, he would be needed. And to be needed had been just what the Marquess of Severne most desired.

But now he needed to know just why his mentor's daughter had vented her spleen upon him. He had only encountered her a few times during that Season five years previously, for he had gone off to the Continent almost at

the same time that she had blotted her copy book so
indelibly that her father had ordered her home immediately. Their lives seemed to run parallel courses, for now
she was back in Town again, just as he was, with a reputation to live down, just as he had. This commonality should
have counted for some sympathy or fellow feeling upon
her part. He thought he had that, from the frequency with
which he'd been running into her of late. He was no
cockscomb, but he'd thought that he had seen that in her
face last night too, as well as something more. Some other
yearning thing that at the worst would have been sensation
seeking, and at best, would have been far more flattering, if
equally impossible for him to satisfy for her.

Even if he'd been imagining things, at the very least he'd
have thought she might have been grateful to him. He thought
he had done her a service once. Though he was not the
sort of man to call upon those he'd aided so that they could
even up accounts, still he would have thought she might
have considered herself in his debt for that past incident,
if not for his abortive attempt at glossing over what he had
guessed to be her inadvertent remark this morning.

Perhaps she'd made a slip of the tongue about his past
history last night at her party, but then he'd been sure that
the incident disturbed her far more than it had affected
him. But this morning, to have so thoroughly rejected the
way he'd tried to mend matters when he thought she'd just
committed another missaying, forced him to conclude that
she was deliberately setting out to insult or enrage him.
Why this should be so was a mystery to him. And he could
not resist a mystery.

So the viscount's dark daughter was very much on the
marquess's mind as he entered his club for his luncheon
engagement, and his own storm-dark eyes were shadowed
by thought even as he absently greeted his luncheon
companion.

"Good heavens, Joss," the Duke of Torquay exclaimed
in mock terror, pushing away from his setting as the marquess took his seat at their table, "I should have hidden the
cutlery if I had seen that look upon your face before this.
At the very least, I shall be sure to examine the dregs of the
teapot before I allow you to pour. How have I offended
you? Is it that I didn't immediately compliment you on your

vest, dear friend? Or was it my failure to note your new boots?" he inquired in very humble tones.

"What? Oh, Jason," the marquess said, grinning, "forgive me. I've just come from one of the roundest setdowns I've ever been privileged to receive, so I suppose I'm still sulking."

"Ah, you've been proposing naughtiness to the minister's daughter again, then," the duke commented sagely in his low, hoarse accents.

"No, to Talwin's daughter, or so you would think from her response," the marquess replied as he took up his knife, but only to deal with his luncheon.

"Talwin's filly? Isn't she the lady whose interest you were complaining of the other night? Why Joss, my dear, first you grumble that she likes you overmuch, and now you become savage at her dislike. Are you quite sure we're discussing the same female?" the duke asked innocently.

His companion sighed. "Aye, well, it is a coil. First she seeks me, then repels me. If it's difficult to fathom, it's harder still to live with, believe me."

As the gentlemen made their way through prawns and soup to beef and burgundy, the marquess told of his morning's incident in a frowning, halting manner. This had nothing to do with the texture of his roast, as his waiter feared, but rather with the fact that he was attempting to interpret his tale even as he related it.

"Come, Joss," the duke said simply when the younger man had done with both his story and his luncheon plate, "you are like a declaration of love in a letter, you've left the best part out."

"How does the duchess bear you?" Joscelin commented, leaning back in his chair.

"With fortitude," the duke answered briefly, for with all his constant banter, his intimates knew that he never involved his beloved Regina in any of his wicked innuendo. Then he added, more seriously, "Come, Joss, you ought to know that you can always talk with me and that I will keep your secrets close as my next breath. I'm old enough to be your father, dear boy, and since that estimable gentleman is rusticating nicely in the West country, I should be happy to stand in his stead."

"It's not my secret precisely," the marquess said slowly,

and then smiled widely and added, "And you must have been a prodigiously precocious child, Jason, to have taken on fatherhood so young."

"So I was, but I shan't make you jealous by documenting it," the fair-haired gentleman remarked airily before he said softly, "But I might be able to help if only because discussing a problem makes it simpler. You cannot always be the lone wolf our foes term you, you know. And believe me, I respect and admire Talwin fully as much as you do. Why, no one else would have been able to lure me from my countrified fastness but he, although my lady is grateful to him, since she's spent all of our visit buying out every shop in Town. I do believe she has secret plans to erect a complete replica of London on the grounds of Grace Hall so she can charge one pence a peek at it, judging from the amount of objects she's sending home from here. Why do you think the girl should hold you in such dislike, Joss?" he asked, becoming serious all at once.

"The only thing I can possibly imagine," the marquess said quietly, although his table was as he always specified, far from any human ear, "is that she resents my having been witness to a foolish moment she had in her youth. Although I can scarcely credit that, for she's no paragon to be so top-lofty. I interfered with her plans once, years ago when she was first out, for her father's sake as well as her own. I intercepted her at Mother Carey's place of business, you see, and detached her from her escort and took her home before any in the admittedly castaway company had time to recognize her face."

The duke's china-blue eyes widened and he gave a low whistle. "Salvation indeed, Joss. Tell me, do you think she knew the time of day?"

The marquess laughed and shook his head. "No, Jason, I do not. Most definitely not. Because she turned the colors of an autumn leaf before she commenced shaking like one as I led her to my carriage. She'd just come in, and all the company was occupied elsewhere, grouped around a couple in the center of the room. She only got one peek at what they were ogling before I intervened. Before she could think to swoon I braced her with some hard words and hurried her away. Still, she had a glimpse of some of the carry-on, and for all I know that may be why such a stunner is still unwed. Mother had one of her famous exhibitions on display that night," he explained as his companion winced.

"Young James Flowers, Wardley's heir, took her there, and you know what he came to in the end," the marquess added.

"Indeed. I had an evil reputation once upon a time, but that fellow's was foul. There is a difference," the duke mused thoughtfully.

"Well I know it," his friend agreed. "But Jason, the girl's attitude troubles me. I work with Talwin because I want to and feel I ought to, and I shouldn't like to have his daughter at daggers drawn with me. I've avoided her because I believed her to be just as wild as she was when she was sent home years ago. I thought her interest in me was caused only by her more lurid fantasies. Well, you can't blame me for not wanting to be the instrument by which she's ordered home again." As his friend began to protest, the marquess raised one thin, well-cared-for hand and said, "No, Jason, hear me out, it would be no strange thing if my presence in a lady's parlor enraged a dutiful papa. I am a divorced man and I'm not welcomed in the best circles."

"Thank you," said the duke sweetly. As the marquess attempted to make a recover, his friend brushed his protestations aside and went on, "I know, and you are right, Joss, but for whatever it's worth, I also don't know a decent fellow in the land who wouldn't want you for his son-in-law, even so. In fact, if my eldest girl were a month more than thirteen years of age as we speak, I'd be marching down the aisle with her to meet you at this moment."

"So if I won't have you as a father, you're set on becoming my father-in-law?" The marquess smiled, before he went on earnestly, "But I did avoid the girl, Jason, and then, when I couldn't ignore her for civility's sake, I tried to be discreet for kindness's sake, and she skewered me. I cannot imagine why. Then again, there's a great deal about her that puzzles me, for she wasn't a madcap at first, you know. I remarked her when she first came to Town and she was docile as a dove then. The wildness was a thing which grew upon her."

"Then I think, my lad, you'll just have to study her more closely, as you would any other wild thing, and so get to know her a deal better. I don't believe her attitude will influence Talwin one way or another, if that's what's troubling you," the duke said slowly, "but I don't think that it is. She's very beautiful," he said off-handedly.

"And it's decidedly not that," Joscelin said, laughing, "for the world is full of beautiful women who do not have fathers I go in awe of. It preoccupies me so because," he said, as though thinking aloud, his hard, handsome face growing very still, "I have always hated enigmas."

"How very odd!", the duke exclaimed, his low voice filled with amazement, "for I thought I knew you very well, Joss, and I believed you always loved a mystery."

The two gentlemen said a lengthy good-bye on the street in front of the club. They were much remarked upon as they stood and joked and reminded each other of when they next should meet. It was not odd that this should be so, on either count. Even though the duke was all impatience to join his duchess again, since he seldom could like being gone from her for too long, and even though the marquess had a delightful afternoon arranged for himself, since he had no present obligations and felt he deserved a treat, the two gentlemen liked each other very well and were often loath to break from such congenial companionship. And since their appearances were almost as sensational as their reputations, it was only natural that bystanders should often ogle them and whisper "birds of a feather" when they were seen together.

But then, the duke mused as his companion at last took his leave, his young friend hadn't needed to expend so much effort as he had in his past in order to earn his bad repute. He had not needed to bed half so many shocking creatures, he had only to wed the one, and then leave her, by decree of divorce. For that simply was not done. Not by a gentleman.

It was a pity it was so, the duke thought as he finally strolled off to his townhouse. Though he was not in actuality of an age to have been Severne's father, he felt that same sort of protective concern for him. Not because the lad was incapable of looking after himself, but because it seemed so wrong that he was deemed an outcast by correct society. There was a legion of gentlemen who practiced far more despicable acts who were welcomed into the highest reaches of the ton because they indulged themselves in secret, thus socially acceptable fashion. The fact that young Joss could not woo or wed where a gentleman who, say, habitually sought the reluctant embraces of underage servants might, was damnable.

But then, thought the duke, his face brightening, even as his pace quickened as he hurried homeward, it was never necessary to wed some social lioness in order to be blissfully happy. Then too, he thought, so amused at himself that he chuckled low in his throat, only an old hopelessly married fellow like himself would even think that a dashing young gentleman like the marquess needed to be wed at all. Joss could accommodate half a dozen lovers this very afternoon and be happy as a man could expect to be, the duke concluded as he reached his own door, although from his own experience, he didn't really believe that at all.

The duke, for all his urbanity, would have been surprised to know that his friend Joss completely agreed with him. For even as the marquess walked to his next afternoon appointment, he regretted having made it, even though it was planned to be an interlude of pleasure with an exquisite young woman. It wasn't that he didn't enjoy such a pastime as he had planned, it was only that in some little corner of his consciousness he wished it were more than merely a pastime. But he quelled that traitorous thought as he entered the carpeted hall of a quiet hotel on Park Lane.

He glanced at his pocket watch once as he took the stairs to the rooms he had previously arranged to let, and when he came to the door to the rooms, he sighed only once, knowing he was fifteen minutes late and she would be very angry with him. He could not blame her overmuch, for there were few men in London who would keep her waiting a fraction of that time.

But when he let himself in the door with his passkey and strode to the bedchamber, she sat upon the bed awaiting him and looked at him longingly, and never breathed a word of censure but only opened her arms to welcome him. As he came into her embrace, even as he took the kiss she offered, he wondered what strange mood she was in today to account for her gentle acquiescence.

"Joss," she breathed at last, playfully, placing a finger upon his lips where her own had so lately been, "you utter beast. To let me wait and wonder at your tardiness, and worry that perhaps you had decided to abandon me forever. It was too cruel, but very like you. But I forgive you, as I always must do."

This was so unlike the lady that the marquess sat back and ceased undoing his cravat.

"I'm sorry I'm late, but come, why not just screech at me for a while and be done with it? These gentle lamentations, sweet, are never like you. You make me quite uneasy, and that will never do, will it?" he breathed into her ear, while his long fingers stroked away the little golden curls that clustered over it.

"Ah Joss," she said, exhaling and treating him to a gust of candied violet scent, "it pleases you to jest, I see. But here I have waited for you, alone and afraid in a strange room in a strange hotel, with never even my maid nearby to help me should I need her attentions."

Aha, that tune again, the marquess thought wearily, the last traces of real desire deserting him, though all he said softly was, "But my dear, we have been through that too often. It is, I feel, enough that I entertain myself with Lord Lambert's beloved wife. It would be too much, I believe, to avail myself of his bed, linens, and liquor as well as I do so, don't you think?"

"Beast!" the lady cried, and struck him smartly across the cheek before she turned and bent her head so that it was so completely covered by streamers of her shining golden hair that he could not see how hard she tried to bring out some realistic tears.

The marquess sighed. It was becoming tedious, he thought, even as he attempted to gently pull the lady back into his embrace. The affair had started well, but was ending badly. Obviously, she wanted her husband to know of the liaison for her own reasons, and his own insistence on keeping their meetings discreet was running counter to whatever plans she'd hatched. Although there could scarcely be two more different females in appearance and style, she too, he thought, even as he assured her of her safety in the hotel and his regret at being late, wanted him mainly for his reputation, even as the wicked young lady he'd been discussing at lunch no doubt had.

But for all of his sagacity about the lady in his arms, and

her whims and machinations, he was entirely wrong about
her reasons for wanting him. As she swept her hair back
from her eyes and turned her face to him again, realizing
that she'd get no further with her importuning today, she
gazed at him. And were she the sort of female wise enough
to understand that gentlemen need flattery too, she would
have told him what pleasure she took in that simple act.

She looked into his searching eyes and even forgot to
look for her own reflection there, they were so deep and
blue and intense. Just staring at that hard young face, with
its clean contours and curiously full lips awaiting her own
mouth's touch, made her want him more than any other
man's presents or flattery or fame ever had. And though it
would have been very good if Lambert did more than
suspect their meetings, just to show him how well she
could do for herself, since he had that shocking Turner
woman's favors now, she would forego that simpler pleasure for the more complex ones she could discover in the
marquess's close embrace.

But, even as he gathered her to himself, as he whispered
a list of her physical virtues for her to glory in, he found
that only a part of himself was involved in the proceedings.
Another, more rational Joscelin had already risen, walked
across the room, and seated himself in a chair, and idly
swung his booted foot and waited for the randy fool to be
done with his foolish pleasures. Or so it seemed, or so it
increasingly seemed to happen to him.

It wasn't that he didn't like females, he did, and had
always done so. He was a devoted son to his fond mama,
and he had looked after his two younger sisters' welfare
with so much affection and goodwill that they'd both grown
to be jolly, confident young girls who were now the delight
of their husbands' lives. Perhaps it was because he genuinely liked females that he was lately so disconsolate in
each of his fleeting affairs. For he was used to valuing those
of their gender as he valued his men friends, as separate
and distinct persons.

And yet lately he'd only had dealings with those women
who, if truth be told, he didn't care for too very much once
they were up and out of his bed. He was not so compelled
to find bedchamber companionship as, for example, his
friend the duke had been in his youth. Yet while not

precisely a rake, it could be said that the Marquess of Severne was also never long deprived of a female's intimate company. But since he was not driven, he exercised selectivity in his choice of partners. Now that he was a grown man he no longer visited those establishments where he could choose a female for the evening as he would a bottle of wine. Nor could he enjoy any relationship such as so many of his fellows did, where a young person was properly housed and clothed and paid quarterly, even as a footman or a housemaid was, in exchange for the performance of personal services that were supposed to pass for acts of love.

But it was never love he sought, or so he told himself. At least he was wise enough to know it could not be found among those he had deceived, as they attempted to deceive him, on his missions upon the Continent. Neither did he expect to find himself such a gentle passion either with or among those ladies he did disport with, those bored and spoiled beauties whose husbands allowed them to stray so long as they reciprocated that privilege. Females of the servant class were too amazed at his attentions, or too conniving at receiving them, for him to become involved with, and respectable young women from any social station, were, of course, quite above his touch.

He was saved from these gloomy reflections before they could hinder his present plans, by his lady's suddenly twining her fingers in his thick hair and wrenching him even closer to her. When he stopped his ministrations to stare in puzzlement at her, and even that other Joscelin, the one that had abandoned him to solitary carnality, looked up in surprise, she breathed, "Ah Joss, do not be so cruel to me. I know I deserve it after my complaints, but please spare me." Since she said this with a look of great anticipation upon her uplifted, lovely face, he sighed deeply. That other Joscelin gave a cough of a laugh and left him alone again.

Games, he thought wearily, whenever an affair became flat, they always thought to recapture his and their own interest with neverending games. He decided to ignore her.

"Joss," she whispered, as though she might be overheard, even though he had difficulty hearing her, close as he was, "go ahead, I won't mind. Be savage with me if you must. I've known you weeks now and you no longer need restrain yourself."

"My dear," he said slowly, "you know I am not cruel, nor do I enjoy cruelty, nor will I indulge you in it."

"So you say." She laughed until her whole body trembled beneath his and then looked up at him wisely. "But you cannot deny the evidence in your face. Nor have you seen that pitiless look in your eyes as others have. And I have heard the rumors. Oh yes. We all know it is not your inability which took you from your marriage. I can vouch for that," she said smugly. "Nor is it any part of your person or personality. Save that. It must be that. That's what everyone says. So go ahead. Don't hold your desire back. I'm not some inexperienced chit, as your wife was. I won't mind. I rather like it, actually. Only don't get too carried away, I have a dinner party to attend tomorrow night."

He stopped completely. And it seemed that a small surviving scrap of his pride, which had escaped the slaughter of his self-esteem five years ago, now quietly stopped breathing as well. The fantasy he had of that other, watchful, safe, and uninvolved Joss died, too, for he was entirely appalled.

He had known her for weeks, as she'd said, which was longer in fact than he had known the wife she mentioned. That this woman who waited eagerly beneath him, trembling not with laughter now, but in excited anticipation of what dark and nameless deeds she believed him capable of, could so misjudge him, could so value him for what he would consider repugnant, astonished and infuriated him.

He did not leave her at once, for he was only human. And though he did not half meet her expectations, as he could never so completely unleash his anger in such fashion, he did not precisely disappoint her, though his callous divorce of his mind from his body more than disappointed himself. And when he left her, he left her for good.

But as he walked home in that London twilight, he thought for the first time that perhaps, just perhaps, it was time for him to marry again. If not for love, then for an end to expecting love. And to anyone who would be willing to have him, and his heirs, and not a great deal more of him than that.

FIVE

The rain had come. It was a fine mist really, pearl gray and opaque, hardly qualifying as a true rainstorm, but it made the morning dim and bleak. Yet no one complained except for the smallest children who knew no better. In a curious way it was comforting to have such thoroughly damp and dismal weathers on the heels of those few glorious episodes of picture-perfect spring. However much that interlude had been enjoyed, a true Englishman knew when he had been given false coin. This day felt more natural, and a fellow could relax now and know the truth, that at last the brief flirtation was over, and it was well and truly springtime.

Leonora sat at her dressing table while Katie did valiant battle with her hair, which she claimed liked to coil and tie itself into knots at night just to spite her while her lady slept.

"Good heavens, Katie," Leonora said, wincing and biting her lip as Katie found and attacked a particularly convoluted snarl, "you make me sound like Medusa. It's only hair. And it's only that it's damp out today."

Katie gave out a grim laugh and bore down harder on her chosen foe, her mistress's heavy, tangled tresses, as if they were indeed hissing snakes she battled with. Leonora declined to mention that part of the problem just might have been that she had tossed and turned the entire night, falling to sleep now and again only to wake immediately, struggling up from the grasp of ghastly dreams. She ought to feel lucky, she thought, as she bit back a little cry as Katie sought and discovered a particularly complex knot, that at least she hadn't strangled herself with her own hair during her restless, sleepless night.

She was in such discomfort now, from the combined effects of the past night and Katie's present crusade against disorder, that she was about to ask the girl to leave off and simply go and get a razor and clear the whole lot off the top of her aching head, when her pain-heightened senses detected the sound of the merest scratching at her door.

"That can be no other but Annabelle," she groaned, annoyed at the sound, but glad of a reason for Katie to lay down her punishing brush. "Go and let her in, please, for I haven't the patience to shout her in. She'll only hesitate and wait until I call her again, and I don't have the head for all that roundabout this morning. Go, go, Katie, do please, or she'll scratch a groove in the door. I wonder what's to do? It isn't like her to come to visit this early. She's always afraid I'm still sleeping if it's before noon, although I've told her a thousand times that I'm always up and dressed by nine in Town."

"Maybe her bed's on fire," Katie muttered sourly as she went to the door. Leonora detected a bit of hope in that sullen pronouncement, and did not think it was only because her maid had been interrupted when she was just getting into her full stride as a champion hair brusher. Katie made very little effort to hide the fact that she liked Annabelle about as much as she did a toothache. But then, Leonora thought, her plain-faced, plump little Katie was very secure in her position, and probably had been secure in the cradle, and so had little patience with a hesitant, shy girl like Annabelle.

Katie opened the door to admit Annabelle and then turned around without a word and marched back to her hairbrush, as though she was eager to seize it up again before the handle could grow cold. In fact, she thought as Annabelle came softly into the room, she would be damned if she would give her breath in greeting to that sly little layabout. Katie was as class conscious as a queen. And, she thought as she attacked her mistress's hair with renewed gusto, causing that lady to gasp as she gave good morning to her relative, there wasn't any reason on earth why Miss Greyling couldn't go out and work for her bread as any healthy young woman ought, for she wasn't a true lady like young miss, and that Katie would lay odds against her own life upon.

"Well, and what brings you to visit me so early this morning?" Leonora asked with false cheeriness, since Annabelle had already done with greeting her and refusing her offer of a cup of chocolate and only stood and stared at her with a dolorous expression.

"I only came to see how you were feeling, cousin," Annabelle said softly, "since you were so very upset last evening. You went to bed early, you know. Are you quite recovered?"

Leonora felt a twinge of guilt, for she remembered that one of Annabelle's chiefest pleasures since she had come to visit had been when the two of them would sit and read aloud through the long winter evenings.

"I'm much recovered, Belle," Leonora began, and then she broke off and said more vehemently, "Oh rot, no I'm not. But at least my wretched night brought me counsel. I was sick with shame at myself last night, Belle, and there's the truth of it. Imagine, to serve Severne such a turn! He doesn't deserve it, nor do I deserve the opinion he must have of me that I've given him with my own rash tongue. I know better, Belle, there's the worst of it. I have all the words in my head, ready and in perfect order and formation, and then I see him, and open my mouth, and they all tumble out like clowns."

"Do you care for him so very much then?" Annabelle asked, her blue eyes wide.

"Why no!" Leonora exclaimed at once, as though her relative had asked her if she plotted against the King. "But, you see, he did me a favor once, and I'd like to show I'm still grateful. Then too, you know, Belle, he is not acceptable everywhere and I should like him to know that I don't agree with that sort of attitude at all. And yet each time I see him I give him cause to believe the opposite is true."

Although her mistress's hair now resembled a dark and flowing silken scarf, Katie gave a handful a little sharp tug as she began to arrange it, if only to pay her back for such a blatant lie. For gratitude didn't bring such a look to a female's eyes, nor did a grateful lady jump as though she'd sat on a tack when she was asked about her feelings for a gentleman she only wished to give her thanks to.

"But he is acceptable here and he must know that,"
Annabelle said reasonably, "because he was here just the
other night as your father's guest."

Katie gave the blond young woman a rare nod of
approval, for someone ought to make her mistress see
sense. If she could overcome her nervousness about the
fellow, she could speak to him and judge him whole and
cold, as a female ought to do, before she made some other
disastrous leap. Not, Katie mused, as she paused in her
work, that a leap toward the marquess would necessarily
have been so ruinous for her mistress, if it were not for the
matter of that shocking divorce.

There was the pity, Katie sighed to herself. If it weren't
for that, she considered that he might have been one of the
few gentlemen in all the civilized world who might have
made a fair match for her adored mistress. But then too, if
it weren't for that, he likely would have been married three
times and over by now, he would have been that eligible.
Still, that was an opinion she would never breathe aloud,
since she believed her mistress to be such an impulsive
female. Better, Katie thought, that she should never think
any other decent female could see a glimmer of goodness
in him.

"That's true, but you see, Belle," Leonora sighed sadly,
"Father has sophisticated tastes, and Mama doesn't necessarily share them. I don't believe Severne would ever have
been one of her guests."

As her relative cocked her head to one side in her
incomprehension, and Katie nodded above her head like a
wise woman reading gypsy cards, Leonora told Annabelle
the pertinent details that she knew about the marquess's
brief marriage and subsequent disgrace.

"It was a writ, I believe, called an 'A Vinculo Matrimonii'
or some such," Leonora went on, wrinkling her brow as
though in deep recollection, as if she hadn't committed the
words to heart the moment she learned of them, "being an
entire dissolution of the bonds of matrimony, which is
more difficult to obtain than a plain separation. But then
again, a mere separation would mean that neither party
could ever marry again in any case."

Annabelle did not lose her quizzical expression, but then,
Leonora thought whimsically, perhaps she never could, her

light brows were so perennially arched above those wide light eyes. But she must have been surprised, for she only said with wonderment,

"Indeed, I have never heard of such a thing, cousin. There were some terrible husbands that I knew of, at home, but their poor wives could never be quit of them. Why," she said, blushing faintly, "I am sure that Mama might oftentimes have wished to be free to wed another, but even though Father left us and never returned, she couldn't ever seek her happiness with any other gentleman while he yet lived. And yet she herself often said that so it must be. And so it must. I cannot believe that this marquess can be so admirable if he was party to such a proceeding."

Katie gave a vigorous nod of agreement as the fair young woman went on to add, before her cousin could cut in,

"And I doubt it matters if it was his wife that sought such, or even if she was at fault in it. For if she sought to obtain a divorce from him, it may be that she was driven to it by unspeakable actions on his part, and if he sought it, what sort of a man must he be, not to be able to bear it as most men might?"

Since this was the longest speech that Annabelle had given in days, Leonora was so taken aback that she could not speak up in defense of the marquess at once. But, she noted from glancing in the looking glass, Katie was actually smiling at her cousin in the fondest way imaginable. That, if nothing else, stung her from her silence. For she knew Katie's opinion in the matter, and that opinion was that Severne was a handsome dog with a heart as black as coal and morals that must make his heart seem lily-white by comparison.

"Well there you are!" cried Leonora heatedly. "Belle, you have said just what so many supposedly proper people say. But you can't have looked at it clearly. For I say that it is far worse to continue on in a marriage that is a mockery of man's and God's laws, simply for propriety's sake, than it is to dissolve such a union for sanity's sake. There are too many persons, right here in London, who lead lives that are blatantly hypocritical lies, who would be better off declaring the truth and—" But here Leonora stopped, for both her cousin and her maid were observing her in horrified fashion. She had raised her voice, as well as herself, she realized, becoming so impassioned that she sprang to her feet without knowing it and no doubt startled them. Worse, she thought as she sank back to her chair, she had almost said, "too many persons right here in this house" instead of "right here in London."

"Well," she said weakly now, "I'm sorry if I became exercised. But you see, it's foolish to think Severne a monster, for nothing in his aspect or his reputation gives credence to that, at least. And I maintain that his was an act of courage, not cowardice."

"And his wife?" Annabelle asked, as much to Katie as to Leonora.

"No one knows," Leonora said sadly, "for she was from the remote North country and not from the West where Severne's principal family seat lies, and she never came to Town at all. She did marry again, but she died of a fever not two years past."

"Unhappy lady," Katie murmured, earning a sharp glance from her mistress, for Leonora well remembered her maid's initial reaction to the news when she had it back at home. Katie had positively slavered over the gossip then, with not a hint of the pious sympathy she was treating them to now.

"Still," Annabelle persisted, more animated in this discussion than her relative could ever remember her having been before, "if it were a meritorious thing, cousin, why are there not more such divorces?"

"Ah well," Leonora said with a shrug, "it is no easy thing. Even our Prince, you know, would give much to be rid of his Caroline. But it drags on in its legalities, and costs the earth. And then one must testify to all sorts of shameful things. Severne, you see, said it was his fault. He said," and here she dropped her voice and looked down at her toes, "that it was his inability to consummate the marriage."

Katie snickered at that and Leonora's head came up, even as her shoulders did. "Well," she declared fiercely, her fine brown eyes blazing, "since everyone and their uncle here in Town seems to know that that's not true, we must assume it was a gentlemanly lie in order to save his wife the agony of testifying in front of a legion of strangers.

"Then too," Leonora continued into the thoughtful silence which followed her words, "a divorce does forever exclude one from certain parts of society. I am not saying that it has made Severne a pariah, for it has obviously not done so. But he did have to join a different club, and some of his acquaintances dropped off. Your reaction, I assure you, is only a fraction of a larger tide of censure. I cannot say who his late wife remarried, but Severne himself may have a great deal of difficulty marrying another high-born lady." Here, Leonora's expression clearly showed what she thought of such lofty ladies.

Leonora fell silent, abruptly realizing that her discussion was showing a knowledge of divorce and all its laws and their repercussions that went far beyond the common. Her listeners might never guess the actual hours of reading and subtle questioning that she had done to obtain her information, but they must if they had any wit, be aware by now of how very interested she was in the subject.

Katie was aware of it, and had been far before her mistress's outburst. The only revelation she had been treated to this morning was the one involving Miss Greyling. For, Katie thought, it only went to show that even she could be wrong once in a lifetime. Because it now was clear the chit was wide awake to Lady Leonora's obsession, and was caring enough to have it out with her. There wasn't a doubt that she'd not budged the lady an inch from her opinions, despite her objections to Severne, but it showed some heart and spirit to at least have tried. Katie thought for a moment of offering the girl some help with that flyaway blond hair of hers, but then stopped herself. There wasn't any point, she sniffed, in going overboard.

"But cousin," Annabelle said softly now, "you said it cost the earth. How is it that the marquess can still live in such style? Could it be that his wife's family was so eager to be rid of him that they willingly bankrupted themselves to do so?"

But now both Leonora and Katie laughed. "Oh Belle," Leonora said, smiling, when she saw that Annabelle hadn't joined in, "No, we weren't mocking you. It's only that it's well known that Severne is very well to grass. Why he could obtain a divorce for himself and all the gentlemen in his club and not feel the pinch. He's very warm in the pocket."

At that, even Katie chuckled, but Annabelle still did not.

All she said, as though to herself, softly, interestedly, and with great seriousness, was, "Ahh!"

Leonora ran her palms down the side of her frock so that they might not show the tell-tale signs of dampness should the gentleman take her hand. She was diverted from her nervousness for a moment by the thought that perhaps a lady ought use her handkerchief for such a purpose, and the immediate ridiculous following thought that a lady, of course, would always have cool, dry hands. A lady, Leonora remembered from her schoolroom days, only required a handkerchief for those infrequent tears caused by her exquisite sensibility.

But she, Leonora grimaced, as she paced her room and waited for the expected summons, would likely need a large sponge for her hands by the time her interview took place. She had sent Katie on errands, which today involved the hastily invented necessity of acquiring a quantity of ribbons, and she had also gently, and then rather more ungently, given Annabelle to understand that she wished to be alone this afternoon. So far as she knew, Annabelle was now cloistered with one of several books that she had pressed upon her, given as much in atonement as in sincerity, since she knew and regretted the fact that her defection would cause her cousin to spend a solitary afternoon. Despite attendance at several teas and simple suppers since they had come to Town, Annabelle had not as yet made any friends of her own to pass the last of this misty afternoon with.

But then, Leonora thought, glad to have a respite from her own pressing problems for a moment, Annabelle was in a curiously difficult position. Having no family or fortune of her own, she could not have a presentation of her own. Since she was a relation of the viscount's, however distant, she could share in everything but the actual riches of the house. Yet again, even though personally impoverished, being of good family, she could scarcely be expected to go out and earn her own way. And so she was neither servant nor cosseted daughter, and she could befriend neither sort of female that she met in Town.

Had it been herself who wore Annabelle's little slippers, Leonora thought, she would have struck out on her own long before this time. But, she remembered, it was easy to say what one would do if one's life were different, quite impossible to know what would actually be true. She was no one to criticize Annabelle, she admitted to herself with a scowl, especially since she scarcely knew what to do with her own life now.

At least she would not remain passive, Leonora decided. And that was why she paced, and sat, and walked the length of her room, and stood again, waiting for her father to have an audience with her. She could not bear inaction. Even if it meant that she must face her father alone to ask a favor of him, she would do that. For no matter how grueling, it would be better than doing nothing.

She must beg Severne's pardon. She might gain no more from it than the felicity of seeing him register her sincerity and penitence in those quick deep eyes of his. But that would be enough. No, she thought suddenly, drooping and dropping into a chair, no, to be honest it would not. But it would be better than nothing.

She realized she was entirely preoccupied with the marquess, but knew from experience that there was not a thing she could do about it. For so she had been for the past five years. It wasn't a morbid fascination because of his unhappy marital circumstances. Leonora's father had a wide circle of acquaintances. There were other divorced gentlemen in the kingdom and she had met them, too. But none of them, not the Marquess of Anglesey nor the wealthy Mr. Rowan, nor even the sensational Baron Hyde, had ever caused her heart to flutter by merely one flicker of their lashes as they gave her an amused sidewise glance. Then too, she wasn't the sort of female whose heart ever reacted so, unless she rapidly ascended a flight of stairs. But so Severne affected her, and so he had from the day she'd first clapped eyes upon him.

Five years is a very long time to maintain an interest, but Leonora had a constant sort of mind. Her sister had included him now and again in the general run of gossip in her letters and on her occasional visits home, and if she sometimes neglected the matter, an exquisitely subtle hint or two would be enough to keep an interested party *au courant*. Leonora knew that her father had continued an association with the marquess, and she regretted that any such business (and business she knew it must be) was always conducted in London. If any one thing had often tempted her to renounce her long exile from Town, it was the notion that there she might see Severne again. The sight of him was about all that she hoped to have of him. Now she had blighted even that little dream.

If things had gone differently, had she not seen and heard her father at his play those years ago, had Sybil not enlightened her as to the truth of her adult world, she might well have set her cap for the marquess then. Her mother's objections wouldn't have weighed with her, her father might have countenanced it, and in those days she had believed in her desirability with all the confidence of youth. She'd been a headstrong girl, he had affected her strongly, and she'd thought she might just snare him.

He had totally ensnared her interest. She thought his looks unmatched by any other gentleman's. His voice was balm to her, his wit, which she stored up examples of, warmed her, even as the tales of his wenching, rather than dissuading her, warmed her in other ways. She secretly wept for his excommunication from society, and the sight of his tall, spare frame held stiffly erect even as he was snubbed at some gathering, brought real physical pain to her. She excused him the divorce without ever knowing its cause, only believing its cause could never have been his doing. For a rational, sensible young woman, this attitude was radical and a little frightening. And thoroughly delightful in its intensity.

She had been in the throes of a full-scale infatuation. Had she had more time, had she remained in Town, she might have plucked up her courage and begun a campaign to catch his eye and heart. But then, too, she might have discovered that no infatuation can ever survive its arch foe, familiarity. Sharing mundane experiences, such as head colds, boring musical evenings, or deadening family gatherings, begins to nibble away at the core of such ephemeral passions. Constant association would have transmuted it, like ore brought to fire, to its essential and true nature. It might have ended in boredom, disappointment, or even true love. But it would have ended.

Instead, alone in the countryside, passing the years reading and dreaming of love when she ought to have been practicing it, her dream of the outcast Marquess of Severne had only grown sweeter. His divorce became more of a virtue in her eyes than any of his detractors had ever thought it a discredit. Whatever else he had been, she reasoned, he had not been a hypocrite, playing out a great charade of dutiful husband, as her own father and brother-in-law did. He was never long absent from her thoughts during her long absence from Town. And there he had loomed so large that perhaps in some corner of her otherwise sensible mind, she almost believed he knew of it and she was embarrassed for it. Because now she could scarcely look at him directly without her tongue cleaving to the roof of her mouth, and every time she'd met him, she'd disgraced herself.

It was intolerable. She no longer had designs on his single state, for she'd given up all such thoughts those years ago. If she couldn't think to wed any man after learning of their common practice of marital duplicity, how could she think of bearing the more enormous pain of having someone as wonderful as Severne constantly deceiving her? She had solved the problem by making such a possibility patently impossible.

When her parents would not let her go home at once as she'd wished to do after what she had witnessed, so as to brood and think the thing out, she had gone and forced them to it. There hadn't been a rogue or roaring boy that she hadn't taken up company with, nor a flat or fortune hunter that she hadn't actively encouraged. She believed that it had only been her confusion and fastidious upbringing which had prevented her from offering them more than her lips then, and her father's fame that prevented them from taking advantage of that confusion to seek more, but she hadn't remained in Town long enough to test her theory. For then, as if by some particularly malign act of fate, it had been Severne himself who had saved her from the worst fix she'd gotten into.

She'd honestly only been thinking of how effectively it would shock everyone if she showed up at a soiree at the type of establishment that caddish fellow James Flowers had described to her. So she'd blithely gone with him to the place he'd called "Mother Carey's house" that day. She hadn't been thinking too clearly about anything at that

point. Up until the time that she had seen everyone in the
gilded room she'd just entered gaping at the handsome
couple in their midst, she hadn't cared about anything but
her escape from London either. But the moment she had
gotten close enough to see more than their heads and the
distant, fixed smiles they wore, she'd realized that the
young man and woman standing before everyone were
not wearing anything else. Then, from the second later
when it registered upon her shocked senses that the rhyth-
mically moving pair were not dancing either, she'd become
aware at last of her own danger and the degradation which
could result from her dangerous self-absorption. Before
more horror could set in, most fortunately, Severne had
stepped in.

But by then, it hardly mattered. She'd ruined her reputation so thoroughly that his witnessing the final touches to its
destruction was unnecessary. If *she* wouldn't think of wedding anyone, why then, she had seen to it there was no
possibility he'd ever think of having her.

Although in five years a reputation might be mended,
and as in Leonora's case, extreme youth, when gone, is a
handy excuse for extreme folly, her own expectations had
not altered a jot. But sometimes dreams are so necessary
for their creators that they do not disappear entirely upon
awakening, but only change until they have become transmuted into something acceptable in the clear light of reality. Now Leonora only wished to convince the marquess of
her goodwill, and she just wanted to have the pleasure of
being able to chat with him now and again, and maybe, if
things went as well as they possibly could, he might someday, perhaps, even call her "friend." And that was why she
must speak to Papa, for he was the only one who could
help her achieve that last humble longing now.

By the time that the viscount had returned from luncheon at his club, Leonora had almost exhausted herself
preparing for her interview with him. She hadn't sought
him out privately for so long that she'd forgotten the look
of the offices he maintained in a small room on the main
floor, behind the library. For all she'd spent so many happy
hours there with him in the past, as she came into his room
when he bade her, it all looked new to her, or at the very
least, like a revisited landscape from some childhood dream.

Thus, as she stood and stared at the familiar yet unfamiliar furnishings and got her bearings, she did not see how quickly he had leaped to his feet, nor how nervous her father was, nor how he looked at her so eagerly. By the time she turned her eyes to him, he had seated himself again and was requesting that she do the same in his usual dry, bored tones.

It was more awkward than she'd imagined. He didn't help her at all, save for interjecting small inquiring sounds whenever her speech faltered. So she held her face as impassive as he kept his, and in as toneless a manner as she could, she told him of how she had insulted the Marquess of Severne the previous night and compounded the insult while attempting to right matters this morning.

"I wish to set the matter straight, Father," she said coolly. "The difficulty lies in the fact that he is scarcely likely to hold still long enough when he sees me coming for me to do so. And I shouldn't blame him in the least for taking flight at the mere mention of my name."

"I see," said the viscount slowly, "so you wish me to have a word with him?"

"No," Leonora said flatly, "for he'd expect you to do the pretty, whether I meant you to or not. I must speak with him, Father, but I can't see how I can do that without your help. I cannot be so forward as to send him a note, and there's small likelihood of our meeting in company, for you know that we don't travel in the same circles. Sybil and Lord Benjamin don't associate with him because of his reputation, and Mama must always follow Sybil's lead. Neither can I lie in wait in the hallways here, hoping to accost him coming out of your offices. Can you think of a way that I might meet him on mutually safe ground, and tender my apologies to him? It is rather important to me," she added with stress, but in as colorless a tone as she had recited all the rest.

An awkward silence followed as she gazed at him and waited for him to speak. He seemed lost in thought. Then he looked up at her. Ah, my Nell, he thought with something very much like anguish, where have you been all these years? Why did you change so all out of recognition? And why did you suddenly turn your face from me? He had wanted to ask her that from the beginning, but anything that he had said to her then had remained unanswered, and then it had grown too late, too cold to ask with warmth.

He had hesitated too long. If the estrangement were due to something he had done, he wanted to know of it, and yet didn't. He'd done many things in the name of his country that he'd rather not explain. He couldn't imagine what else it might have been, or if he could, he shrank from discussing such with her. For her good opinion had always meant so much to him. How he missed her, his dark, proud, laughing, headstrong daughter with her passionate beliefs. She had been his delight.

She looked back at him serenely, her calm matching his, while all the time she yearned for him to throw back his head and laugh with her at the two silly persons in his office, staring at each other inscrutably, like opposing mandarins across a chessboard. Oh Papa, she thought, how I have missed you!

"I think," the viscount said coolly, at last, "that perhaps I may be able to arrange something."

"Very good," Leonora answered levelly.

And then they sat and nodded at each other, since there was nothing else to say.

SIX

He saw her at once, almost immediately after he had entered the room. It hardly mattered that he had been expecting to see her, and was prepared for the moment with fatalistic curiosity. That was forgotten when he saw her. She was easily the most beautiful creature he'd seen in years. It wasn't only the unexpected brilliance of the silken scarlet frock she wore which glorified her luxuriant contours, or her elaborately dressed dark tresses that transformed her and disarmed him utterly. It was the look upon her lovely face when she caught sight of him, that radiant look of glad welcome, of whole and joyous greeting, that warmed him entirely and made him feel as though he were coming home at last.

"My lady," he breathed, as he went to her and took her hand in his.

"My lord," Leonora answered, daring to look in his eyes and then, seeing the interest there, not daring to believe his reaction to her.

"If I say that you are in magnificent looks tonight, I become a plagiarist, for I'm sure every gentleman here has told you those exact words already, but I will risk it." The marquess smiled as he regretfully relinquished her hand. "You are in great looks tonight, my lady, you may add my sincere compliments to your list."

For that moment, Leonora only stood and gazed up happily at him, no immediate words of reply came to her, and for that one moment, none seemed necessary. But then Annabelle, beside her, shifted her little slippered feet, and someone, somewhere else in the room, laughed loudly, and the moment was past. Then she became aware that she and the marquess were standing, arrested and silent, in the midst of a throng of interested persons. It would never do for her to continue to stare stupidly into the gentleman's face, she thought dazedly, so she blinked her eyes and sought the words she had rehearsed.

When he saw her about to speak, his face changed as well and he said immediately, with a touch of rue, "Ah. But forgive me, for I fear I overstepped my bounds. I recall that you have not exactly been seeking my company of late. Please permit me to just leave my compliments and move on. I give you good evening, my lady."

He smiled again, and sketched another bow, but she stopped him by saying quickly, in an urgent, hushed whisper that held more than a touch of desperation, "Ah no! Please, my lord, stay a moment."

Since she had also reached out to touch his sleeve as she spoke, he remained still and kept his expression politely blank. He had no idea of what the lady sought to say to him, but however welcoming her smile had been, her past record caused him to fear the worst. When he had received the invitation to the Lord and Lady Benjamin's soiree, he accepted the fact that he must show his face here tonight. The Benjamins, he knew, were not in the habit of including him in any of their social schemes. But the hostess was the Viscount Talwin's elder daughter, and the Lady Leonora her sister, and no doubt the invitation had been arranged to smooth out the uncomfortable matter between them. He still had no idea of precisely what that matter was, or so much as a clue as to why the Lady Leonora should detest him as she did, but he had known that to refuse the invitation to make peace was to refuse to be a gentleman.

He had intended only to stop in for a momentary visit, had in fact come rather late so as to achieve the briefest possible encounter. But her face had caused him to forget that this was only a courtesy invitation that he had accepted for the sake of politeness. Now, the lady's silence caused him to remember, and he suddenly wondered if she were actually going to dress him down for his presumption. So he held his breath as she opened her lips to speak.

"I wrote the thing out," she said at once, her eyes

searching his face, "but I thought it would seem foolish to drag a paper from my purse and read you a prepared statement. Foolish and cowardly. But you see," she went on in low tones, dropping her gaze to his cravat, "every time I say a thing to you it gets garbled somehow. So I committed it to heart."

Now he wore a look of bafflement, so she closed her eyes so that his confusion would not daunt her. Even as he noted how thick and dark her lashes were as they lay against her cheeks, she spoke, and her voice was so hesitant and the words so obviously rehearsed, that for a moment he thought that he was attending to some sweet child at her bedside prayers, rather than to this impossibly haughty and beautiful young woman at a fashionable soiree.

"My dear Lord Severne," she began seriously, and at that, his lips twitched, for it did sound as though she were reading something she had printed out on the underside of her eyelids, "I know that in the past days it has appeared as though I were deliberately setting out to insult you. But I assure you that if I had done, I would have been far more successful and said far worse things to you, for I am not a fool, you know."

But then the lady frowned and opened her great dark eyes and fixed them on the marquess and said in deeply grieved tones, "I almost did it again there, didn't I?"

He only smiled and nodded at her. At that, at the sight of his barely contained amusement, she sighed. "Then I'll leave off the prepared text, for it goes on at some length, you see, and I begin to realize that the more I say, the more difficult I will make it for myself. Lord Severne," she said in a great rush, "I never meant to slight you. Indeed, I admire you very much and have always done, and as you'll recall, I even owe you a debt of old, so there was never any reason to bear you the slightest ill will. What I said at the bookseller's was all twisted about, for I was the one who was forever running into you and I didn't wish you to apologize to me for something that was never your fault. Your speech was lovely. In trying to emulate it, I fair hung myself though, didn't I?"

She never waited for his reply but only raced on to say, "But I've passed the last few years in the countryside, and have had little practice in social discourse, so I suppose that

accounts for it, though I well know that nothing can excuse
it. I wanted so very much to avoid discussion of your
divorce when we first met at my father's house that of
course I brought it up and then pretended I didn't and
made a cake of myself. Then I compounded the error at
the bookseller's. In my attempts to right matters, I continue
to wrong you. So I'll only say it the once: Please forgive
me."

He gazed at her thoughtfully and did not answer immediately. But before she could become too anxious, he
broke the silence by saying, softly, musingly, "Years ago,
when I was away at school, I had a schoolmaster who had
the reddest nose. Even redder than your exquisite gown,
my lady. And it was all pitted and pocked as well," he
continued blandly, as she looked at him curiously. "Since
the fellow dipped deeper into his port than his lessons each
night, he had grown himself a true grape-lover's probiscis.
One afternoon I was mentally tracing the topography of
that amazing beak in an effort to stay awake during one of
his interminable lectures on Greek history, when he called
upon me for an answer. I promptly said, as near as I can
recall, that the Greeks effected their entry into Troy by the
remarkable device of hiding in a wooden nose."

He paused to give his listener time to absorb his words,
and then waited for her to fail in her attempts to contain
her giggles. Then nodding, he went on, "After I recovered
from my caning, I went to him to apologize. Of course, I
then told him I had meant a wooden horse, since everyone
knows you can't look a gift nose in the mouth."

"But you were only a boy then," Leonora said when
she was able.

"Yes, and isn't it fortunate that you are not?" The marquess smiled. "For now I can ask you to stand up with me
for this dance. And if you were, I could not. You see? You
are not the only one who can become so entangled in your
words when you wish not to say something very badly,
that you do precisely that. Perhaps I ought to have written
it down so that I could get it right. But from the moment
that I first saw you this evening, my lady, I have been
yearning to ask only one question: May I have this waltz
with you?"

When she did not reply at once, but only gazed at him dazedly, he asked again, softly, "Do you waltz, my lady?"

"Yes," Leonora breathed, and then dared only add, "but not very well."

"Good," he said with satisfaction as he took her hand to lead her into the dance, "then you won't notice how maladroit I am. And since you are in such a penitent mood, you'll probably apologize when I tread on your toes. I *am* in luck."

He bore, she was always to remember, the clean scent of soap, with a faint overlay of the lavender which his valet had probably kept his linen in, and another crisp, distinctive scent very much like lemon mixed with sweet ferns. And his arms were very strong, and his body lean and strong as well, and she could not find the courage to look up into his eyes as he whirled her around the room. For in some fashion, there within the protective circle of his arms, she felt safe from the power in his gaze, much as a tree at the very heart of the storm is spared its greatest fury, even as the surrounding landscape is not.

He did not press her to speak, but only held her as close as was correct and looked down at the top of her dark head and saw her lashes fall over her downcast eyes, and not for one moment did he believe that she was merely watching her steps so as not to lose count with the rhythm of the dance. For she danced superbly, or was it he, he wondered, just as all the seated couples and dowagers and chaperones did, as they watched the dark, distinctive couple move gracefully across the floor. They were as suited in looks and motion as a "demmed fine pair of matched blacks stepping through their paces in the park on a Sunday morning," Lord Kilburn remarked bibulously to the lady's father as they observed the couple, before his comment caused him to wax sentimental about his own fine pair of chestnuts.

When that dance was done he led her into another. And he would never have relinquished her while the musicians still breathed if he hadn't caught the astonished eye of a watchful dowager just as he was about to draw the Lady Leonora forth with him into the dance once more. Then he recalled that to do so would be to declare his interest in terms he was not even thinking of, and though he was relieved that he had not committed a misstep, he was even more pleased that she had been willing to commit it with him. For, as he told himself as he stood quietly with the lady at the edge of the dance floor, he of all people did not believe in instant rapport, since he of all people could not dare to do so.

"We can't dance together again tonight, you know," he said softly then. "It just isn't done unless you're prepared to name the day."

Her head shot up at that, and as she gazed at him the color came and went in her cheeks. But as she still did not speak and would not meet his eye again, he said on the barest whisper, "And if you won't look at me or speak with me, perhaps you might be interested in stepping out into the garden with me. For there's only one other thing left to do now that doesn't require speech, that I know of, at least. And we must do something, or part company, and that I find I do not wish to do at all. Do you?"

He was smiling, she saw. And those pale plum-tinted lips were so near that she could almost feel his warm breath upon her cheek. It was the fact that she suddenly did feel it, and realized that he was drawing closer, that woke her from her inaction. This encounter, she realized, was very real, and not just another phantom one of the thousand or so that she had shared with a fantasy Severne during all the years she had passed alone in the countryside. And even as she knew that the touch of his lips would far surpass anything that she had imagined in the countless times she had envisioned just such a meeting with him, she knew that this, tonight, was too soon, too simple, and too good to possibly be true, in any fashion.

Her annoyance with herself brought her wits back, and so she told him immediately, adding,

"For you see, I feared that saying something to you might lead me into another ghastly misstatement. And we seemed to get on very well so long as I remained mute. But you're right, of course, so if you'll promise to understand my difficulty, and not flare up if I commit another gaffe, I think I'll do very nicely."

"Ah," he said sorrowfully, "then there's to be no rapturous lovemaking in the moonlight for us tonight, then?"

"No!" she said vehemently, a bit too vehemently, for the

merest hint of regret had come into her eye the moment after he had done speaking and she very much feared he had caught it, as of course he had.

"Very well," he sighed, "but I doubt there'll be anything further for me to forgive, for I've discovered that once you own up to such a difficulty, it generally tends to go away forever."

"You never mentioned noses to your schoolmaster again then, I take it?" she asked.

"Never again. Not so much as even a syllable of a word beginning with "no." As a matter of fact," he exclaimed, "I became the most charming scholar he had. It was my answering eternally in the affirmative to every one of his foolish comments which earned me my highest grades that year, I suspect," he said thoughtfully. "I do wish you had that same difficulty with me," he added fervently.

It was delicious, she thought, to be able to stand and banter words with him. For he was right, once having admitted to her inability to deal with him, she was as glib as she could wish to be. And she did wish to be facile, to be witty, to be clever with him. Any other way of conversing with him would have been too unnerving. He had a way of looking directly at the person he was speaking with, as if he could see into their souls through their eyes, and for all she knew, he could. It was far better to amuse and be amused by him, in turn. Shared laughter was a rare thing, and easier to cope with for her than any other sort of sharing that she could imagine herself involved in with him.

So they laughed together about their own foolishness, as the dancers formed their sets around them. and they made merry gossip when the musicians rested. He took her in to a late dinner as she laughed about an anecdote from his university days, and he had some trouble managing his dessert plate as she told him of the antics of a local farmer and his errant daughters.

They had asked Annabelle to join them, but she had declined. It was Severne who had spied Annabelle's hesitation as he had led Leonora to her chair. "Your little companion looks devastated at the way that I've dragooned you for the night," he whispered. "Is it that she particularly disapproves of me? Or could it be that she expects to join us?"

"But she is not my companion, she is a distant cousin, and newly arrived in Town, and I'm sure it is only that she doesn't know where else to sit," Leonora declared, clearly appalled, but only because she had so completely forgotten her relative's very existence. And thus the marquess had gone to ask Annabelle to join them. Annabelle refused the offer with a pretty show of confusion. Leonora might have felt more regretful had it not been for the fact that it was so strangely gratifying to see such an otherwise smooth fellow make such poor work of concealing his relief at Annabelle's decision. Still, Leonora had paused in their raillery to have a serious word with him about her relative.

"I?" he asked in such mock confusion that she had grinned despite herself. "Come, Lady Leonora, you have been in the countryside, to be sure, but not, I think, on another planet. I am the last person who might know some earnest, wealthy, decent young chap who is hanging out for a poor, virtuous, portionless wife. Now," he added consideringly, "I may be able to call a few 'friend' who are fortunate enough to be earnest, wealthy, and decent. And I might just be acquainted with someone who'd be interested in a female who was unfortunate enough to be poor and portionless. But that 'virtuous' you mentioned," he'd sighed, shaking his head in regret, "there's a formidable stumbling block."

Even in the midst of her laughter, a glance toward Annabelle, who sat mute and unbefriended, caused Leonora to be half inclined to go and fetch the girl to them despite her refusal, because it was Annabelle for whom she was supposed to be acting. It was Annabelle who had brought her to London in the first place, and thus it was Annabelle who had, in a very real fashion, brought this entire evening about.

But for this one night, she thought, oh just for this one night, she would be selfish and she would laugh and talk and enjoy herself to the fullest. Tomorrow she would doubtless repent having behaved in such giddy fashion, but then by tomorrow Severne would be able to report to her father that he had patched matters up between them, and by the next day he would doubtless have forgotten her as well.

For her father's sake the marquess might well mend fences, but she knew very well that for her father's sake he

would go no further. She might have tarnished her name
by association with notorious gentlemen five years before,
and she might well at the very heart of her heart not care if
she lost even more in an association with Severne now, but
he was still, whatever his history, a gentleman. And a
gentleman did not bring about the ruin of a friend's daughter. But that was a thought for tomorrow. For tonight, the
marquess sat across from her with a quizzical smile and
waited for her reply to some sally he had just made. She
laughed to cover her involuntary sigh. Tomorrow, she decided, would be Annabelle's. Tonight, then, was hers.

But it was the future that he spoke about with her, even
as she prepared to end the most delightful evening she
could remember ever having passed in her life. He stayed
her for one moment as she was about to join her father,
whom she had been surprised to see emerging at last from
the card room. She was astonished at how quickly the
night had come to a close, for now that she was aware of
the hour, she could see that her mother was already making her farewells to Sybil and Lord Benjamin, and a great
many of the other guests had already left. At least, she
thought with relief, Severne would think that she had only
forgotten the hour because as a relative of the hostess, she
was expected to stay until the last. But, as usual, he had
missed very little of her reaction.

"It seems wrong somehow to end a conversation only
because they threaten to close the room up around one,
doesn't it?" He laughed. "But for myself, I wouldn't mind
in the least if they threw a dust cover over me and blew out
the candles, so long as they allowed me to continue to stay
on here through the night with you."

Because this was a subject so near to her heart and what
he had said so very close to the truth, Leonora could say
nothing in reply. But after a pause, when he nodded as
though satisfied with what she didn't say equally as much
as he might have been with what she might have said, he
went on, casually, so entirely casually that she doubted
how easily he said it, "Do you go to Lord and Lady
Swanson's musicale next week, my lady?"

"Why yes," she said at once, immediately deciding to
cancel the impending headache that normally would have
prevented her from ever setting foot in the Swansons'

parlor to hear the youngest Swanson debutante grind up
sonatas in her pianoforte.

"Why that is excellent," he said, smiling down at her
with such warmth that she wondered how anyone could
ever have called that lean face austere or threatening. For
the amusement in those dark blue eyes and the power of
that quirked smile quite banished any hints of coldness or
cruelty from the angular planes of his face. No, she amended,
tearing her gaze away from those knowing eyes, not austere in the least, but yes, oh yes, she thought with a
panicky sort of delight, still threatening.

"But that is delightful," he said as he took her hand,
preparatory to taking his leave, "for I am promised there as
well. Perhaps you will care to sit with me?" he asked
quickly, as though he really did not care in the least. She
answered as quickly, so that he would not think it an
important decision, "Why yes, my lord."

He frowned, as though he had felt a momentary pain.

"Ah no. Please, at least Severne or better still, Joscelin,
or best of all Joss. 'My lord' is for strangers, and Severne
was for schoolmasters. You don't wish to remind me of
noses, do you? But then, with your family history, perhaps
you consider even Joscelin too fast. "Well," he said reasonably, "I note that your sister and Lord Benjamin seem the
most devoted couple, and yet I'll swear he's never told her his
Christian name." Before she could chide him for the liberties he took with her sister's idiosyncrasies, he went on
obliviously, "So, Joscelin, if you must, and Joss if you will,
but if you hedge it and name me Lord Joss at the Swansons',
I warn you, I won't reply at all. You understand," he said
suddenly, "this is all so that I may call you Leonora, as
your sister and mother do."

"I wish you would not," she said with the beginnings of
a laugh, but stopped when she saw how quickly his smile
vanished and how cold and still his features suddenly became. She rushed on to say, before he could note how
appalled she was both at his misjudgment of her intentions
and his instant reaction to it, "Not Leonora, please. Mama
and Sybil are very correct, you see. And Annabelle very
shy of informality. But father dubbed me Nell when I was
little, and so I shall always be to those who . . . know me
and my preferences," she finished, now horrified at how

close she had come to saying a wrong word, making a slip she had hoped she would never make again with him.

"As in Nell Gwyn," he observed as he relaxed. "Then I see their objection, although I don't share it."

"Just so," she said, relieved that the potentially disastrous moment had passed.

Then they made their good nights and he went home grateful that he had waited to hear out the rest of her sentence so that the misunderstanding had not remained. And she went home relieved that she had caught herself before she uttered the one disastrous word that would have ruined her night. Although it was an innocent enough word, it only being *love*. And they both looked forward to the musicale at the Swansons' stately townhouse.

The Swansons' evening, designed to provide music for friends and potential suitors for their daughter, was a disastrous failure for all but two in attendance. Miss Swanson botched her Bach and forgot half her country songs and then proceeded to thrash Haydn within an inch of his musical life. The gentlemen in attendance fled into sleep, the dowagers, who should have been used to such little musical murders, gossiped in low voices when they weren't wincing from the discordant notes, and the young people squirmed in their chairs as they had not since their earliest days in the nursery.

But Leonora sat beside the marquess. And when they could not speak it made no difference, for when they looked at each other the evening became uproarious. Though Leonora did not once laugh aloud (although she felt that effort nearly cost her life, even though she had never actually heard of anyone strangling on repressed hilarity), she could not remember a more enjoyable night. And so she told Joss when she could, and so he agreed that it was.

They seemed so much in agreement that night, though they had so little chance for words, that Leonora was surprised that she did not see him the next evening at the theater, for he had said that he admired Kean and she felt sure that he would have understood her reference meant that she was to be there. So she saw very little of Mr. Kean's splendid portrayal of Shylock, or any other goings-on upon the stage, she was so busy scanning the audience in hopes of catching sight of the marquess.

Nor did she see him at the dashing Lady Armintage's soiree at week's end, though he had, in passing, mentioned that he had also received an invitation to that crush. There were upward of two hundred at the affair, and Leonora looked at no person more than once, and scarcely attended to a word that was addressed to her, and behaved in such distracted fashion as she sought to catch a glimpse of the marquess's distinctive form that her mother said quite crossly that her sojourn in the country had turned her into a veritable bumpkin. And she did not find him at his London neighbors', the Pruits', dinner party the next night, although she could have sworn he'd said he would be there.

Only when at last she sank to her lowest ebb, and lost the battle with herself, and forced herself to go to Hatchard's, creeping veiled through the aisles of that great bookshop as though she were seeking pornographic literature instead of only a glimpse of him again, did she admit that she already knew. He was gone. And the years had changed nothing for her. For she couldn't cope with loss any better now than she had then, even if this time it were only the loss of something she had really never had. Even if it were only the loss of a particularly fond, recurrent dream.

SEVEN

There was very good reason for the fact that saints were so often martyred, Leonora thought on an afternoon a week to the day after she had met the Marquess of Severne at her sister's house. The way they inspired others with an irresistible urge to kill them precisely when they were at their saintliest, she reasoned, even as Annabelle sat and stared sadly at her, was likely only another integral part of their heavenly make-up, a divine device to ensure that they would not fail to get speedily to their just rewards.

For though only Annabelle seemed to know or care about what was bothering Leonora as the days went on, it seemed that only Annabelle continually irritated the sufferer. Oh Katie knew, for there was little that Katie did not know, but Katie's idea of helpfulness was only to sniff and say once if she said it a hundred times, that it stood to reason that a gentleman who threw over a wife would have even less thought of constancy to an acquaintance. But Annabelle, in her quiet fashion, seemed to genuinely grieve for her relative's disappointment, and was so tirelessly solicitous that she made Leonora feel even worse. Her constant presence was a constant embarrassing reminder that Leonora had forgotten her existence entirely when the marquess had but smiled upon her. Thus, her oversize, omnipresent concern soon wore on her cousin's already frayed nerves.

Leonora gave a guilty start when she realized that Annabelle had addressed a question to her even as she had been brooding about the murderous proclivities such unrelenting kindness provoked.

89

"I'm sorry, Belle," she said at once, "but what was that you said?"

"I only wondered, cousin," Annabelle said softly, "if you would like to read some more today? We were up to Act Three, Scene One, when we left off this morning, before luncheon."

"A very good idea," Leonora said with false enthusiasm. "Why don't you start, and I'll listen a while. My eyes are rather bleary and tired today. I believe they always appear to be so when the apple blossoms come into bloom."

Since the park was several blocks away, and nothing that remotely resembled a humble apple tree would be given leave to grow anywhere near the Talwins' town-house, Annabelle could be forgiven if she had raised a skeptical eyebrow at her cousin's excuse. But not one of her pale brows was lifted as she replied, sincerely.

"Ah no, cousin. I'm sorry you feel unwell, but I'm content to wait. I cannot read half so well as you do. My voice is too soft, I can't put such passion into my reading of those lines. I should much rather wait until you are feeling more the thing."

Annabelle, seated on a small gilt chair, sat erect, her hands folded neatly in her lap, and continued to stare at Leonora, who lay back, with one hand shading her eyes, against a gold velvet settee.

After a brief silence, Annabelle spoke again. "Then what should you like to do, cousin?" she asked hesitantly.

Leonora bit back the words, "Hang myself . . . or you," and finding herself amused at her unspoken reaction, realized that she was feeling rather better. One thing that Annabelle's constant mournful presence had done, she thought, was to help make her thoroughly sick of herself. If every patient got themselves an irritating doctor, Leonora decided, sitting up and looking around her with renewed interest, they might all make themselves well a great deal faster. She found herself wishing she had someone to share this idea of a medical advance with, and then, looking toward her relative's concerned face, she realized that her lack of humor was perhaps Annabelle's most singular lack of all. And then, now feeling very guilty as well as bored with herself and her languishing, she said briskly.

"But I'm not blind in the least. So I'll just go fetch down

the book and we shall read a bit, and then, why if I continue to rally, we'll go for a stroll."

"To Hatchard's?" Annabelle asked at once.

"Most definitely not!" Leonora declared as she rose from the settee, "for I've enough books to read to last me through a confinement, much less a simple headache."

Annabelle blushed at Leonora's remark, but got up from her chair with alacrity and was at the door to her cousin's chamber before Leonora had taken her first step forward.

"Oh no!" she cried softly, with something very much like horror in her expression. "You've been unwell, cousin. I cannot let you carry the book. I'll be back in a moment."

Leonora sank back on the settee and smiled to herself. There it was. For no one else would consider the fetching of a book, sizable though it was, as some kind of Promethean task. But Annabelle had stationed herself at her beck and call since she had declared herself feeling poorly, going so far as to offer her fresh handkerchiefs each time that she so much as frowned, and a fresh cup of tea each time she sighed. And even when she had clearly not been needed, she had seated herself a space apart and fixed her cousin with such a basilisk stare that Leonora could swear she could see her great blue eyes continuing to gaze at her in the night, long after Annabelle herself had crept off to her own room.

It was that, as well as her own resilient spirit, which caused Leonora to declare her period of mourning over. For it *had* been precisely that, she realized, as she awaited her cousin's return. She had been in at the death of an illusion, and it was only proper that she had grieved for it for a decent interval. It had not only been the demise of all her fantastic dreams of a knight errant (and as she laughed to herself now, there scarcely could have been a more errant knight than Severne), but it had also been the end of the last silly lingering hopes of her girlhood. But all things must die in their proper time, Leonora thought fiercely, and as she was three and twenty it was time and past it for her to be done with such idle foolishness.

So it was that when Annabelle came back to the room, slightly flushed and more than a little winded, burdened as she was by the huge volume she bore in both arms, Leonora greeted her immediately by saying,

"Now that I'm feeling more myself, Belle, we shall finally complete our arrangements for that little ball we were to give. You know, the one where we were going to show you off as a bit more than Lady Leonora's dutiful companion. Don't look so shaken, Belle, we talked about it at length when we were back in Lincolnshire."

Annabelle put the volume down on a tabletop and brushed down her dress, all the while never taking her great-eyed gaze from Leonora's face.

"But cousin," she breathed, "your mama . . . your sister . . . your papa . . ."

". . . will all think it is for me, and since they fear I'm past all prayers, they'll be thrilled to provide such a showcase for me. It won't be deception, Belle," she explained kindly, seeing the apparent fright in her cousin's face, "for I shall let them hose and shoe me, and ring me round with mayflowers as well, if they like. The only difference is that I shall insist we do the same for you, and that instead of seeking a life's mate for myself at the ball, I shall instead be alive to all possibilities for you. And who knows, my dear, if you capture the interest of someone that Papa fancies, perhaps he'll even arrange some sort of dower for you."

Leonora paused to muse on this new theme, but after her cousin's continuing silence she realized that in this, she might be building impossible expectations, so she hastened to add, "Never mind that. In any event, I have funds of my own, and trust me that I shall not let you go penniless to a husband."

"Oh cousin, how ever shall I repay you?" Annabelle whispered, so overcome by emotion that her little nose became pink-tipped, and her eyes began to grow red and fill up with what seemed to be shining pinkish tears.

"Good lord" Leonora cried, growing embarrassed, and feeling curiously rather like a great hulking huntsman in contrast to Annabelle's dainty white rabbit. "Don't weep, Belle. I thought you wished to read with me," she said at last, in an attempt to forestall any sobbing.

But that remark turned the trick, for Annabelle did no more than give a little shaky sigh and then she turned her complete attention to the book she'd brought in from her room. It was one of a set that rested in the library at home

in Whitewood Hall, but they were such particular favorites
of Annabelle's that when the family removed to London,
Leonora insisted they be brought with them. In fact, Annabelle took such pleasure in each book that Leonora insisted
the girl keep whatever volume they were currently reading
on hand in her room so that she would not have to
constantly dash downstairs to the library. It was not only
because the books were heavy, it was also because Leonora knew that her father was often to be found in that
room here in his townhouse, and believed the less reason
there was to cross his path, the better for them both.

All her past rancor was forgotten when Leonora saw her
cousin standing, looking down at the book in anticipation.
If it was often difficult for Leonora to remember that only a
year of age separated herself from her new-found relative,
times like these made that fact almost impossible to accept.
For how like a happy child Annabelle appeared at such
moments. And almost like a child, she was always attracted
to books with large and interesting pictures. She'd been embarrassed when Leonora had noted that about her when
she had first come, and had blushed and ducked her head
when her cousin had spied her interest in time-worn favorites that had been retired from her own nursery days.

But Leonora had only been amused that first week when
she'd seen Annabelle take refuge from a dreary day by
thumbing through her old copies of Mrs. Dorset's delightful
illustrated booklets. She had watched in silence as Annabelle perused *The History of Mother Twaddle and the
Marvelous Achievements of Her Son Jack,* with all its lavish
copperplates, remembering what a particular favorite it had
been of hers. When she had seen Annabelle engrossed in
her old copy of *Beauty and the Beast*, she had been
touched, remembering how her father had used to read
her a bit of the story each night from that handsome book
before nurse took her off to bed.

So it was not at all surprising that Leonora had hit upon
a happy idea even as Annabelle, becoming aware of her
presence, had blushed and stammered and tried to make
light of her literary tastes. Leonora had said not a word but
only stepped up on the ladder and taken down Volume
One of Mr. Boydell's beautiful edition of Shakespeare.
Annabelle's eyes had widened as Leonora had struggled to

lift the book down gently. For it was a formidable looking thing, all covered in fine floral-embossed black leathers with gilded endpapers, and it was fully a foot wide and more than that in height.

"There!" Leonora had announced triumphantly, opening the book at random, "Now this is one of my favorites and it has equally as many pretty pictures as any you've chosen. But here, you see, is a picture book for those who like to pretend to be adults. For these words are the match of any picture for beauty, but there is a great quantity of both."

Soon Annabelle had been gently leafing through the book, exclaiming over all the lovely page-high illustrations. And as she had been enchanted by one particularly amusing one from *Measure for Measure*, showing Falstaff with a great pair of antlers upon his head, it was only natural that Leonora should begin to read the pertinent passage aloud. Annabelle was enchanted, and Leonora soon secretly appalled when she discovered that the poor girl's education had been so haphazard that she knew very little Shakespeare at all.

Nothing would do but that Leonora must sit down and read more of the play, from the beginning. Annabelle sat by her side with her wide eyes shining, and listened, and looked at the amazing pictures by Mr. Fuseli and Mr. Smith and the other artists whose engravings filled the volume. When Leonora paused and asked her cousin to read, Annabelle took fright, and she only humbly asked that Leonora please go on, for she could never do half so well. And so the pattern was established for them.

On some rare occasions, when Leonora had done reading and insisted that Annabelle have a go, the girl would approach the book as though it had teeth and she'd begin to read the last bit that Leonora had just done with. But she'd speak it flat, the way a tone-deaf person might sing, without expression or conviction, as though she only just heard the sound of the words and not their meaning at all. Then a combination of the flattery implicit in the request, and Leonora's own love for the bard would cause her to pick up the book and read again, just as Annabelle had wished her to.

Now Leonora winced to see the page Annabelle's marker

fell open to, for they had left off in the midst of *Romeo and Juliet*. It had been a choice made over a week ago. As Leonora eyed the page unhappily, she devoutly wished she had opened the book to something different on that past, carefree morning, something that she could have coped with more easily now. Something less poignant, like *Hamlet* or *Othello*. Because she knew she would have been more at ease this morning with any emotion as simple as revenge or jealousy, than she could possibly presently be with love.

But she soldiered on to find herself becoming engrossed in the words, just as she always did, taking refuge from her own harsh reality in the equally cruel but safely fictional world, just as she always had.

"Ah dear," she sighed at length, closing the book, running a knuckle beneath her nose and sniffling rather loudly, "I daresay I'm the only person I know who actually weeps when Mercutio is slain. But he is one of my favorites. Everyone else saves their tears for Romeo or Juliet, of course, but not I. I *always* weep for Mercutio. He's such a lively, brave fellow, so full of jest and wit. 'Ask for me tomorrow and you shall find me a grave man,' he says, even as he's dying. How I always miss him when he's gone."

"But why," Annabelle asked softly, her clear white brow marred by a frown, "should anyone weep for either Romeo or Juliet?"

"I think," Leonora said after a pause, "that we will read on a bit more today, if you can bear to let your tea wait, that is?"

"Oh yes, thank you," Annabelle said happily, sitting up in her chair again. "I should like that very much, cousin."

Leonora would have been content to read on until her voice shredded away to a whisper, she was so anxious to enlighten Annabelle as to the fate of Master Shakespeare's star-crossed lovers, but after a long while she noted that whenever she paused for breath, she could hear her listener turning in her chair as though seeking a more comfortable perch. It was her own voice that bred the boredom, she thought, shutting up the book as sorrowfully as though she had betrayed a friend instead of a poet nearly two hundred years dead.

But no, she told Annabelle all the way down the central staircase as they went to tea, she did not mind in the least, and yes, she insisted, as they paused at the foot of the stairs, she had wanted the break in the reading, for it was her voice that had grown fatigued. She had begun to promise, upon pain of several forms of violent death, that they would pick up the book again the next day, when she became aware that her father had come out of his chambers and was saying farewell to a visitor.

The dashing gentleman was immediately introduced to the two young ladies, as was proper. He made his bows, confessed himself devastated that he was unlucky enough to be off to the Continent the next day, so soon after finally meeting two of the most exquisite females in London, and then, promising his eternal admiration, was gone through the doors. He had done no more or less than was strictly proper, but though Leonora looked after him with an amused smile, Annabelle hung her head as though she had been offered a carte blanche instead of common pleasantries.

But Leonora had no time to sigh over what a thorny path lay ahead of her in her plans for her cousin's social advancement, for her father hesitated, and then said,

"Ah . . . it's as well that you intercepted me as I was bidding Baron Stafford adieu, for I had a message for you and my appointment with young Nicholas today had put it right from my mind. But now that he's gone, if I might have a word?"

Leonora nodded, then put her head to the side and waited for him to continue. She noted that he hadn't prefaced his remark with "Nell," as he hadn't in years, and neither had he said "Leonora." But since he looked at her sadly and steadily, she assumed he meant he had a message for her and not for Annabelle. Indeed, she wondered if he had forgotten the girl's presence in his house entirely.

But then he said, "It was from Severne," and she stopped all her idle ruminations and only listened very closely.

"He's only just returned to Town, you know," her father explained. "Well, he had a sudden errand to run for me, I sent him off to the coast for a few days. But almost the first thing he told me when we met again this morning at his club, was that he regretted missing you at the theater far more than he missed seeing Kean there."

When his daughter said nothing but only stood still and watched his lips as though she were waiting for the next word to form there so that she could seize upon its meaning at the moment of its birth, he went on almost apologetically.

"I've spoken with your mama, and understand that you are thinking of having some sort of little ball here soon, not a formal presentation, of course, but something gala nonetheless. I hope you will invite Severne, Leonora. If for no other reason than as a favor to me. I know," he said quickly, although she scarcely breathed, much less tried to interrupt him, "that he doesn't enjoy the favor of your mama or sister, but I think him a decent fellow, even with that divorce action against his name. And he's done me a few services. You don't have to smother him in kindness for my sake, of course, but I would count it as a favor if his name were to be included in your list."

The viscountess was more than a little surprised when her daughter roused her from her afternoon nap to insist that they immediately begin to set up the very same ball which she had been urging her to finally put into motion, with a singular lack of success, since they had arrived in Town. And though she was quite naturally gratified by Leonora's compliance, she could not understand why the girl was on fire to get to the stationers to order up the invitations. Nor could she fathom why her daughter then passed more time worrying about how quickly the fellow could print up the formal summonses than she did about what she was to wear for the occasion, as any normal female might do. But the viscountess was not one to question why her miracles did not come gift-packaged. It was enough that the plans for the ball began to go forward more swiftly than she had ever dared hope.

Leonora lay down her pen and stretched out her arms and heaved a great sigh of relief. Then she applied the blotter and sanded the note and looked at it with great satisfaction. An observer, had there been one in the lady's chamber, might look to see how many other invitations she had just done with writing out. To judge from her outsize relief at the completion of the task, one might have expected to see half a hundred or more similar ones newly penned. Then, seeing her smirk and gloat as she eyed the single invitation upon her otherwise empty writing desk, the same observer would have to conclude that this particular invitation must have been addressed to no less a personage than His Royal Majesty himself. And from the look of dreamy pleasure upon her face, one would have to further conclude that His Highness had not only recovered from his incapacitating illness enough to promise her personally to attend, but that he had vowed to bring her his son and a dozen glass slippers as well.

But it wasn't any one of the Hanovers that Leonora was thinking of, it was only Severne, as it had only been Severne that she had thought of for the past days. They had met for the briefest times at a dinner, in the park, at a concert, and in passing, at the Opera. Now the Season was winding down, and now she would have her ball, and now she would have the chance to have him by her side for an entire evening. She could not have mistaken the warmth of his smiles, nor the look in his eyes, nor the caress in his voice, she thought as she rose and took her precious invitation with her to the door. But even if she had, she thought with glee, still she would have him by her side for an evening. And that would be more than she had dared dream of a week before, and more than she'd hoped for when she'd first come to Town.

She made her way down to the hall so that she might see the invitation, her ticket to one evening of realized fantasy, safely into a footman's care. Her father's secretary had addressed all the other cards, but this one, oh this was the one she had, for the sake of her own future restful nights, to see correctly and safely launched.

Leonora paused, with a sudden discomforted, sinking feeling, when she spied Annabelle standing irresolute in the hallway. But then she relaxed as she recalled that she had made no plans with her cousin this afternoon and so had nothing to feel guilty about. Indeed, she had been so in command of herself these past days, so pleased with her world and easy in her mind, that she had forgotten none of her obligations. She'd deliberately thrown Annabelle in the way of several eligible young gentlemen in their travels around Town, many of whose names already adorned the invitations that lay stacked upon the reception table awaiting the footmen who would bear them to their destinations.

"Where are you bound, Belle?" Leonora asked merrily as she shuffled through the pack of neatly sorted cards of invitation, nodding at some names, pursing her lips at the sight of others.

"Oh," Annabelle said as she untied her bonnet, "why I've only just returned, cousin."

"Lucky thing that," Leonora said absently, "for it's going to pour soon." Then, looking up, Leonora frowned. "Belle, I hope you didn't go sailing out of here without a maid or a footman in tow! You cannot go out alone here in Town, you know that."

"Oh," Annabelle said in a tiny, cramped voice, "I almost did, but then I remembered your warning. Then too, when I saw the sky so black I came right back after only a few steps out the door. So no harm was done. What is that you have there, cousin?"

"Trying to evade the subject, eh?" Leonora said with a great mock scowl. But her mood was as light as the afternoon sky was black with impending rain, so she soon laughed and said in a stage whisper, "Only *the* invitation. Well," she said more briskly, remembering from Annabelle's blank expression, that she did not care for the marquess and his reputation at all, "it's the Marquess of Severne's. Knowing that father specifically requested his presence, and knowing that Mama don't care for him by half, I decided to write the thing out myself to be sure of it's being done. And I've brought it here to be certain of it's being delivered in time."

And with a great show of nonchalance, Leonora tossed the invitation on top of the pile on the table. And then she absently stroked it into alignment with the neat stack beneath it with the tip of one finger, as she told her cousin she was going back to her room to pass the rest of the stormy afternoon in a little nap. She was greatly relieved to hear that her relative planned to catch up on some stitching in her own room, for Leonora had no desire to read aloud this afternoon, nor even to bear anyone else's company. But she also had no intention of sleeping this day away, not when her wakeful dreams were so exciting. She only

wanted time alone, so that she could sit and hug them to
herself.

Then she gave the invitation one last lingering look as
though she could scarcely bear to let it out of her sight, and
then she gave her cousin good day and fairly skipped up
the stairs to her room again. Annabelle, however, stood
quite quietly alone in the hall, even after her relative had
long disappeared from her view.

Leonora thought at first of the strong hand that would
take up the invitation, and the deep blue eyes that would
quickly scan the words she had written with her own hand,
and then of the curved mouth that she hoped would quirk
into a pleased smile of reminiscence and acceptance. Then,
as the rain began to drum upon her windows, she thought
of the evening to come, and then as the wind drove the
rain in rhythmic hisses against the panes, she closed her
eyes and slept as she had never thought to do.

So it was that she was startled and a little confused when
Katie burst into her rooms and said grimly, "You'd best
come downstairs, my lady, for there's the devil to pay."

EIGHT

He had been reading in his study but the lowering atmosphere of the day blunted his attention even as the steadily darkening sky dimmed the pages he'd been turning with increasingly less frequency. And instead of calling for the lamps to be lit, he'd closed his eyes several times and almost dozed off over his book just like any one of the old campaigners he'd recently left to their slumbers in the library at his club. But then his butler entered the room and cleared his throat until he saw the firelight reflected in the startled open eyes of his employer.

"My lord," his retainer said softly, "there's a message for you."

He blinked several times as he reacquainted himself with reality, for though he was never a sound sleeper, still the stolen half-sleep of day is more difficult to rouse oneself from than the normal slumbers of the night.

But when he took the slightly damp card from the butler's proffered silver salver, he blinked several more times as he read it. There must be some joke behind this, he thought as he raised his eyes to the butler's unreadable face.

"What's this, Wilkins?" he asked, a smile already hovering at his lips, for he expected some rare jest from one of his friends to follow and was pleased to discover some leavening of this dismal afternoon. In fact, he peered as best he could into the gloom beyond Wilkins' shoulders, expecting to see Torquay or some other companion hovering in the shadows of the rain-dimmed study, about to spring some delicious mischief upon him.

"A reply is awaited, my lord," the butler replied stonily enough, but with some trace of discomfort evinced by his barely perceptible shifting of his weight from one foot to another. It was a simple enough movement, and in any other mortal it would have been unremarkable, but in someone as highly trained as Wilkins, his employer realized, it was eloquent and a sign of high excitation or deep distress.

So the Marquess of Severne turned his full attention to the note and read it again, and reread it with a frown.

"A reply is awaited?" he asked, disbelieving.

This was singular, he thought, wide awake now, but as confused as if he were still in a tangle of dreams. For it was only an invitation to a ball to be given at the Viscount Talwin's house, in honor of his daughter Leonora. Although, he mused with a rare sensation of simple content, the word "only" was highly inappropriate in this case. The sight of her name written out on the card before him was as ironic as it was pleasing. For he had just been thinking of her. But to be fair, he mused, that could have truthfully been said of him at any time during this past week. Still, the pleasure of seeing the name that was on his mind written out before his eyes, and written, moreover, on an invitation that requested his presence at her side, was obscured by the fact that he hadn't the slightest idea of why the lady would ask for an immediate answer of him.

It wasn't done. Not that he believed that the lady was a conventional creature, but still she could not be gauche enough to invite a chap to a ball in her honor and let him know that she breathlessly awaited his answer. Yet again, he thought with the merest smile replacing his frown, she might do just such a shocking thing by way of apology for her past missayings. If she were serious, then he could never approve such rashness, it was just the sort of wild behavior that he'd originally been wary of in her. But since he could not believe that she could seriously be awaiting an answer from such as himself with any degree of impatience, he smiled more widely.

And because past circumstances had caused him to so thoroughly murder his self-esteem, and since he so very much did not wish to believe her guilty of any further misjudgments, he allowed himself to appreciate her jest more fully. For since jest it had to be, he decided, then jest it certainly was. He tapped the card upon his hand as he mused on how he could reply in kind.

The Marquess of Severne did not often delude himself. But like the frog in the children's tale who turned the cream to butter in his efforts to prevent drowning in the churn, precisely because he was unfamiliar with the process, he was able to accomplish what was absolutely necessary without becoming aware of how he did it. At this time the marquess would have been able to exonerate Lady Leonora from an accusation of murder, even if he entered a room to discover her fretting about how to pluck her favorite scissors from out of some unlucky fellow's breast. He had been a good agent in the service of his country because he had a uniquely cautious mind. If she had not precisely ruined him for future work with her father, still the Lady Leonora had unwittingly accomplished a singularly unusual thing herself. For if it had been a very long time since he had wanted to trust anyone quite so much, it had been far longer than that since he had wished to trust his judgment of any female at all.

It had been almost eight years in fact, he realized, remembering, as he stared at the invitation in his hand without seeing it, for his had been an early summer's wedding.

And it wasn't that he had trusted little Sylvia so much as that he had no reason in the world not to trust her. They had stood there, that bright morning those eight years ago, and they'd taken the congratulations of all the invited guests. And she'd smiled and laughed even as he had, and there wasn't a reason why they shouldn't have been the prettiest, happiest young newlyweds in all the land, just as each of the enchanted company had sworn that they were.

If not a love match, it could not be denied that they were a fair match. They both were young and comely. She had been blushing and fair as the sunrise and he, dark and bright as a starry night. She had always admired him, from the cradle upward, or so her papa had said to encourage his offer. He had known of her since he had been breached, for his brother had been promised to her at birth, but his brother had died shortly after that only happy event in his abbreviated life. And just as he had taken on his brother's title and tributes at his own birth, it had been easy enough to be convinced that she was another duty it was his privilege to shoulder for his phantom sibling. And they were both good, dutiful children, that no one could deny.

There were, however, some things that it was best not to refine upon, for those few things spoiled the symmetry of the picture of the newly married pair, and a few spiteful relatives or jealous neighbors whispered them in certain shadowy corners of the church's reception room. She was almost three and twenty, and he, two years her junior. She had never made a come-out, or even been to London. And though they had known of each other forever, if all the actual time they passed together were actually tabulated, it would total only a few days of concentrated time.

But then there are always sour wedding guests, her papa said laughingly, they are as much an ingredient for a successful reception as a pinch of salt is in the wedding cake. And there are always envious guests, his papa agreed, which was well, he said sagely, for too much jubilation attracts the spiteful fates. The two fathers certainly seemed to be in need of something to balance their outsize happiness, for they were in raptures all the day. For they had been friends since they had been in short coats, the two dukes, Burlington and Stroud, and it was exquisitely satisfying for them to see their boyhood dreams of becoming true family become reality at last as their children were joined as they had been pledged.

The fathers had a ready explanation for everything. And he, the young bridegroom, had believed it all, as why should he not? Her father said that she'd always loved him and wanted only him for her husband, and had known that he would, in time, make his offer. So naturally, there had been no point or need to her having a come-out, or going off to London town. And that made perfect sense.

And of course, she was older than he, hadn't she been betrothed to his late brother when they both had been in the cradle? In fact, after a conversation with his new father-in-law, and after a few cups of excellent punch at his reception, how sorry young Joscelin had felt for his long vanished brother, for to be deprived of life seemed this day to be no less pitiful than to have been denied the love of such an exquisite bride.

So if he did not precisely love his bride, why then what of it? his father had whispered, as the two had last words before the young groom prepared to go off on his wedding trip. It might be that they would be as blessed as he and his own wife had been, his father confided, to have been picked for each other as man and wife by their respective families, and to have eventually discovered that they would not have wanted to have chosen any other for themselves. The fathers had seen to it that young Joss had met with little Sylvia now and again through the years, but it was as well that their homes lay half a kingdom apart. In fact, her father and his would have deliberately kept them apart if that had not been the case, so that shared childhood would not breed a shared contempt when they grew up.

Seeing the happiness so large upon his father's face, Joss could not regret what he had done. He didn't love his bride, but he was young enough to expect that love would come to him as easily as every other good thing in his life had so far done. She was very pretty, and if she only giggled and looked at him with her great blue eyes large with awe and admiration each time they had met during the past weeks of their engagement, why then, that was as good as love to a lad scarcely past twenty. And if they'd never had any privacy, what with his father and her father and her family and her chaperone always hovering about the pair, why then, the ceremony today would remedy that. She certainly wasn't the only lady ever wooed and won in society's front window.

A gentle, thoughtful boy, brought up in the shadow of a dead brother who might have been anything his devoted parents would have wished, Joscelin Kidd was ready to take on his several responsibilities. He wed where they bade him just as soon as he finished with his schooling, even bypassing the obligatory grand tour that most young gentlemen were treated to, so as to ensure his parent's pleasure. It was never that he lacked heart or passion, it was only that he had been trained to put duty above all else.

Only weeks after his university days were done, he was outfitted for his wedding day. There was only one thing done for his own convenience, and even that, he convinced himself, was for the success of his marriage. He'd been careful to complete all aspects of his education before his wedding day. He'd paid a visit to a certain famous female in the university town who had seen to a different sort of lessons. It had been such an enlightening experience that he had gone back several times to other instructresses in the same abode to be certain that he had got the information right.

So as he rode off in the flower-decked carriage with his new wife, the young marquess had high expectations for his future. He smiled at his suddenly silent bride, and still warmed from the glow of the punch, seeing the light from the setting sun giving radiance to her sweet pale face, he believed in that moment that he might very well learn to love her, and even remain faithful to her, and beget several descendants with her as well. For today everything seemed equally unreal and possible.

Three days later, he brought her home to her papa and left her there forever, and rode down the wind to get home to his own father before the gossip did.

For on his wedding night, after dinner in the remote hunting lodge that his father-in-law had prepared for the honeymooning couple, Joss had sat and watched the fire for a long while after his bride had gone off with her maid to prepare for bed. Then he went to his own chamber. When he came to her door at last, in his dressing gown, it was only so that he could tell her not to be concerned. It was foolish and pointless, he believed, for them to try to consummate the marriage as yet, for they didn't know each other at all. And though he had been enormously successful with the professional young females he had obliged on even shorter acquaintance, he could not like the notion of visiting his own wife in the same spirit. They had their lives before them, he thought, there was no need to rush their fences. Having decided this, he felt it was a gesture Sylvia would appreciate, and then he discovered himself to be greatly relieved by it as well.

So he told her all his reasons, as she sat up in her bed in her demure white gown that did not totally conceal the mature swelling of her breast, her golden hair all around her, and her great blue eyes fixed upon his face in wonder. She looked so charming he almost regretted his decision, and he told her that as well as he came to sit beside her and take her hand. As she did not reply, he brushed his lips against her slightly blushed cheek and breathed in her light perfume and sighed as he said again that he felt love

was best attempted between lovers. At last she spoke, and
when she did it was to say in her small high voice,

"But aren't you going to get into bed, Joss? Mama and
Nurse said that you would, you know."

He repressed a smile at her naiveté, silently congratulat-
ing himself on his correct decision, and only told her again
how it was with them. For, he explained patiently, they had
only spoken of trivialities in the past when they had been
together, and now they had all these days and weeks to
become better acquainted, so that when they came together physically as man and wife, it would be a natural
thing that grew from their emotions for each other.

A slight frown marred her serenity and she said, a bit
petulantly, "Does that mean you will not? But Mama and
Nurse will be very angry, for they said that you would
come into my bed tonight, Joss."

He had never felt less like a lover, especially since she
had summoned up visions of her invisible but watchful
mama and nurse and their eventual absorption of every
detail of the union's consummation, and so he told her, with
a laugh to lighten his disapproval.

But now she frowned, and her lower lip began to jut out,
and she said peevishly, "Well, of course I shall tell them. I
must, Joss. For they want to be sure I've done everything
right so that you won't be angry with me. Now you must
come into bed with me, or they'll think I've been a naughty
girl. They told me what you must do," she said sadly, "and
they said that while you are at it, I mustn't mind. I must
only think of all the good things that they will give me if I
behave while you do it. And then," she said, brightening, "I
shall have a new white kitten when we get home. Just like
Puffin. Do you remember Puffin, Joss?" she asked eagerly.
"He grew up and then he began to scratch up all of
Mama's chairs, so he was sent to the barn. But I shall have
a new one if they are pleased with me."

He remembered Puffin. Suddenly he also remembered
that each time that they had met, she had been very shy of
speech, only asking him innocent questions, to which he
had been pleased to reply endlessly, to all her family's
approval. And when he had coaxed her to talk, it had
indeed been about Puffin, or her singing bird, or her new
musical box. He had thought her as unspoiled and ingenu-

ous as a child. Now he only sat and stared at her, and
hoped against all hope that he would soon see a twinkle
come into her eye, or her lips quiver at the jest that had
become too rich to contain a moment longer.

"But Sylvia," he said softly, "we scarcely know each
other. And if we are successful this night, there is every
possibility that we might become parents by spring. I scarcely
think it right that you take on the duties of mama before
you properly know the babe's papa."

He smiled at her then, a gentle smile of sweet reason
which softened his stern face and had always won him
hearts in his past. But the smile slowly slid off his lips as she
said, with just as much sweet reason,

"Oh Joss, I know that we may get a baby. We're married, silly, and married people get babies from the good
angels. But babies are very pretty and you can dress them
up like dolls. Anyway, Nurse will take care of them, she
promised. And I was promised a white kitten if I lie very still
for you tonight. And I promise I won't cry if it's nasty or if
you hurt me. I shall name it Snowy, for Papa named Puffin
and I didn't like that name at all."

He promised her a kitten. In the end, after speaking with
her until her eyelids grew heavy and the fire in the grate
died down, he understood it was no joke, he realized there
was nothing amusing in it at all. Then he promised her a
white kitten, and a singing bird that you could wind up,
and a new doll to take the place of the baby that he would
never give her. All so that she would not cry. For she was,
just as he had thought, a very sweet, ingenuous child. And
always had been, and always would be.

It had been the raging fever when she was five, her papa
told him as he paced and blustered in his study after
Joscelin had returned her to him. They had almost lost her
then, and were grateful even when they eventually discovered that though she had held on to her life, she'd lost the
ability to ever grow any older in her mind.

They had never thought to tell anyone, but then, the
duke had cried, wheeling about red-faced and angry to
confront his new son-in-law, they had never lied about it
either, had they? And there were worse things, he said,
downing another brandy, than having such a biddable
wife. And he'd had a chance to see for himself, hadn't he?

And *they'd* all grown used to it, and loved her so much that they honestly hadn't seen any problem. And, he muttered eventually, as much to himself as to the back of the young man who strode from his house, she was their only child, their only chance at posterity.

His own father had only grown very silent, and said, "Are you quite sure, Joss?"

"Yes, Father," he replied, and then, because he knew no other road but obedience to his parent, he said, while all his soul writhed, "I'm sorry. I expect I shouldn't have flown off like that. I'd no right to burden you with it. I'll go back with her, sir, but I won't, I cannot have children with her. I know that Burlington is right, and that she'll throw true and have normal babes, but I will not father them. I'll not get a child with child. I'm sorry, sir, but that I cannot do."

But all his father had done was to throw him a startled look and say, "Don't be a fool, Joss." Then he had ordered up his horse and had traveled to see his old friend, alone.

When he returned, he called his son to his study and told him of the divorce proceedings that would be set into motion.

"But the scandal, sir!" Joss had said, aghast at how casually his proud father was proposing that the family's good name be irrevocably stained.

"The name is nothing against your life," the duke said sternly. And during the next weeks and months and years, as the case dragged on, and more palms opened for more funds, and more mouths opened for more gossip, Joss came to understand that whatever else he had wrongly judged, at least he had not erred in his attempt to please his parent. For his father would not allow him to sacrifice himself on society's high altar. So his father-in-law was persuaded, by means Joscelin never discovered, to allow the dissolution of the marriage to go forth. But one sacrifice Joss insisted on, for his own honor's sake.

A writ of *A Vinculo Matrimonii* was filed for in his wife's name. And so that she would never have to testify, the Marquess of Severne swore before God and his peers that she was yet a virgin because he himself was impotent when he married her. Which was not precisely perjury, he told himself, for on that one night, at least, it had in a sense been true. Whatever it cost him to avow such a thing publicly, at least in this fashion she might have a chance to wed again. For she was, withal, undeniably a sweet child.

Of course, it made his life difficult. So difficult, in fact, that he left his home for the grand tour, after all. Only this tour was arranged by a spymaster. And it may well have saved his life. For it is no easy thing for a young man to attempt to prove repeatedly to a sniggering world that he was, whatever else he had claimed in courts of law, yet a whole man.

Even taking into account his extreme youth, the Marquess of Severne did not want to remember a great many things he had done during that time of his life. But he would never forget what the Viscount Talwin told him he thought of his actions the morning they had first met. As the older man persuaded him to drink his fifth cup of strong coffee, he had mused, looking about the parlor of the brothel where Joscelin spent so much time that he could almost be said to have taken up lodgings there, that he considered the marquess's way of life ". . . a valiant, amusing, but foolishly slow form of suicide." And just as Joscelin had begun smiling at the jest, Talwin had taken a pistol and laid it on the table by his cup.

"If you wish to do a clean job of it, so that your loved ones' mourning will be over and done with sooner, you may avail yourself of this," he had said, and as the shocked young man gazed at him, he had gone on casually, "but it seems a waste. Now, if you don't mind risking your life, I might have a need of you. But only if you care to gamble with your life. *Not*, I repeat, *never*, if you only wish to lose it. I have placed a neat suicide within your grasp with my pistol. But I offer you only the possibility of death, as well as honor, if you choose to live, and work with me."

Talwin had saved his life by giving it meaning, and now the gentleman he owed so much had a daughter who requested an immediate reply as to whether or no he would attend her ball as his guest. She was a female who would have caught his eye if her father had been the dustman. She had such pure physical beauty she made him eager as a boy to touch her, and her wit, spirit, and style delighted him as a man. She had attracted him so completely that he had been glad of the excuse her father gave him to leave Town on some trifling business before he committed the unpardonable crime of trying to attach her.

He'd borne the viscount no malice, even as he'd obeyed him, shrugged, sighed, and packed his bags. However much he may have desired furthering his interest with the lady, he could scarcely blame her father for placing her immediately beyond his reach. Because, of course, he knew that a divorced man was not a fit suitor for a decent, well-born young woman.

But was she so very decent, the marquess wondered? There had been that strange wildness that had forced her home her first Season. And that protracted stay in the countryside. Most peculiarly of all, it seemed that her father countenanced their continued relationship. For when he'd returned to Town, he had only mentioned Leonora once to her father, to end his own doubt, so that it could be out in the open and he could be warned away from her once and for all. But the viscount had only said, "Yes. We're giving a ball for her soon. She'll want you to attend, and I tell you, Joss, I should like to have you come as well. She's a determined young woman with her own mind. But in this case, lad, I think you should know that I shouldn't mind if she had you in mind."

But why should he not mind? the marquess thought, studying the invitation again, as though those simple, formal words might hold the answer for him. Did they think, for some reason he didn't know, that she could not do better for herself? Lord knew he didn't look for perfection in a female, as he didn't believe it existed in the human condition, and he certainly could not offer it in himself. But it had been his bad fortune that every female he had involved himself with, from his child bride to his cheats of mistresses, had been disastrously flawed. Still, with all his dark misgivings, he couldn't find the flaw in Lady Leonora . . . no . . . he couldn't perceive the flaw in Nell, he corrected himself with a smile. For he admired her entirely.

So when he at last looked up at his butler to give him a reply, he was grinning widely. He'd decided that for once, for this one time, he would believe again, despite all the good reasons why he knew he should not. Because he had discovered that he needed to believe again. Just as her father had given him a new cause for his life those years ago, now again, when he required it the most, another member of the viscount's family was gifting him with new hope for his future.

"I'll pen an instant reply," the marquess said, rising and going to his writing desk. As he wrote, he smiled to himself at the light phrasing he used, thinking of how she would appreciate it, and when he handed the note to Wilkins, he said, "Give this to the fellow, and a few pieces of silver as well. It can't have been pleasant, coming out on such a grim day, but he's lightened mine so much he deserves a reward."

Wilkins hesitated, and then said, "I shall give the note to the young woman, my lord. But I don't believe we ought to offer her money for her pains. I don't," he continued reprovingly, "consider it fitting."

"What young woman?" Joss said angrily, for one wild moment thinking that it might be Nell herself, out on some spree.

So when he first saw the drenched young female standing, shivering and dripping, in his hall, he felt a queer relief that it was not Nell, that she was not so abandoned as to take leave of her senses and defy society again. If she had done so, then she would have given the lie to all that he was beginning to feel for her and think of her. Were she to act the madcap sensation seeker now, she'd become just another example of his wretchedly mistaken notions of those of her sex. His relief, however, was short-lived.

"Why it's Lady Leonora's companion . . . cousin," Joss said at once. "Whatever are you doing here . . . Miss . . ."

"Greyling, Annabelle Greyling," the girl said through chattering teeth. "But my cousin insisted that you receive this note without delay. And you mustn't blame her, for it wasn't actually raining too hard when I left the house."

"By God, girl, where were your wits?" the marquess demanded after he sent his butler for a towel. "Why didn't you let the driver deliver it?" he asked angrily.

"Why," she said as if amazed at his question, "there wasn't one. It is not for someone like me to dare order up the coach. I walked, of course."

He stared at her and then asked with barely suppressed

irritation, "Why not just hand the note to a footman in any case? That's what they're paid for."

She hung her sodden head and said softly, regretfully, "But my lord, that is what I am paid for as well, in a manner of speaking. For I'm only a poor relation, and it's very kind of my relatives to take me in, so I must do my best to please my cousin."

He looked down at that white, drowned face, and held in a sigh for foolish young women who overdo good deeds.

"I'm sure she didn't need you to perform tasks that are man's work," he said as he watched the puddle widen about her feet. The girl was drenched. Her dress clung to her body in a fashion that might have been lascivious if it weren't so pitiable. The thin wet white muslin outlined her small high breasts, their nipples pointed and prominent from the cold, and beneath them he could see her ribs, and lower still the spiraling spiky curls of her pubic patch between her sharp pelvic bones was clearly delineated. But she was such a beaten, starveling thing that nothing but his pity was aroused for her. He gave a sound of annoyance and did not wait for Wilkins, who for all he knew was ironing the towel before he considered it fit to bring to his master. Instead, he threw one of his own capes over the shuddering girl.

"She said she wished the note to be delivered," the girl said softly, gazing up at him with fright in her wide, pale eyes now. "And there were no footmen available. I have learned not to disagree. Please your lordship," she said urgently, "just give me an answer to bring to her, and disregard the rest. Oh please," she asked on a rising note of fear.

He did not want to believe what he thought he heard that she left unsaid. And it was not until he had gotten her into his carriage over all her protestations that she should walk because her cousin would be furious that he had been inconvenienced, and they were almost at the Viscount Talwin's house, that he dared question her further.

Thus, when he saw the Lady Leonora as she stumbled down the stairs to her front hall, obviously awakened from an afternoon nap, brushing back her witch-wild, witch-black tresses from her rosy, sleep-warmed cheeks, he could

not contain his anger. Or his anger with himself at his own
desire for her.

He did look like the devil, Leonora thought dazedly, as
he stood before her and scorched her with fury playing like
lightning in those wild, deep blue eyes.

"Get her out of those clothes," he commanded, and
then remembering to whom he spoke, his lips quirked, but
not with the humor she'd lately been imagining, rather they
twisted into an expression of scorn that seemed to find a
corollary knot within her own stomach as he added, ". . .
my lady. For if you don't, you'll have a funeral here in a
week, rather than a ball."

He dripped rain from his high beaver hat and from his
cloak, but when Leonora tore her horrified gaze from his
grim features, she saw Annabelle at his side. The girl looked
shrunken, for she too was draped in a gentleman's volumi-
nous, streaming cloak. As Leonora watched, Annabelle unbut-
toned the cloak and took it off, handing it back to the marquess. And then she looked like some sort of drowned creature, almost a caricature of the picture of the drowned Ophelia
that she so admired in Leonora's book of Shakespeare.

Her fair hair lay like wet seaweed plastered to her cheeks
and neck, and her dress was so transparent with moisture
that it clung to her as though it were the covering for some
half-human, half-sea creature dragged up from the ocean
floor, and her lips and face were white with chill.

"But never fear," the marquess said coldly, never taking
his stare from Leonora's shocked face, "for she did your
bidding before she drowned. She delivered the invitation
that could not wait for a sunny day or a footman's leisure
. . . as you wished."

"Oh Annabelle!" Leonora cried. "How could you? Why
did you?"

And Annabelle, in a voice as lost and plaintive as a gull's
cry, but with her eyes as wide and empty as a shoreless
sea, said at once, "But cousin, what are you saying? I was
only trying to please you. It was what you wanted, wasn't it?"

Leonora met the marquess's blazing eyes and then without a word, looked away quickly to her poor drudge of a
cousin. It was then that the Marquess of Severne knew,
with a dreadful sick sense of triumph, that he had, at last,
found the flaw that he had been seeking and never wishing
to find.

NINE

It was undeniably an unfortunate trait, he thought as he handed his cloak to a footman, for a lady to be carelessly cruel to her underlings. And certainly, such behavior might well signify a certain overall callousness in the lady's personality. But then, there were worse things, the Marquess of Severne thought as he greeted his hostess. There were a great many far worse things he decided, as he took the Lady Leonora's hand, than simply being a bit thoughtless in one's dealings with some insipid, insignificant little chit that had been landed upon one by an act of charity by one's family.

As he spoke with her, and heard her delighted, musical laughter, he believed every unspoken word of his silent rationale. As he gazed down into her lovely face, so clearly filled with relief and joy at his presence at her ball, so pleased to reflect back his own smiles, it was easy for him to forget all his disappointment and chagrin with her. But it was a brief respite. No sooner did she reluctantly turn her sunny countenance away from him to greet her next guest, than the shadows of doubt descended again.

For after he'd greeted Talwin and the viscountess and Leonora, of course, there was Lady Sybil and Lord Benjamin, and then, standing a little apart from the rest as though even here she feared a sudden blow for her presumption, was Miss Annabelle Greyling. She, too, greeted him with an immediate look of sheerest joy. But that expression was as unfamiliar to her face as it was transient. In a second she had recovered herself and she wore a look of trepidation as she tentatively offered him her hand, as

115

though she believed her elation would bring punishment upon her.

When he left the reception line, the Marquess of Severne acknowledged several old acquaintances, accepted a glass of champagne from a wandering footman, and ignored the steady stares and sibilant hiss of whispers that his appearance always caused in the section reserved for the aged, infirm, and subservient: the seated dowagers, chaperones, and companions who were ranged against the wall.

"We were fashionably late," a familiar hoarse voice said at his side, "but you were, as always, fashionably later. How I wish I had your timing, my dear Severne. Now Regina, my only love, pray do not echo my sentiments, or my feelings shall be wounded. It is enough that this creature comes loping into the room like a wolf upon the flock and takes all the attention away from me, it would be more than I could bear if you were to begin to entertain fantasies about certain other rumored aspects of his excellent timing as well. I give you good evening, Joss. I knew you had arrived from the moment the wallflowers began to sound like a snakepit at feeding time."

"Good evening, Jason," the marquess replied lightly, giving his friend the Duke of Torquay his hand but not his attention.

For, "Good evening, Duchess," he breathed next, taking the lady's hand and never taking his eyes from her face. "You grow more lovely each time I see you. It's no wonder that this selfish gentleman keeps you mewed up in the countryside, safe from all of us desperately enamored fellows."

"Good evening, my lord," the Duchess of Torquay said, coloring up in a becoming fashion, as though she'd not had such a compliment in years, when there was little doubt that she was praised each time she took one graceful step into company. With her striking sunset-colored tresses, bright green eyes, and a form that was still shapely after bearing two sons, it might have been significant, the gossips thought with a little thrill, that the lean young marquess still stood gazing at her, seemingly eyeing her hungrily even as her husband looked on.

But experienced social lions shook their heads and turned away. They knew that this duke and his duchess were so unfashionable as to be constant to each other as the tide was to the shore. And the marquess would no sooner think of seducing the lady than he would his own sister, and he was no Byron. It was merely a game the trio played each time that they met, only a gentle sort of raillery between friends. Since each of them had difficulty in winning true friends, they perhaps each feared altering any rituals that had sprung up between them, lest they inadvertently give offense and lose the fellowship that was so rare and valuable to them. The marquess and the duke had earned their relative isolation from the highest sticklers in the ton. But the lovely lady who had wed the infamous duke had done nothing but wed him to ensure her name's becoming notorious.

To be absolutely fair, the marquess thought as he smiled down at the duchess, she had also done a few other things to have merited her notoriety. She'd been born beautiful, clever, and also penniless and of obscure parentage. Then she'd compounded her sins by constantly defending and praising her wicked husband. She'd also presented the widower duke with a fine brace of boys to accompany his motherless young daughter, and kept his interest so well that he'd never sought another female since the day they'd wed.

"I'm relieved and delighted to see you here," the marquess said to his friends when their customary spate of mocking mutual flattery was done with, "and surprised, as well. But evidently, when Talwin says 'Do this,' it is performed."

"It's not just because he is our great Caesar," the duke replied thoughtfully, "it is because we genuinely do enjoy seeing him. Of course, we cannot say as much for all his exalted company present tonight. But then, the duchess and I feel that we don't have the opportunity to do charity work often enough at home. So when we come to London, we believe it is our obligation to inject some interest and amusement into the miserable lives of the senile, otherwise addled and terminally bored. Hence, our attendance at such affairs as this one."

"I applaud your missionary zeal," the marquess said with an admirably serious expression, "and hope for your sake that we are far from the ears of any of his intimates."

"We are never far enough from the ears of Talwin's intimates," the duke replied with a smile, "that is what makes him the valuable sort of fellow that he is. But if it is his family that you're worrying about, we've had a word or two with Lady Leonora, and she, of all this lot, would we believe, agree with our attitude completely. A delightful child, a rare find, a credit to her papa, as well as a beauty, and still unattached. How odd."

"Not in the least," the duchess said softly, "not if she is looking for a true match for her heart, as well as her mind and her spirit."

The duke looked down at his wife fondly. "Such touching sentiment," he breathed. "That is one of the joys of marrying a much younger female," he confided sweetly to his friend. "And I get to read her fairy stories each night before bed as well."

But then, finding himself to be the object of a particularly fixed and speaking look from his duchess, he shrugged and said on a grin, "And now I must have this dance with her, for having had a dance alone, I must pay the piper. The tune will probably cost me another visit to the Pantheon Bazaar tomorrow. Oh Joss, take care what you say to Talwin's lovely daughter. Domesticity looks economical enough, but it costs dearly."

As the marquess watched the duke lead his duchess into the opening dance of the night, he thought that he might have reminded his friend that he, of all men, perhaps knew better than most just how high the price of marriage really was. But the duke was his friend and would doubtless have been pained to know he'd caused pain with a thoughtless remark. But then, Joscelin realized, the remark would not have bothered him one whit so much as a few weeks ago. Somehow, sensation was returning to his sensibilities, something was causing the ice about his emotions to crumble and sheer off. Then, seeing the bright glow of the pink of her gown as her father led her into the dance to open her ball, he believed that he saw a glimpse of some of the dark radiance that had begun to thaw him.

He watched her through the first set of dances, and once she looked across the room and saw him as well. The smile she gave him caused him to begin to take a pace forward before he caught himself, and he was relieved to see her

father's surprise when she missed her next step as well.
When the music ended, he made his way to her side. And
in the one pause between her answers to other admirers,
he bent close and said only, "Do not look for me to
partner you in the country dances, nor in the gavotte, nor
the minuet. I have only two opportunities to take you in
my arms, and be sure I shan't waste them. I'd like two of
the waltzes, please, my lady, the first and second ones. If
you would be so kind," he added humbly, like a small boy
ordering up pastries at a baker's shop.

Her radiant smile was her only answer before she turned
to reply to a question had been put to her by a frowning
Sir Phillip.

He took pleasure in observing her grace as she danced
past him, and might have passed the rest of the night thus,
for the duke was partnering his lady, his host was busy
putting his guests at their ease, and he himself was content
to only wait and watch until he could claim his turn with his
dark lady.

But he had not been successful at his chosen avocation
because he was oblivious to the world around him. So
much as he might have tried to deny the nagging thoughts
which nibbled at the edges of his attention with the sharp
rodent teeth that unpleasant recollections always employed,
he could not escape their insistency any more than he
could continue to pretend to ignore the long and watchful
gaze that had been fixed upon him since the dancing had
begun. He turned then, and opened his eyes and his mind
despite all his disinclination to do so. And so he admitted
Miss Greyling's unblinking stare even as he acknowledged
the unwelcome, unhappy thoughts which it brought to his
mind.

The moment that their eyes met, she, of course, dropped
her gaze and looked down at her slippers as though they
were of paramount interest to her. He made his way across
the room and took her hand.

Her fair hair was brushed into a lacy aura about her pale
face, and she was dressed in a blue gown the same soft
color as her wide eyes. But she only looked a bit neater
than usual to him. Her coloring was too bland, he thought,
for a man whose eyes had become transfixed by contrasts.
For who would trouble to stare at the shy blossom, no

matter how delicate, when he had a chance to watch a
dark and vivid dancing butterfly?

"Miss Greyling," he said as he made his bows, "I'm
happy to see that you've taken no harm from your ill-advised
excursion the other day."

"Oh no!" she said, her wide eyes opened wider than
usual, as though he'd proposed some shocking thing to her
instead of merely inquiring after her health. "I have a very
stout constitution, my lord. I didn't take chill at all. And so I
told my cousin originally. For I would not have undertaken
her errand if I had thought it would make me ill enough to
take me from her service for any length of time."

He didn't wish to hear the reply, but he knew he must
ask the next natural question of her.

"Oh no," she replied in her wisp of a voice, "Cousin
Leonora did not remain too angry with me for too long. As
you see, I am here tonight, and I have been allowed to
dance. In fact, she bade me promise a dance to both Mr.
Plumb and Mr. Wood."

As Mr. Plumb was so stout it was a wonder that he could
walk, much less dance, and Mr. Wood was a gentleman
who barely qualified for that title, being both ill-mannered
and clutch-fisted and old enough to be her grandfather as
well, the marquess felt his spirits sink. Was she being
punished for her disobedience, as she had told him that she
feared she might be? For she had begged him, all through
her shivering ride home, not to refine upon the matter too
much, since her cousin would be outraged that she had
mishandled it. She was only to have delivered the message
to him promptly, and bring his prompt reply in return. The
fact that he had discovered her acting as messenger and
then rescued her from a cloudburst was gallant, she'd
whispered, but might do more harm for her than the good
he so evidently wished her.

But he didn't wish her good, he thought now with a
surge of annoyance and guilt. Her presence reminded him
of all he realized he should care about, but didn't wish to
know. She was so fragile, vulnerable, and clearly beset
with woes that he knew he ought to be her natural protec-
tor. Yet she summoned up not so much gallantry in him
but rather a weird amalgamation of pity and impatience
with her. From the few hesitant things she'd let slip on that

ride home, he had learned that she was put-upon, deni-
grated, and treated like the lowliest lackey by her imperious
cousin. But lord, he thought with regret, that cousin was a
sparkling blend of wit and fire and passion, and she, by
contrast, a natural whey-faced victim. Which made it no
more excusable, he knew, only more difficult for him to
deal with.

At least, he thought with a trace of humor as he looked
down upon that delicate, bent, white neck, she didn't bear
the marks of a whip or cane upon the pitifully thin and
narrow shoulders that her fashionable gown left exposed.
Perhaps, he thought with a certain sense of weariness, they
starved her instead. But no, she'd said that she was well
housed and clothed and fed. What was it then that she had
said in that sad, flat tone that afternoon that had made him
take in his breath sharply? Ah yes, he remembered . . .
"My cousin is used to command. And it is not so difficult,
my lord, for me to obey. I have no other place to go. So
please, oh please, say nothing of this. For I should not
have mentioned it if you had not gotten so upset with me
for only doing her bidding."

He gazed at her downcast head and for a moment
wanted to tell her to pick up her head and look him in the
eye, speak up for herself and leave off her hesitant, shy,
and backward ways. No, he wanted to shout that at her.
But then, he grew ashamed of his bizarre reaction to the
poor chit's unhappy situation, and even more angry at his
own willingness to blind himself for the sake of a lovely
illusion. So as reparation for the insult he had not given,
and as penance from the crime he hadn't yet committed,
he asked her to stand up with him for a dance.

As the dancers were at the moment beginning a very
complex set, they waited by the sidelines for it to be ended.
As much to pass the time as to divert his own attention
from the lightly stepping, prettily swaying form of a familiar
figure in glowing pink upon the dance floor, he casually
asked the silent blond girl beside him.

"And do you enjoy your stay in London, Miss Greyling?
I imagine as a recent arrival, you must find it filled with
wonders."

"Indeed, who would not?" she answered quickly. "But

most of all, I enjoy the fact that there are so many booksellers convenient to my cousin's house."

"Ah, and are you a great reader, then?" he asked, not expecting more than a hesitant "Yes indeed" from her. So he was surprised, and not a little ashamed of himself, when she answered with more enthusiasm than she had so far shown.

"Yes, and what a joy it was to find that the viscount had such a full library. I am particularly fond of a set of Shakespeare that he has let me read. I know that there are a great many worthy new writers, but somehow I enjoy those works the most. How fortunate that my cousin likes to hear them read aloud on dull afternoons," she said with great satisfaction.

They had something to talk about then, as the long courtly dance wove on around them. For as he confessed to her, he often frequented the booksellers as well as book auctions, as it was his pleasure and pastime to constantly add to his own library. And he was pleased as well to discover that once they were off the subject of her own life and onto the topic of Shakespeare, she was so clear-spoken, confident, and coherent of thought as to be almost a different person.

"Yes," she concluded, noting the way he'd raised an eyebrow to something she had just said, while a small smile played about her lips in a manner that he suddenly discovered to be charmingly self-effacing, "I know it is odd to prefer Mercutio. But he is one of my favorites. I *always* weep for Mercutio, he's such a lively, brave fellow. For he's always so full of jest, and witty as well. 'Ask for me tomorrow and you shall find me a grave man,' he says, even as he is dying. How flat the rest of the play always is for me when he is gone from it." She ended her comments on a sigh as filled with emotion as though she had just seen brave Mercutio fall in front of her very eyes. He was amused and charmed by her perception and the depth of her sentiment.

"The Boydell edition, you say?" he asked with interest.

"Yes," she said, coloring up and then giving him a roguish smile. "I know what you are about to say. It is a picture book for those of us who like to pretend to be adults. But the words are the match of any picture for beauty, and there are a great quantity of both, so I confess, it is my favorite."

"Oh pray don't apologize," he said laughing. "We have a set at home as well. I particularly enjoy looking at the Fuseli engravings, and you?"

"Oh yes!" she said immediately, ducking her head in her old way again, but this time he found her gesture to be more explicable. Clearly, he thought in almost avuncular fashion, the chit was unused to the ways of gentlemen, and unused to being in society. But as this thought only led him again to wonder at how she was treated, he went on at once, as much to escape his own train of thought as to hear her response,

"Ah, you like illustrations then? But I have other delightful volumes at home with both words and pictures that match in their virtues. The particular ones I'm thinking of are rather odd little works, and I doubt that many people have read them, but I have always enjoyed the fellow's poetry. He's not so dashing as our Byron, there isn't a corsair in sight, but then, the fellow illustrates his books as well as writes them, and I should like to see George attempt that. He's also not a bit as well known by half, I'm afraid, but have you read any of this fellow William Blake?"

She gazed steadily and wordlessly at him, as though she were having some difficulty framing her answer. She paused, and looked around her as if in search of something. It was that hesitation that made him aware that the music had stopped and that new couples were coming to the dance floor. He smiled at how subtly she'd called that to his attention, and took her hand.

"Come then," he said. "We'll talk of Erato and her disciples later. Now's the time to exercise the arts of her sister Terpsichore, just as you've promised me you would."

The dance that began as they took their places was a waltz. Even as he took Annabelle Greyling into his arms, he realized his error. Looking past her head, he could see Leonora searching for him in the crowd at the sidelines. He could not explain a thing to her, neither could he now lead Miss Greyling off the floor, especially since he noted, as if from a distance, that she came into his arms with an audible little sigh, like a happy child coming to some reward. So he stepped into the dance with her.

Two surprising things diverted him from his worries about
how he'd explain his desertion to his hostess. They were
both things he became aware that his present partner
lacked: shyness and grace. He'd thought Miss Greyling
might be so leery of him that she'd stand, as many a young
miss might, at the furthest allowable perimeter of his cir-
cling arms. But he was astonished at how close she allowed
herself to drift to him. As they moved, now and again he
became aware that her breasts, or her hip, or some part of
her torso often grazed against him. Then too, he also
quickly realized that as she had little feeling for the dance
and less knowledge of the steps, her inadvertent bumping
against him must be just that.

If he smiled while he danced with Miss Greyling, it was at
the thought that this was becoming one of the few times in
his life when he could totally sympathize with his sister's
tales about put-upon young females and their overbearing
suitors. For all the while that he danced, his partner was
treating him to all sorts of intimate contact that he devoutly
wished would cease immediately. At last, he thought he
could understand why it was that females so often complained about a fellow's straying hands. Although he knew
that nothing dire could possibly result from all the intimate
contact he was experiencing, it was decidedly unpleasant
to have that sort of contact visited upon oneself when one
didn't expect or request it. And since Miss Greyling's hard,
sharp little breasts and keen hipbones did not stir him in
the least, it could be said that he suffered from their touch,
as well as from the lively fear that she might, in some
fashion, think it was he who engineered their constant
jostling.

It was the ludicrous thought of Miss Greyling as some
sort of notorious molester of innocent gentlemen that made
the marquess grin widely. It was the wide grin that Lady
Leonora first saw when she at last discovered where her
promised partner was. And it was that lost, utterly desolate
look upon her face that her cousin saw in that one moment
before Leonora remembered who and where she was, and
erased it, trying valiantly to replace it with an unconcerned
expression.

When the dance was done, the marquess bowed and
thanked Miss Greyling. She murmured the proper reply,

and then, as he was about to take his leave of her, she did an improper thing. She put her hand upon his arm, and said in a hurried undervoice filled with all the old hesitation and fear, "Please, oh please, my lord. Tell my cousin that you danced with me out of pity. Oh pity me, please, and tell her that, won't you? For I saw her face, and she is very angry with me. Very. Please?"

It was appalling to have her beg, but unthinkable for him to refuse. So he nodded, and when she dropped her hand from his arm, he turned to seek out her cousin. And saw her watching him and Miss Greyling with a hard, cold expression upon that damnably lovely face.

When he approached her, he was so very angry with her and yet so very attracted to her that he could find nothing to say but, "May I now have this dance, my lady?"

And she, her eyes glinting in the bright gas and candlelit room, only put up her head and gave him her hand and said, "Yes, of course," when she knew that she ought to have said, "No, damn you for a liar and you may not."

They danced in silence, each filled with growing rage with each other, each finding respite in the motion and the music from the growing desire that seemed perversely to be fed from that rage, motion, and music, just as all the moralists had warned when the wicked Vienna waltz had first swept society. Onlookers again murmured at their matched beauty and grace. The Duke and Duchess of Torquay glided by and nodded at the viscount, who was thoughtfully watching the couple. And Annabelle Greyling refused Sir Phillip a dance, all the while never taking her eyes from the pair.

When the music was ended, they simply stood and stared at each other until they noted that other dancers were forming for a set of country dances. Then the marquess led Lady Leonora to a corner, well away from the others. The company's attention then focused on Lord Bigelow, who was partnering Miss Turnbell in the set, for there were wagers laid that he was, at last, actually going to offer for her hand this night.

So it was relatively simple for the marquess to draw Lady Leonora from the room, out the partially opened side doors, and to the darkened garden behind the house. It was a star-struck night, bright even in contrast to the glittering ballroom. It seemed to Leonora as if some black and mottled cloth had been hastily flung across the daytime sky, so much brilliant light escaped through the myriad random holes in the fabric of the night. She noted, as though in a dream, that an unidentifiable intertwined couple started as they approached, and then seemed to melt away themselves into the deepest shadows, but she never hesitated as she went with him.

He still said nothing to her. Not even when they stopped and he looked down at her and took her head between his hands and gazed down through the star-struck darkness into her dark eyes. She did not speak as she searched his stern visage for some hint of his intentions, nor did she pull back when he lowered his head to hers, nor did she seek to escape his lips when they came to rest gently upon hers, and then less gently seemed to insist on some sort of answer to his next harsh unspoken demand. Though her heart thudded so loudly that she was sure it echoed throughout the garden, and pulsed so wildly that it galloped beneath his hand, still she sought to give him what he asked of her. So that when he was finally done, he held her closely, and they rested there against each other in a tense embrace that was never restful in any fashion.

When he spoke at last, it was in a low voice of shaken wonder. "Lord," he said, as he strained her silky hair through his fingers. "I find that I want to take you with me into the bushes, and to the devil with all the conventions of civilization. And that, with all that I know of you. What is it that you do to me, Nell?"

And since there hadn't been a word of affection, though she hadn't really expected protestations of love, and since she discovered that she understood what he meant so entirely that it shocked her to her soul, she only said, with an anger that threatened either to cause her to strike him or to drag his lips down to her own again,

"I do nothing. What is it that you want of me?"

"I'll swear that you know better than that, Nell," he breathed against her ear.

It was her own desire that she struggled against as much as she did against his callous use of it. For she knew that if he had breathed one word, just one word, of warmth toward her, or of respect for her, or of fascination with her as a person, she would have gone with him anywhere on the face of the globe itself, no matter what the consequences.

But tonight he was different toward her. He approached her as though he knew how she burned at his touch and did not care, and used her as though he expected her absolute compliance, which, she realized with sorrow, she had given him entirely. Yet even as he angered her, he drew her as he always did.

Catching at straws to save herself, she thought of how he'd deliberately sought to take her down a peg. He'd promised the first waltz to her, and even as she had waited for him, she'd seen him blissfully clutching poor, frail, foolish Annabelle to his breast. What manner of man was it that she'd lost her reason to? So she said at once, out of hurt, and out of great fright for what she continued to feel even though she was hurt,

'I know only that if I am not available, little Annabelle will do as well for you, won't she?"

"Is that what you're afraid of?" he asked incredulously. "You seriously compare yourself with that innocent little creature?"

Into that one sentence she read contempt for herself and the ease with which she had returned his embraces.

"You seriously think that I believe you either know or care about the difference between us?" she cried.

Into her reply he read the scorn she felt for her cousin's lowly position, as well as what she thought of the morals of gentlemen who had thrown over their legally wedded wives.

They stood and glowered at each other wordlessly. Until he pulled her into his arms and kissed her angrily and thoroughly even as she clung to him with the same furious despairing desire. When they parted, she put a hand to her lips and only stared at him. He stood and waited for her to offer him some sort of reaction, as though there was a thing which he was waiting to utter but could not just yet trust himself to say to her.

It was Annabelle's hesitant voice which cut into the loud silence that had fallen between them.

"Cousin?" she called in a wavering little voice as she came groping out into the darkened garden like a woman blinded by the starlight. "Cousin Leonora?"

"Oh lord help me," Leonora said through clenched

teeth, "what does she want now? Or did you promise her an interlude in the moonlight as well?" she asked him.

Whatever he had been about to say died on his lips. He gave Leonora one long, expressionless look, and then led her to her cousin. Then, bowing, he left her.

But he did not leave the party. In fact, it was noted and much commented upon that the Marquess of Severne danced with the obscure Miss Greyling once again after he had taken her in to dinner, and that he lingered over her hand for a very long time before he left the Talwins' ball.

TEN

"Kind of you to stop in to say good-bye," the viscount commented as he filled his visitor's glass once again.

But his guest put up one white hand as he was proffered the drink, "No, thank you," he said in his husky, whispering voice. "Since my duchess will have my head when I come late to tea, I shudder to think what other parts of my adorable person she would revenge herself upon if I came to her merry with drink as well."

The viscount had to turn his head as if he were wondering where to replace the glass in order to conceal his smile. Those few who knew the Duke of Torquay well were constantly amused at how often it pleased him still to say "my duchess," as though he were only lately wed, as though there were some special magic and merit in that proud possessive phrase. But he soon sobered, remembering how few of his own friends and acquaintances derived any sort of similar pleasure from mention of their own marriages. That thought quite naturally led him to the business at hand again.

"The invitation was kind," he said gruffly, "and unexpected. I hope it's not too much for you. I know how seldom you and your delightful duchess entertain."

The duke's lucent blue eyes lit up at that, as though he well knew how much his phraseology had amused his host, but he only said softly, wonderingly.

"You shock me, Talwin, you do. It's very bad ton, you know, to chide a fellow for inviting you to his home even as you accept his invitation. And we are not precisely hermits, you know, my duchess and I. No, no," he went on, ignoring the viscount's attempts to explain himself, "never think it is all for you. It isn't a bit of it, you know. We want to go home, you see. It's time. In the past weeks, we've seen every outstanding new piece of theater and heard every fresh scrap of enthralling gossip, and have managed to be noted by every person of unimportance in London and have doubtless contributed to half a hundred delectable new scurrilous tales ourselves. But we have to be careful of our reputations, you know, lest familiarity take the shine out of them. Well, even a circus must eventually move on. So the ton will just have to soldier on without us for a space, I fear. But perhaps Boney will take up the slack and liven things up for them by invading this summer," he mused.

"Surely you don't believe that Johnny-come-lately can replace you?" the viscount asked dryly.

"Jacques-come-lately actually, and no, though it's kind of you to fret over it," the duke answered agreeably. "But we must go anyway. Still, though we're headed home, we do hate to part company with our closest friends. So we hit upon the happy idea of having a festive week at Grace Hall for a few of our intimates. It's warm enough for picnic parties, and water parties, and riding parties—we can make ourselves dizzy with our revelries."

"Just what you most wished," the viscount said quietly.

After a pause, the golden-haired duke shifted in his chair and went on thoughtfully, "Well, you did mention that you could scarcely give another ball, and I don't wonder that Lord Benjamin and his good Sybil balk at it. It looks mightily odd for the Talwins and the Benjamins to suddenly become such demons for society. And then too, my duchess and I worry over Joss. We have few friends, perhaps that's why we take such undue care with those we do have. He's a very good man, and deserves better than he's gotten, and far better than what he appears to be going after. And though we don't understand or approve of what he seems to be doing at the moment, we're enormously fond of him. As we are of you. And of your delightful daughter, although we don't know her too well."

"Nor do I anymore," the viscount said sadly, "but I do want her happiness."

"It's happiness we're both after, then," the duke agreed, and then smiling widely as he rose from his chair, he said,

"Talwin, if you find it amazing that I am become such a paragon of husbandly virtues, you may find it even more delightful when I tell you that I know myself to be perhaps the most unlikely cupid that ever picked up a bow. And I can't ascertain," he mused, "whether it's my advancing age that has made me so interested in the trivial, or whether the wisdom that comes with age has shown me that affairs of the heart are what is essential, and all the rest, trivial."

As the viscount took his guest's hand, he said, "Whatever it is, Jason, I'm grateful for it. And so would Leonora be, I'm sure, if she knew of it. If I dared let her know of it, that is." He grinned. "Oh, and before I forget, I've some papers for you to look over," he said, turning to take some correspondence from a desk drawer. "There's some nastiness on the coast that I'd like your opinion on. It may well be trivial compared with my daughter's love life, but I think our Prince should know of it, and I'd like your recommendations. I doubt Boney's going to fly over Dover in a balloon, and don't think for a moment that he's about to tunnel under the channel neither, but I don't like the look of this report of beacons on the cliffs. See what you make of it," he said as he handed the letters to his friend.

"Of course," the duke said. "So then we shall see you, the viscountess, and the Lady Leonora as well, on the twenty-fifth?"

"Thank you, and gladly," the viscount replied.

The duke hesitated, and then asked, after a pause, "And her companion Miss Greyling accompanies you? I inquire," he said carefully, "because Joss specifically asked me if she were coming as well when he received his invitation."

"She accompanies us," the viscount said on a sigh. "How could she not at this point?"

"Do you have that report on her history as yet?" the duke asked casually, glancing down at the gloves he was donning.

"I only just sent for it, on your urging," the viscount answered glumly, "and I doubt it will come to anything."

"Oh doubtless," the duke said carelessly as he took up his walking stick and prepared to take his leave of the older gentleman, "but I'm nevertheless glad that you acted on my suggestion and are proceeding with the inquiries. I've always followed my impulses, and see what they have got me. *My duchess,*" he said on a laugh that was all self-aware, and aware of his friend's embarrassment even as he laughed with him.

The fair-haired young woman stood looking down silently at the great book which lay open upon the table. She ran one finger gently across the page, brushing it slowly across the picture which showed two little boys embracing while their spaniel played at their feet and a king looked down upon them.

"No," commented the dark-haired woman who'd come into the room behind her to look over her shoulder, "I'm never in the mood to follow the awful chronicles of Richard Crookback today, Belle. In fact, it's become so warm today, so summery actually, that I scarcely feel like doing any reading at all. Why don't you read on without me? Then later, if you like, we can go for a stroll. Or," Leonora said lightly, as she turned her back to her relative, "there may be no need for me at all, for you may be invited out for a ride again."

The chamber grew very still, and then Annabelle said in a soft, hurt, and puzzled voice, "Cousin, are you angry with me? For if you are," she said at once, when the lady spun around with a deep blush upon her cheek, "I'm sorry for it and want to know what I can do to remedy the situation. A carriage ride," she said quietly, "can never make up for my losing your esteem. Is it that you dislike my associating with the Marquess of Severne? But that is nothing, for I can always tell him no, next time that he calls. I can always refuse politely by telling him that my friendship with you, cousin, is of paramount importance to me."

Annabelle stared at Leonora expressionlessly, awaiting her answer. But it was a time in coming, for Leonora was too appalled for immediate speech. Trust Belle, was her first acutely embarrassed thought, to bring the thing out into the open without hesitation. The girl has no shadows in her soul, Leonora thought, feeling very small and crabbed. I am a spiritual troll compared to her. No wonder he has chosen her, she is light to my dark, in morality as well as looks. Who would not choose day over night? Then she rushed to say, almost stumbling over her words in her haste, "Oh, Belle, no never. Whatever gave you that impression?" while all the time she thought, I did, heaven help me, I do.

"But cousin," Belle replied, "you looked so very unhappy when I accepted his offer to ride around Town to see the sights the other day, that I almost refused him until you insisted that I go. And then, when he came to call that first time, you left the room at once, or at least you did when you realized that he had come to visit with me and not you. Then too, when we met at the Winthrop house that night, and he came to sit with me, you frowned and then left us. I do enjoy his company. He is amusing and very kind, and handsome, too, but I owe you so much that I would forego his company for you if you wish. You have but to ask me to do so. I cannot say," Annabelle went on, cocking her head to one side in thoughtful consideration, "that he would then take up with you. But I could ask that he do so, for my sake, if you wish me to."

Had any other female of her acquaintance but Annabelle said what she just had, Leonora felt that she would without doubt have slapped the chit soundly across the face, or even done more complete mayhem with whatever stray objects were at hand. Or if not that, she thought sadly, remembering that her passions, while strong, were usually ridden and reined by strong conventions, she would have at the very least dressed her down and slammed from the room.

But Annabelle, she sighed, Annabelle had no malice in her. Just as it had turned out to be impetuous rather than presumptuous of her to take matters into her own hands and deliver Severne's invitation personally, so too, what might appear to be vicious behavior, this gloating over Severne's apparent courtship, was only the innocent reportage and observation of a child. Or a childlike adult, she corrected herself.

She gazed at Annabelle sadly as she tried to frame a politic answer for her. What was it, she wondered, as she had since Severne had taken up with Belle, that attracted him to her? If she herself were a gentleman, Leonora thought, surely she would not wish to make love to a female who behaved more like a girl than a woman. But

then, she admitted that she hadn't the sightest idea of what
gentlemen truly preferred in their choice of females.

She'd once believed, hadn't she, she remembered, that
her father would prefer to remain faithful to his wedded
wife rather than taking up with sluttish baggages that he
encountered in public parks. Although, Leonora thought
again, as she had in her recent uncomfortable nights, she
could see how a man might be drawn to a vulgar tart like
the one she'd seen her father embrace far more readily
than she could understand interest in such a meek, obedi-
ent creature as Annabelle, no matter how lovely she appeared to be. But then, she decided, bizarre as it seemed,
perhaps the gentlemen wanted Annabelles for their wives
so that they could then go out and betray them with
females who were low harlots.

And if so, why then it might well have been her whole-
hearted response to his kiss, she thought wearily, that had
convinced him to begin his courtship of Annabelle. He
might have thought her an experienced cheat, he might
have had a wife who cuckolded him, or he might have
thought her delightful to dally with but nothing more, and
had known that one did not trifle with a viscount's daughter.

It might have been a dozen other things she could not,
and would never know about. But Talwin's daughter had
certain obligations to her position and to herself. So Leonora drew herself up and steadied herself.

"Please say nothing to the marquess," Leonora said
humbly, "for though it's true that I once liked him, I cannot
say that I know him at all, not really. And I think that if he
prefers your company to mine, you certainly ought to allow
him to continue to see you. He would be a wonderful
catch for you. And that is what our trip to Town was all
about originally, wasn't it?"

"Yes," said Annabelle, "but I thought you'd forgotten
that."

Leonora looked at her sharply, but the fair-haired girl's
expression was bland and she only trailed her finger over
the opened page again.

"You said you did not wish to read Richard Crookback
today, as though it were an unpleasant chore. Is it? And if it
is, why is such a work included in such an entertaining
volume?" Annabelle asked suddenly, leaving off the other

conversation with the unconcern of a child. And so, Leonora, glad to forget all her painful ruminations, gave her a brief lecture on King Richard the Third, which became so interesting to her that it was not long before she was reading aloud from the book after all.

She looked up at her audience just about the time that Richard was beginning his treacherous courtship of the Lady Anne. Annabelle was patting at the dust motes that were set spinning around her like golden fairy dust in the stream of light from the window each time one of the great pages of the book was turned. Leonora dropped the smooth and unctuous voice that she had adopted for her characterization of Richard, and said simply, as she closed the book, setting up a draft that caused the golden specks to whirl in a blizzard of activity, "It really needs a man's voice to do it justice. I don't blame you in the least for losing patience. Richard is such a lovely villain I'm sure I'd enjoy his company more than I would most heroes'. But a woman reading his lines gives him a dimension I'm sure was not intended, for I don't believe that a woman could ever be so entirely evil, so wholeheartedly concerned with only her own advancement, so brutally self-interested as to blithely destroy all those closest to her. Richard is gentle here, to be sure, for he must be so, but it is a particularly seductive, dangerous gentleness, and I do think a man ought read the part. Then again, men did act all the parts when it was first performed, and I often wonder what other connotations the roles had then."

Annabelle did not answer. She only looked steadily at Leonora. In those moments, when she was fixed with her relative's wide, unblinking stare, Leonora often felt uncomfortable, for she liked a face that gave one a clue as to what was beneath.

"I think you are right," Annabelle said at last, "and it is too sunny a day for Richard Crookback. The other day, when we were at Lady Sybil's tea, one of the ladies mentioned another poet, one I didn't know about. I wanted to ask you about him immediately, but I didn't wish to interrupt your conversation then. For you know everything, I think, cousin."

"Oh well, oh really," Leonora said, speechless because she was so unexpectedly flattered and pleased. For if she had lost everything else, it was good to be reminded that there were some things that fate and fickle gentlemen could never rob her of, that there were some things that were entirely her own: her wit and her erudition.

So she turned an interested face to Annabelle, who said, furrowing her brow in remembrance, "The lady asked me what I thought of William Blake, and I didn't reply, for I'm sure I've never heard of him. Have you?"

"Why how delightful!" Leonora cried. "But who was she? The lady that asked, I mean. Because I've always loved his little books, and I've never met another who had enjoyed him, aside from my father, that is to say, and I should love to know her."

"I can't recall," Annabelle said apologetically. "There were so many ladies there, and all talking at once, I recall."

"Well, no matter," Leonora said happily, "for I've not read him in years, and just the thought of his work cheers me. He's a very simple fellow, Belle, and his poems are so slight that you think them childish until you begin to think about them, and then you realize that like a child's statement, they have all the wisdom in the world within them, only not done up in all the flowery trappings that some of our poets like to use. And he illustrates his books as well. My father keeps his copies in the library downstairs, I believe. Come, let's have a look at them."

There were two volumes in the library and Leonora first read some selections from one, and then gave the book to Annabelle to scan while she picked up the other.

"It's the contrast," she said, engrossed in riffling through the little book, "the marked contrast between the two books, between innocence and experience, just as he says, that I find most interesting. For example, you recall that one about the lamb? Well, here is one about a tiger, and—"

But she wasn't fated to finish her statement, for a faint background noise she hadn't attended to before resolved itself into the undeniable sound of a throat being carefully cleared. When she looked up at the second impatient, "A-hum," it was to see the butler awaiting her attention.

"The Marquess of Severne has come to call, my lady," he announced, "and your father wishes you to join him in the little salon, if you would."

"Oh," said Leonora, as she snapped closed the book and lay it absently upon a library table. "Then you must go to him, Belle. Go on, I'll just stay and read for a bit," she added, looking about her awkwardly, and then gesturing stiffly to the rows of books upon the wall.

"But cousin," Annabelle said with something very much like amusement, "it is not my father who requests my presence."

"But it is you that Severne has doubtless come to see," Leonora stated bluntly.

"Yes," Annabelle said reasonably. "So then, I think we must both go."

He must have been surprised that she had come, Leonora thought, for he looked hard at her the moment she entered the room. She was perversely glad that she had worn a bright gypsy crimson gown this afternoon, for it did make her seem more blatant than Annabelle, in her soft dawnblush pink frock. And if that is what he thinks me, she told herself, lifting her head, then that is what I shall appear to be. He had come to call for Annabelle three times in the past weeks, twice to pay proper morning visits, once to take her for a sedate ride about Town, and he had monopolized her conversation at two social affairs. And all the while he had studiously ignored herself. Then let him have his milk-white maid, Leonora thought, and when in time he begins to lust for his spicier wicked ladies, I shall be glad that he can never have me.

They made their curtsies, and they made their bows, and the viscount made polite chatter for the four of them. It was he who took on the major burden of the conversation since his wife was occupied with her afternoon nap, and neither young woman seemed about to speak, and the marquess appeared for once to be uneasy. He answered his host readily enough, and commented sagaciously about the weather, just as he ought, but his face was still, and he never turned his head in Leonora's direction again. In fact, she thought with a spurt of anger, she'd like to have fired off a pistol over her head just to see him startle and stare at the one place where she knew he would not.

Since he was not observing her, she had time and to spare to covertly gaze at him. He wore a dark gray jacket over his white shirt and silver and gray waistcoat, his breeches were a dark gray, and his high black hessians gleamed. He seemed rapier keen, even leaner than she'd remembered, and when he smiled at something her father said, she saw the angular planes of his face shift, and when he looked at her cousin, she saw the brilliance of his eyes soften.

"Oh would you, cousin?" Annabelle asked.

"Well, I certainly can't offer objection to Severne's plan to take you ladies in his new barouche for a short spin about the park," her father said at once when Leonora did not reply. She understood again why it was that he was considered such a perfect diplomat, for she'd been so busy watching the marquess, she'd never heard the conversation at all. Then she had time to gather her wits as her father added, "Of course, as it's an open carriage, there can't be any gossip about such a jaunt, and then too, from the way he's been going on about those new cattle of his, I doubt he'd be interested in anything else, even if it was to be a ride at midnight in a carriage with black curtains over each window."

After the marquess had done denying such a lack of appreciation for beautiful ladies, Leonora said coldly, carefully, and concisely, "Ah, too bad. For I've a mountain of correspondence to catch up with. But Annabelle, you go, please do."

As Annabelle looked to her cousin, with a great deal of shy hesitation, Severne took up the fair girl's hand and echoed, with great warmth in his rich, deep voice, "Oh yes, Annabelle, you go, please do."

Even as Annabelle dropped her lashes over her eyes and flushed prettily and hung her head, Leonora looked at their linked hands and took in one steadying breath. For she noted that it was a strong and slender hand that captured Annabelle's. And when he raised it, to bear Annabelle's hand to his lips, his soft white cuff fell back, exposing his wrists. Then she saw that his wristbones stood out prominently, almost like those of a boy who'd come into his growth too fast. That one unexpected glimpse of him made her remember that it had not been so very long since he'd left his boyhood behind and that he was, no matter how aloof and mannered he appeared to be, yet vulnerable, yet very human.

Leonora saw him reluctantly loose his grip from her

cousin and, still gazing at his hand, she remembered its touch upon her in the darkened garden. Then she thought, just as a gentleman she'd recently read about had thought of his lady, and with fully as much longing, "O that I were a glove upon that hand . . . ," before she recalled herself and was shocked and sickened to her soul by her own unlooked for, uncalled for, and passionate reaction.

Leonora was very glad to see him assist Annabelle up to his carriage's high seat, and she did not need to pretend her smile of relief as she waved good-bye to the pair when the equipage went off down the street. Only then, only when she let the window curtains fall back into place, did she hear her father's voice.

"We've been invited to Torquay's house for a week in the country. Severne's to come as well."

"I don't wish to go," she said stonily, not looking at her father, but only gazing empty-eyed at the empty street.

"I want to go," her father said softly, "and he's asked if Annabelle may come. I'm afraid," he said, pausing to note how her eyes closed momentarily, as though in pain, "you must come as well. It will not look right if you do not."

"The devil to what it looks like!" she blurted, opening her eyes to give him a look of blazing rage and sorrow.

His own eyes held anticipation as he suddenly recognized the spirited girl who stood before him. She stared at him and said in a rush, as though the words sprang unbidden from her lips, "Father! Father, I . . ." And then she looked more closely at him. Her shoulders slumped and she said quietly and patiently, on a long exhalation, "Yes. Yes, of course you are right."

He began to explain the arrangements that had been made for the visit, while all the time she stared out the window. And he thought, with a rising of his own spirits, that for the first time in a long time, he'd almost had his daughter Nell back with him again.

"Thank you very much," Annabelle said quietly, "for asking for me when the viscount was with us. My cousin could not help but to allow me to come when I was asked when he was present. Not," she said suddenly, putting her gloved hand to her lips in horror, "that she would have denied me the treat, of course. Please forget what I said, my lord, oh please do."

"Consider it forgotten," the marquess said in subdued tones, never taking his eyes from the street in front of him, though his horses handled as easily as trained animals from Astley's circus. But then, he had not said very much to her, nor looked at her at all since they'd driven away from the viscount's house.

"I was glad that you asked me to accompany you to-day," Annabelle said at length when he did not attempt to speak with her again. "The morning had been so lovely, and yet I could not leave the house to take in the air. My cousin needed my services, of course, and that always, must always," she corrected herself, "come first with me. But you mustn't think I've been dull. Fortunately, I had some time and so entertained myself by reading last night. And again fortunately, you came to ask us out today."

"And what have you been reading?" the marquess asked dutifully as they approached the park.

"Rereading Richard Crookback," she said with more enthusiasm, in the spirited fashion she often employed when discussing books, he noted.

"Richard Crookback?" he asked with a smile, glancing over toward her. "Whoever composed that work?"

"Why Master Shakespeare," she said a bit uncertainly.

"Ah yes," he breathed, smiling at her, "*that* Crookback. And what was a nice child like you doing up all night with a villain like that?"

"Why," she replied with a pretty show of her teeth, "I must confess that I prefer his company to many heroes'. He's so dangerously seductive, you know."

He laughed aloud at that, and glanced at her as she sat beside him, so simple and neat, this poor oppressed child, with her unexpected depths.

They chatted about Shakespeare's immoral king as they drove through the gates of the park, and passers-by smiled at the charming couple the dark-haired gentleman and the pretty fair lady made, until they saw that it was Severne and some unknown young female, and then they either pitied or envied her heartily, depending on their age and gender.

"Then," the marquess said as he relaxed and let the

horses step lightly down the park drives, since there was no
room or need for them to hurry, "I can understand why
you took up my invitation. It's only natural, since you have
such a fondness for wicked fellows. But you must certainly
have a care for old Iago then as well, confess it, don't
you?"

She grew very still and then said softly, "But I haven't
met him, so I could not say."

He laughed at the queer, quaint way she related to
literary characters, before he saw the quick look of rue
that she shot toward him. Poor victimized child, he thought,
of course she would find such fictional company as real as
life, considering her lonely circumstances. But before he
could gloss over his laughter, she spoke up again.

"But I did spend some time with your friend Mr. Blake,"
she said.

"And did you two get along well?" he asked.

"Oh yes!" she enthused in her breathy little voice, becoming animated again. "But we are old friends. I have
always loved his poems. They cheer me. They seem so
simple, slight, and almost childish at first, until you begin to
think about them, and then you realize that like a child's
statement, they have all the wisdom in the world in them,
only not done up in all the flowery trappings some of our
poets like to use."

" 'Little lamb, who made thee?' " he quoted softly, gazing at her, this odd, sad little Sit-by-the-cinders with her
unexpected wealth of emotions and sensitivity, and taste in
literature which so neatly matched his own.

And seeing the particularly fond and warming gaze he
bent upon her, she ducked her head before she looked up
straight into his knowing eyes, and gave him back a knowing smile.

ELEVEN

The anteroom was so magnificent, Leonora rationalized, that anyone might understand why a person might be reluctant to leave it. Certainly, she thought glumly, as she paced its salmon- and green-, gray- and gold-patterned mosaic tile floor, a guest might be expected to admire it, and so would not be considered to be sulking or hiding, or even brooding if she were discovered hovering here alone, rather than being out on the wide lawns in the bright sunlight with all the rest of the company.

In fact, she remembered distinctly that when Annabelle first stepped into Grace Hall, she'd stopped in her tracks, disregarding her host and hostess, and stared about as if she were entering the kingdom of heaven for the first time, and not merely a duke's country house. Although, to be fair, Leonora thought, gazing about the huge anteroom with its gold-figured canopied ceiling supported by marble columns, there was nothing "mere" about the Torquay home, not in any nook or cranny, or for all she knew, mousehole of it.

The thought of a great gilded ducal mousehole cheered her a bit, and she wore a slight smile as she slowly paced across the inlaid floor again, just as she'd done only moments before. Her own home was stately and she'd always cherished a tiny but steady flame of pride in its comforts and long history of service to family and country, but, she thought, there was no question that it wasn't a patch on this place.

It wasn't only the size and luxury of Grace Hall which struck a visitor, it was the warmth that seemed to permeate every inch of it. There was such happiness here that it was almost a tangible thing, a light that supplemented the spring sunshine that shone through the long windows and a glow to increase the effect of the fires laid in the many hearths to take the chill from the long cool evenings. If there were few homes in the land with the splendor of Grace Hall, there were doubtless fewer still that held such a merry, loving couple as its duke and duchess.

Leonora had never seen the duke do more than touch his lovely wife's white hand in public, nor had she seen the duchess more than smile wistfully at her golden-haired husband when he wasn't looking. But still they managed to convey their mutual adoration far better than had all the titled lords and ladies Leonora had ever seen subtly fondling each other in all manner of places in exhibition of their infatuation. They showed their devotion even better, Leonora thought, than did all the footmen and their wenches she had seen at their usual slap and pinch and giggle when they walked out together. And they displayed their interest in each other even better still, she decided spitefully, than Severne and Annabelle did when they played at cards together in the long evenings, or when he walked with her in the gardens in the late afternoons, or when she spoke low and lingeringly with him in the last hours before they parted company for the night.

"I want to go home," Leonora thought then, with a sudden, sharp pinch of sorrow at her heart that momentarily took her breath away. But it really was too much, she thought, turning her face to a small window and looking out sightlessly at the radiant day, far too much for her to bear even for nobility's sake. Because, she realized, though it is never good to run from one's problems, one doesn't have to take up lodgings with them for life either.

Severne wanted Annabelle, Annabelle desired Severne, that was all she knew, and that was all she needed to know. She didn't have to watch that lean, graceful form bending over that big-eyed, white-faced girl like a willow over a reflecting pool, each day and every night, in order to constantly feel the exquisite bite of the exquisite irony of their meeting. Nor did she have to see the look in those dark blue eyes when they rested upon the light blue ones of her cousin to realize that she must soon rehearse all the congratulations she'd thought to visit upon some other gentleman, any other gentleman, who she thought would have spoken for Annabelle.

And there were times, and often, when she knew he looked upon her as well. Perversely, those were the worst times of all. She winced at what he must think then. If he hadn't held her in his arms perhaps she might be able to accept the thought of him embracing Annabelle. If she hadn't tasted his lips perhaps she could bear to think of them framing his declaration to Annabelle. But as it was, there was no doubt in Leonora's mind that in order to have accepted Annabelle, he must first have totally rejected herself.

It was not pleasant to remember that one night in a darkened garden she had let him know without speech or reservation, that she could not withhold anything of herself from him. It was, however, far worse to know that he rejected all he'd been offered, which was only all that she could possibly give. Although she'd never done more with any man than she had done with him that night, she'd never before wanted more from any man either. Yet on that night she'd realized that she would have been willing to have him know her entirely, not only in body, but in mind and heart as well. But as it transpired, he'd gone on to show her that he quite literally wanted no further part of her at all.

So though she'd only been at Grace Hall for four days, it was four centuries too long for Leonora. It might have been that the loving atmosphere of the great house increased her own feelings of loss and loneliness. It might have been that she couldn't have borne the sight of her fantasy lover carrying off her poor cousin no matter where she was. She no longer knew, or cared. She only knew that she did not care to watch it go forth for one day longer.

That was why she continued to pace the anteroom while all the others were at some great mock archery tournament upon the broad green lawns. She had come this far only to discover that like an insulted child at a birthday party where she'd not been included in all the games, she simply didn't want to play with any of them for one moment longer.

Leonora was wondering whether a sudden attack of

stomach distress or a spuriously strained ankle was a better excuse for the packing she meant to begin as soon as the sun set, when her sister came drifting into the hall like an animated tall cool white fountain, spilling lace and scent all about her.

"How tiresome," Lady Benjamin sighed, "to find you actually mooning about the house, just as Katie said. I'd thought it only her usual impudence, but it's no more than the truth. Heavens, Leonora, where is your backbone, my girl?"

"I must have left it in London, so I'm going back for it tonight," Leonora said gloomily, not looking at her sister at all, but only mindlessly tracing the lead in the glass around a knight's head in one small side window, with one finger.

"Absolutely not," Sybil said firmly. "Nothing could be more disastrous. It would be gauche, it would be ill bred, and it would be foolish as well. A general does not desert the field until the battle is clearly over."

Leonora spun around at that and looked at her sister. For a moment Leonora had thought that she was actually referring to her problem with Severne, but then she realized, seeing Sybil's expressionless face, that she was only indulging in a bit of metaphor. Sybil, Leonora thought, with some annoyance beginning to tinge her overall feeling of despair, was a very civilized person, and so would only concern herself with what was done, rather than with what was actually felt, by all those who surrounded her.

"I don't regard a social week in the country as a battle-field," Leonora said testily, "and so I don't mind losing such skirmishes. I'm leaving, Sybil, and I don't expect anyone to accompany me either. I'll take Katie, and leave Annabelle here with you and mother, and see you all when you return to Town. Then," she said darkly, "I'm going home to Lincolnshire for good. London's not for me."

"I see," Sybil said thoughtfully, coming close enough to Leonora so that she felt enveloped in a cloud of patchouli. "Then I am to assume that Severne's not for you either? Don't gape at me like a startled owl, Leonora. I don't know why it is that whenever I speak with you about anything that is not to do with gowns or fashions, you stagger back amazed. And as it is, any sensate being would be aware of your emotions for Severne."

But since Leonora hoped that she'd been extremely circumspect and terribly subtle in relation to her feelings for the marquess, she only said at once, and somewhat stiffly, "I haven't the slightest idea of what you're talking about, Sybil. It's only that I'm most awfully bored here."

"Don't be childish, Leonora," Sybil snapped. "One of your better qualities is that you so seldom lie. Which is all to the good, since you do it so very poorly. I'm very disappointed to find you exactly as your impudent Katie said, 'moping about like you'd just lost your looks.' Leonora," Sybil said, fixing her sister with a steady stare and showing her concern by the uncharacteristic forceful gesture of raising one finger for emphasis, "the duchess sent me to find you, and now I find myself most disturbed at what I've discovered. I cannot believe that you are content to hide away while that Greyling creature snatches Severne out from under your nose."

Leonora looked away to where she'd been fretfully fingering the design of the window. "But I thought you did not care for the marquess," was all that she could think to reply.

"I cannot care for his history," Sybil admitted, "but father admires him greatly. Lord Benjamin himself says that he's a worthwhile fellow, despite his past. Then too, he is titled, wealthy, and intelligent, and I do not deny that his looks and manners are very taking. You could do worse, my dear. And so I should be ashamed of you, sister, if you allowed that wretched chit to outmaneuver you in this."

Leonora knew that it was useless enumerating Annabelle's qualities, since Sybil thought the girl both underborn and underbred. And though she thought that her sister might be a very good tactician, she doubted that she knew much of the workings of the human heart. Still, she was touched by her concern and tried to frame an honest answer.

"Dearest Sybil," Leonora said, as she tried valiantly to keep her voice level and her eyes dry, "I am pleased that you care. But if you cannot get a horse to drink even after you've led him to water, how can you assume that the gentlemen are any less opinionated than those noble beasts? Dear Sybil, don't you see, Severne has a care for Annabelle." Then she had to pause to bite her lower lip so as to steady it.

"So it would seem, would it not?" Sybil replied calmly. "But then I have seen how much of a care he has for the chit when you are in the room, and how much less he has when you are not. Yes. My dear Leonora, if you assume such expressions repeatedly, in the fullness of time you may well be mistaken for an owl. Were I Miss Greyling," she mused, a pleased expression coming over her serene countenance, "I should not be pleased at all at how my suitor's attentions waxed and waned at the entrances and exits of another lady. And though it would not be the first time that a gentleman declared for one female simply to get the attention or the angry reaction of another, I should hate to see it happen in this case. For Leonora," she said with emphasis, her voice becoming stern, "I would consider it a reflection upon our family name, were you to meekly accept this."

Leonora gazed at her sister for a long moment. She couldn't believe half of what Sybil had said, but there was so much to be hoped for in it if she did, and so much humor in it, even if she didn't, that she felt her sorrow retreating before Sybil's proud stare.

"Well Sybil," she said at last, "if it is a matter of family honor . . ."

"I believe that it is," Sybil said calmly, and then adroitly turning the subject, before the mistiness growing in her sister's eyes resolved itself into something embarrassing, she went on, "And I recall you were always adept with the bow. They are having an archery tournament and I let our family down very badly. I never took to the sport, you know, for fear of developing unsightly musculature. You didn't seem to care, although, to be sure, you were very young then," she said handsomely, willing to give Leonora some credit since she herself had won the most important point.

Their father had been mad for the sport when he was young, Leonora recalled nostalgically, as had every gentleman of the quality, following their young and handsome Prince's lead. But even as Prinny had grown stout and sedentary, interest in archery itself had died, along with all the other dreams of that golden youth. Yet though The

Royal British Bowmen society had disbanded decades earlier, the passage of time had done nothing to blunt the
viscount's enthusiasm for the sport at which he excelled.
When his son had been too small to pass the skill along to,
the viscount had been pleased to tutor his daughters on
long summer afternoons. Though Sybil had always es-
chewed any sport or activity which might present her at
less than her smoothly perfect self, Leonora had taken to
the bow at once, for it was inextricably linked in her mind
with her father's interest and approval.

"Annabelle and Severne comprise one team, Father and
I another," Sybil went on, noting her sister's interest. "The
duchess is entertaining her children, and so won't come
within leagues of the target area, and Torquay has said that
he will only play if the teams are even. You, of course, will
be on Father's side. And then the duke must take Severne's
team. They protested that the odds would be uneven, with
two men on one side and only one on the other, but
Father only agreed, saying that once you took up the bow,
all the others were lost. Severne," Sybil said, as she began
to step out into the hall, and Leonora followed, so anxious
to hear what was going to be said next that it was as
though she were drawn from the house on a long invisible
lead, "Severne did not believe this, and has offered to bind
up one arm to make the odds more even."

"Oh has he?" Leonora said militantly, forgetting that it
was a gentle spring afternoon, and that all the words, as
well as the tourney itself, were jests.

"Yes," Sybil replied, nodding, as they walked across the
rolling green lawns, and she looked with approval at the
high color in her sister's cheeks, and the proud way with
which she stepped across the evenly scythed grass. Leonora wore a classic draped white flowing frock and as she
approached the impromptu tournament grounds, she took
off her sash and tied it about her dark hair in a circlet
above her forehead. So that after she greeted the others
and took up her bow, she looked, as she stood upon that
sunlit sward and took her position, and raised her dark
head haughtily as she sighted the target, like some incarna-
tion of the huntress Diana herself.

Or so the Marquess of Severne thought as he watched
her draw her bow. It seemed to him that she had all the

voluptuous and savage beauty of the goddess. The play of
sunlight and shadow that chased over the dappled lawn
betrayed the filmy material of her gown and outlined her
high full breasts where they rose from the clean line of her
slender body. And yet as she bit down upon her full and
rosy lower lip and frowned in concentration, she looked
fierce. The glint in her deep brown eyes shone through the
lacy curtain of her lashes as she narrowed her eyes to study
the target, and there he saw the classic contradiction of the
wondrously feminine body steered by the strong and forceful mind that personified the huntress deity.

He held his breath as the bow tensed. Then, when the
arrow flew, it went straight and true and to the heart of the
target. He cheered just as the others did, forgetting that she
was his foe in this game, and that such marksmanship must
surely defeat him.

The duke was a strong athlete. But as the viscount said,
in his white shirt, with his glowing hair reflecting back the
sun, he made a prettier picture than he did a competitor.
The marquess had always prided himself on his ability, but
he too hadn't held a bow since he was a lad, and when he
went to the mark it wasn't long before the viscount remarked wistfully that he wished the pretty fellows would be
done with posing for marble busts so that he and his
daughter could get down to some real sport.

When Annabelle's turn came, the viscount held his tongue.
She had to be shown how to hold the bow and nock the
arrow into place. In the end, the marquess had to stand
behind her and help her draw the bow taut, as she had not
the strength in her slender arms to do it. He stood behind
her in his shirtsleeves, with one hand upon hers to pull the
string back and the other around her to steady her hold
upon the bow. As they stood thus, in the instant before he
let her let the arrow fly, Leonora saw that the lines of
strength in his arms were no less taut than that of the
bowstring.

Annabelle's pale hair blew in drifts across his shoulders,
and her wan face lay close to his even as her frail body
seemed to nestle within the cage of his arms. Even at the
moment of highest tension, before they loosed the arrow,
she seemed to languidly float within his encircling arms. Leonora turned away to see the arrow's flight, so that she

would no longer look upon what seemed to her to be a curiously intimate moment.

With all of Severne's help, Annabelle still could not even touch the target. Leonora knew that it was only that Annabelle had never had the leisure to learn such sport. And she knew that there was nothing remiss in her relative's having entered into the tournament despite her lack of skill, since it was quite proper and even desirable for a young female to be utterly incompetent in such matters. But as Leonora went up to her mark again, she did not recall the poor showing of skill at all, but only remembered the luxurious way in which Annabelle had leaned back into the marquess's embrace, and how he had gently sheltered her there.

"Three dead on center!" the viscount exulted. "My girl's not forgotten her touch. You chaps will have me in champagne for the rest of my life unless you stop wagering on us. The House of Talwin is unbeatable, my lads!"

"Another wager? I'd not offer up a button ever again on our chances against you two, Robin Hood and his merry maid." The marquess laughed.

As they grouped around the target to marvel at the accuracy of the father and daughter who had just so roundly routed them, Leonora was so busy noting how Annabelle stayed close to the marquess, as though he were already her partner in life rather than just an archery match, that she was not aware of her host's approach until he breathed, "Well done." Then he added, with every evidence of vast amusement in his clear blue eyes, "It was as though you were inspired."

"Ah well," Leonora answered, bowing her head, "it was only luck."

And so she replied to the duchess's and her sister's congratulations as well. For she had not the strength to say any more. She felt curiously weak now that the rage had swept over and past her. And she was certainly unwilling to admit that when she'd needed it the most, inspiration had indeed come to her—when she'd suddenly seen the red center of the target become blue. As light and mild and staring a blue as Annabelle's wide, unblinking eye.

*   *   *

It was a quiet hour in the countryside. Cattle were coming in from the fields, birds were returning to their nests to salute the oncoming night with soft regretful evensong. At a gentleman's country house, the day was ended gently as well. Dinner was being prepared, ladies of fashion were being prepared for their dinners with as much close attention as the main courses were being given, and gentlemen were either washing or shaving or napping to be in readiness for the evening to come.

But not everyone at the Duke of Torquay's country estate was abiding by fashion's rules. The duke and duchess themselves did not. The pair, who always dispensed with Nurse at this hour, having read their two sons half a tale of ogres with the remainder promised for the morrow, and having kissed and cuddled the gentle blond-haired one before tucking him into sleep, and having just done with giggling and wrestling with the rowdy red-headed one before splashing him from bath to bed, were now occupied with making lazy love together in their own rooms in the long hour before dinner.

The duke's daughter was having dinner in her rooms with her dear companion-governess, Miss Pickett, and laughing over how silly her friend Mary had been at that tea party at her house today. The viscount was strolling the grounds deep in thought, and his daughter Leonora was ghosting about between the library and the back garden and back again, looking for a book or a refuge and wishing that the week was up.

Only the viscount's wife and elder daughter and her husband were behaving precisely as they ought, as they always did. The viscountess, having woken from her afternoon nap, was being massaged and powdered and dressed for the main event of her day, her evening. Her daughter was debating over whether the azure or the apricot frock was more flattering, and the noble Lord Benjamin was dozing and blissfully dreaming about a wicked little minx in Curzon Street, whose name he'd dare not mention if awake.

And the Marquess of Severne was strolling in the rose garden with Miss Annabelle Greyling, and wondering why in the name of thunder he could not bring himself to give her a word of encouragement as to their mutual future. She'd given him every excuse and opportunity, he thought,

as he paused to watch some golden fish bubble up at a
petal that had fallen in the basin of a wide white fountain.
She'd mentioned she didn't know how long she'd be staying
with her cousin, she'd made it painfully clear that since her
time was measured in insults and tears, it might not be too
long before she'd be off about her sorrowful travels again.
And only just now, she'd sighed that she'd miss a great
deal once she'd gone, and looked at him, and then ducked
her head and sighed again.

Now, he knew, here in this soft garden in the scented
twilight, was the time and place for him to catch her up in
his arms and promise her surcease from her weary travels
and a safe port for the rest of her life. Wasn't that why he'd
been visiting with her, and visiting his attentions upon her
for these past weeks? He'd raised expectations that he
knew he ought to try to fulfill, for her as well as himself.
The problem was, he thought, as they walked slowly and
wordlessly, that he hadn't the slightest desire to catch her
up in his arms for any reason.

She walked, as she so often walked with him, with her
head bent and her eyes averted, so that he could look
down upon her unobserved. She was intelligent and kind,
and poor and oppressed, and very sweet, he thought,
nerving himself to say the first word. But even in her thin
white dress, even here in the dying light that softened
every outline, there was nothing about her that enticed him.
There was, he had discovered, even something about her
that repelled him. Now there, he thought, angry with himself again, was a true perversion of spirit.

But when he waltzed with her, and then again today,
when he held her and her bow for the archery contest, her
bones had felt so small and brittle, her body so light and
hot, that he had felt only a shamed sort of discomfort at
their intimacy. Perhaps it was that she made him feel so
fatherly toward her that the idea of making love to her was
as abhorrent as the idea of that aberration would be. Or
perhaps it was that she appeared to be so beaten that the
notion of making any advances made him feel like a perse-
cutor and not a lover. No matter what the reason, there
was no doubt that his unwillingness to take her physically
would be, he thought now, on the rising of a bizarre

chuckle that he quickly suppressed, some obstacle to their marital success, at the very least.

Was he fated, he wondered sadly, watching the young female he felt he ought to feel some passion other than pity for, to marry females who bred this reluctance, this impotence in him? But he argued to himself, this female was no Sylvia, for this girl was learned, well read, and had a mind that dovetailed with his own in her every choice of art and literature.

Was he then, he brooded, as he watched the delicate girl pause at the fountain, doomed to always endure this split between the longings of his mind and his body? For when he thought of who it was that he would wish to be holding tightly against himself now, here in this dim garden as he had in that other nighttime garden, he felt an arousal so strong that it was as if it was she who stood before him, and not this good pale girl whom he knew he ought to desire.

So when Annabelle looked up at him with a reasonable question in her mild eyes, he knew he could give her no answer. Not now. Not until one way or another he had exorcised the dark passion the dark lady had aroused in him. So he took out his pocket watch and pretended to read it in the vague light, and exclaimed over the hour, and walked her back to the house, and left her to go to her rooms to prepare for dinner. And was so furious with himself for his need to conduct the elaborate charade that when he strode into the gardens again to think, and he instead encountered Leonora as she was about her agitated pacing, he stood and glowered at her as though she were some sort of infernal visitation.

But so she was in that moment, to him. He continued to gaze at her as she halted and stared back at him. He knew how subtly malign and infinitely cruel she could be from all of poor Annabelle's hesitantly told tales, and he knew from his own knowledge of her history how reckless she was. So then as he saw her there in the deceptive fading light, with her dark hair and eyes and impossibly ripe figure, it wasn't hard to imagine that she was some mythic personal succubus, sent to drain his soul and turn his life inside out.

They did not speak a word to each other. But it was as though they didn't have to. For then he came to her, and took her into his arms and swept the hair back from her brow and looked down into her wild eyes and then closed his own to keep from drowning there and then kissed her plush lips as he had wished to do since he had seen her in the morning. And she moved against him like dark water flowing to carry him away. Until she ended the encounter as all such desperate acts end, with pain

For she bit down hard upon his lip and pushed him away from herself.

"Damn you," she hissed at him, as wild in words as she was in appearance now. "I am not here for your taking when you weary of my gentle cousin. I am not here for your entertainment. And I know no more of such matters than she. I am not the creature all this makes me appear to be," she wept with fury, holding her hands wide to display her body.

He stared at her, still without saying a word. She looked up into that confused, angry, dear face, still suffused with desire and frustration, and seeing the blood well up on his lip, she shuddered and, weeping openly now, said, "Take her if you must and be done with it, but leave me. Leave me, if not for my sake, then for hers."

Only then did he move. He blinked as though awakening. Then he bowed, as though he'd just left her at some formal affair, and then, turning upon his heel, he left her alone at once.

When the Duke of Torquay's guests at last assembled themselves in the drawing room for their cordial before dinner, there was a certain tension apparent among some of them. The viscount appeared more thoughtful than usual. His younger daughter was as white and silent as though she'd borrowed her companion and cousin Miss Greyling's complexion for the night, as the duke remarked *sotto voce* to his dear duchess. And that young woman, he begged his lady to note in the same whisper, went about the room as smoothly and sweetly this evening as if she ran on small greased wheels.

But it was not until they had all seated themselves at the great table that the more interesting transformation came over all of them. For as they were shaking out their crested embroidered napery, their host said in his hushed tones that made everything he uttered sound deliciously clandestine, "Oh, yes. I suppose you've all noted that we have one less among our number tonight. Yes. The Marquess of Severne is regrettably no longer with us. No, no, dear gentle people, he yet breathes, but alas, not in our vicinity. He came to me not an hour past, and said that he'd received a summons home to clear up some family business with his father. Nothing dire, only estate matters, and he bade me make his good-byes. But surely, we can make merry, even with our diminished numbers," he smiled, noting how each of his listeners remained silent at his news. And seeing how some of his guests still sat stunned even though the soup was being served, he added sweetly, "But my friends, it is still springtime, and we are only one less in number."

It was while the duke was happily undressing his duchess that night as they prepared for bed, that he remarked reminiscently about the reaction of some of his female guests at the table that night. "I felt," he mused as he raised his lips from her creamy shoulder, "rather like the host at a Christmas dinner when the turkey got up and slowly walked away."

TWELVE

Joscelin Peter Kidd, Fifth Marquess of Severne, approached the door to the Viscount Talwin's London townhouse with a book in his hand and an offer of marriage upon his lips. The book was for the young woman that he felt was one of the few in the world who would appreciate its truth and beauty precisely as he had. But however lovely a gift, he believed it to be but a poor shadow of what he might have given her if his world and circumstances were different. For the offer that should have gone with the book was for a different young female. And where the book was to be given gladly with a free and open heart, the offer, he told himself, had to be made simply because he saw no other honorable recourse open to him.

There was a limit, after all. Strictly speaking, he ought to have offered for the lady after he'd embraced her so passionately at her own ball in her own garden. But society seldom concerned itself with such strict speaking. There were always mitigating circumstances that stretched truths, and softened liabilities that allowed certain interesting peripheries to exist. The Lady Leonora had been well over the age of consent, and she'd also been sent home from her first Season years before because of some interesting behavior. Even if that were not the case, the polite world would politely look the other way at any liberties taken with a young woman of her age and wisdom who choose to step out into the blatant moonlight with a divorced gentleman of dubious repute. There were, after all, limits to any protection policy, and the social contract was no different in that benefits were revocable if the injured party had acted in a markedly unwise and irresponsible manner.

But accosting the young woman again, this time when under another nobleman's roof, put an entirely different construction upon matters. There were other, more telling differences. Even though she had eventually responded, it was undeniable that he'd not stolen kisses this time, but had thrust them upon her. And her denial had the ring of truth. Provocative or not, once she'd left his arms he'd realized it was her very existence, not her vast experience, which had ignited him. It had been his best friend's home that he had dishonored as well as the young lady, and her father had also been a guest at the time, and her father was a gentleman to whom he owed a great deal of respect and fealty.

The marquess had taken a week to review his situation, and had opted to make the only honorable and sincere restitution that he could. Even though he had thought to wed another, he would take the young lady in holy matrimony.

His spirit should have been heavy as he approached the lady's door, but instead, it bore less weight than did the slim volume he held in his hand. This absence of despair perversely bothered him, since he saw it as another example of his perverse desires. Though he told himself over and again that today he would be giving up all hope of wedding a gentle, intelligent creature who was a match for his intellect, he could not help remembering that he was about to procure himself a wife who was equal to all his darker desires. This, to the detriment of all his good opinion of himself, did not displease him at heart as it ought to have done. For search as he might, he could find nothing but excitement at the thought of her being entirely his.

He glanced down at the book in his hand. Mr. Blake, he thought as he raised the door knocker, would understand the situation very well. Within this house there was a pure lamb of a girl, all meek and mild. And then there was the other, a tigerish female indeed, who burned bright with the promise of sensual delight. He would have chosen the lamb, if it were not that he had failed to resist the lure of the flesh eater. That his failure did not depress him utterly, depressed him considerably.

In the best of worlds, he thought, in the due course of time he might have found one female who had within her both qualities, to spur desire as well as admiration. But this was not such a world, he was not such a man, and since he had made a misstep, he'd used up all his time for further search. So when the door swung open, he wore an ironic, skewed smile as he realized he had joined Annabelle in the fold. For today he was presenting himself to the butler in preparation for presenting himself as a sacrificial lamb.

He wouldn't first ask her father permission to pay his addresses, as he might have done if things had been different between himself and the lady he awaited as he paced the salon. He liked the viscount too well to offer him false coin. It would be better that Talwin never knew of the furtive embraces that had won his daughter her offer of marriage. Then, too, he could hardly declare his undying love for the Lady Leonora and still keep the distaste for the lie from his voice. Neither could he state that if he did not have her soon, he would run mad. Aside from the fact that it was not quite the thing to let another gentleman know the urgency of the pure lust his wicked daughter provoked in her prospective husband, he did not wish to admit as much to himself.

She entered the salon hesitantly, and kept her distance from her guest to the extent of making sure that there was a small chair between herself and him. She placed her hands over the back of it as she gave him good day as though it were the most natural thing in the world, and all at once, despite his lowering mood, he found it difficult not to grin as he agreed that it was a wondrously clement spring. He wondered if she thought he would have come all this way simply to spring out at her again. And had to admit that he was tempted to, even here, even now, even knowing what he did of her, and what the price was that he was about to pay for her.

She wore a lavender frock, and instead of the color subduing her, he thought that it drew attention to the faint lilac in her cheek and the deep succulent berry of her lips. Before he could set to wondering at what scent she wore today, and as he awoke to the unbidden, unwelcome but ever present visceral response she stirred in him, he spoke.

"You know, of course, that I've come to apologize," he said.

She did not reply at once, for there was no apology in

his tone. Instead, he appeared to be stiffly correct. Though he wore casual clothes—a cream-colored jacket, buff breeches, and gleaming hessians—there was something excessively formal about him today. She had known he would call, and had been awaiting this visit since she'd returned to Town. She'd expected an apology, for whether or not he believed himself to have been right or wrong, he was a gentleman. And what he'd done was not done.

But because she couldn't stop thinking of what he'd done, or stop herself from wanting him to do it again, which was decidedly not done, she avoided his searching gaze now. She'd had a week to wonder why he'd taken her in his arms that night after having taken Annabelle into his company all week, and had come up with a dozen possible reasons for each day of that week. The only thing that she knew for a certainty now was that it hadn't been drunkenness, for she'd tasted his mouth and couldn't have been deceived in that, and it hadn't been love, for she'd seen his eyes and couldn't have been mistaken in that either. That night, his face had borne the traces of every emotion she could tease herself with save for the one she'd been looking for.

"Your apology is accepted," she said quietly, studying a thread at the back of the chair.

"I haven't made it yet," he replied, in a more natural tone. "But be sure, I shall, and more, at once."

He drew in a deep breath, and stood before her with his long booted legs slightly apart, as though for better balance, and he turned a small brown paper packet in his hands as he spoke,

"I'm aware that my behavior was despicable. And I've spent the better part of a week putting my affairs in order. No, don't worry." He laughed briefly. "Your papa has not challenged me to a duel. But the only reason he hasn't, I assume, is that you have not told him of my wretched behavior. And for that, believe me, I am grateful."

"You needn't be," she said at once, wanting him to know that he had gotten no special treatment. "I am not close with my father, you see, and wouldn't be likely to confide in him in any case. I've told no one, in fact," she said truthfully.

But he scarcely attended to her last words, and felt no

more than a passing relief that neither the viscount nor Annabelle knew what had occurred. He was too busy being appalled at the lack of heart in this creature he was soon to take to wife. It was hard to comprehend how a universally admired gentleman such as Talwin could have spawned a child unfeeling enough to be unappreciative of his several special virtues.

"I'm surprised. He speaks of you often," he answered quickly to cover his shock.

"We were close once, there was a misunderstanding—" she began to say, starting to defend herself before she cut herself off abruptly. But it was he that was in the wrong, she reminded herself sharply. And this was an apology that he was supposed to make. He had no right to stand there before her, accusation implicit in his aggressive stance and explicit in his every word. She raised her head and tried to stare him down, and was happy to discover that she could do this easily enough if she remembered to focus her eyes only upon his shirt points, since looking upon any part of his actual self disconcerted her.

So she only heard the hint of regret in his voice when he said in a low, thoughtful rumble, "That's rather too bad for you I should think, for your father's advice and counsel is much sought after by a great many people who would very much like to claim it as a matter of course, as his relatives might."

And since she still dared not to look the fraction higher that she would have had to in order to see his face, for her pride's sake, she completely missed his expression when he went on to say in toneless fashion, "But that is not why I am making you this offer. I ask you to be my wife, my lady, because I believe it to be the right thing to do. And," he added when she did not reply, "I believe that when you think on it, you will agree."

The words, "You have made me very happy," were on his lips. He had only to remember to put the correct slight inflection of sarcasm into them to finish the thing off to his own satisfaction. Then he could request audience with her father, then events would be set into motion, then she would soon be his. He was trying to quell the slight smile he discovered rising at the thought, or at least to turn it into an expression of resignation rather than jubilation, when she spoke.

"Are you mad?" she said.

Now she stared directly into his eyes because her anger had blinded her to his reaction, and her reaction to him.

"Are you serious?" she asked.

"Quite," he said, very stiffly, for he hadn't expected anything but her acquiescence, given grudgingly perhaps, but given instantly. It was never that he considered himself a prize upon the marriage market. He knew all too well that his divorce had excluded him from most alliances. But she wasn't an ingenue, she had a rather difficult reputation to live down as well, her father approved of him, and she, and this he would swear to, she was not indifferent to him. She might not love him, for all he knew she might not be able to love anyone, if her attitude toward her father and poor Annabelle were any gauge. But she was drawn to him, and she desired him fully as much as he did her. That, he would swear to.

In all, unless she wished to remain single and embark upon an affair with him, which was almost never done in her circle, there didn't appear to be any reason why she should not accept him. It wasn't only that she could do worse, it was that he did not see her attempting to do better.

"I compromised you, surely you know that," he said coldly, "and you must just as surely know that I am not so lost to decency that I would not remedy that which I had done. I know the rules, and I play by them."

"But I was not playing in your game," Leonora said, "or so you made abundantly clear to me. It was my cousin you were courting, was it not?" She asked this in the chilliest accents she could summon up. She absolutely refused to let a hint of emotion show in her voice as she voiced that which she knew she must if she were to ever have peace of mind about her decision.

"Yes," he said at once, for he could not deny it. There was, at any rate, he believed, little need to do so. Not for a moment did he seriously think she'd ever considered poor sad Annabelle competition, though originally he'd often hoped she would. But even on the mad chance that she had, the sort of female he knew her to be would doubtless deem this offer a stunning victory over her unfortunate opponent, and consider it payment in full for her wretched cousin's presumption. No, he thought, dismissing the thought, that could never be the reason for her present scorn.

So then, he, badly insulted and wondering now if he were being refused because of his divorce, or something about his person, or perhaps even because he had been entirely wrong about the mutuality of their physical attraction, only said again, in as frigid a manner,

"Yes. So I was. But then, I didn't attack her, did I?"

"No," Leonora replied in a tight, high voice. "But then, we shall forget that incident, I think. No one else knows, and so if we choose to forget, it will be as though it never occurred. Then you need not sacrifice yourself. And so then, neither do I."

"Very good," the marquess said through thinned, taut lips.

"Yes, I think so," Leonora replied in a voice several octaves higher than normal.

Then they both stood rigidly, facing each other and breathing as heavily as though they had just chased each other around the small salon. As, in a sense, they had done.

"Yes," he said at last, now recovered at least enough to speak normally, "A neat solution. Then please, let us forget this interview as well. We cannot be at daggers drawn in public, and tonight I had arranged to accompany you and your family to a musical performance." He neglected to mention that he had planned it to be a celebration, an occasion to show the world their engagement, and only went on to add, "I should like it if we were to go on in as normal a fashion as possible . . . for your father's sake if nothing else."

"And my cousin's?" Leonora asked, though a second later she could have bitten off her tongue for letting him think she cared.

"Yes, that too," he said with an effort to remain casual, remembering that any enthusiasm in his answer might cause Annabelle real distress and possibly retribution from this lady.

"And that parcel you've been holding since I came in," Leonora asked quickly, grasping at conversational straws to make him forget her last question, "was that for me?" She managed a smile and essayed a jest in an attempt to reestablish the normalcy he'd mentioned. "Or did my negative reply cause me to forfeit it?" she smiled.

"No," he said bitterly, for he could see no humor in her rejection, "this would have been for you, my lady." And he took a small tissue-wrapped packet from his inner vest pocket and unwrapped it so that she could see the shining blue stare of a great sapphire as dark as his own eyes, set in a golden ring. He put it back at once, as though he regretted having shown it, and gesturing with the brown paper package he held, said negligently, "This little parcel was for Annabelle."

Forgetting that she had just refused him, Leonora could only feel rage that he had thought to bring a gift for another female even as he offered for her hand. So she immediately said, "Ah. A consolation prize, I see."

"Not quite," he replied. "A book. But yes," he mused, his hard face taking on a softer expression for the first time in the interview, "she would find it consolation, yes."

"Well then," Leonora said, tossing her dark hair back, "I will not delay you in your visit with her. Now you can be her consolation."

"Yes," he said, "of course. Thank you, my lady."

"No. Thank you," she said. And they glowered at each other for a moment before he bowed, she curtsied, and they parted.

But once she came out into the hall and the door closed behind her, she almost sank to her knees. She did not think of her sudden weakness, she only thought with sorrowing wonder, as she attempted to reach her room before Annabelle emerged to join Severne, "Only because he thought he must." And armed with a gift for another woman to let her know he'd been forced to his offer for her. And that offer made with not one word tossed to her in charity to make it more palatable. Not one word of affection, not a word of respect, nor one of admiration. Because she'd listened closely, and had he offered up just one such with his offer, she would have been promised to him at this very moment. And she would have been, she thought with pain, even if it had only been the one word that decided it, happier than she had ever been.

The Marquess of Severne scowled as he waited for Miss
Greyling to join him. He had come to the door of this
house bearing two gifts and now he was about to divest
himself of the second one. This one he knew would be
accepted, and gladly. Then, unburdened, he should feel
lighter. He did, though he could find no pleasure in it. For
he was free, he had been set entirely free, and he felt not
so much unencumbered as confused. For he knew he
ought to feel something other than this terrible sense of
loss.

It was a large pier mirror with gilt cherubs all around it,
and it held a clear reflection with never the slightest ripple,
for the viscount bought only the best for his family. Katie
stood back, as proud as a cook displaying a four-layered
cake with candied flowers on top.

"Now there!" She sighed. "Now there, my lady, is a
sight that will take the shine out of every other female in
the place." And especially that curd-faced little cheat, she
thought, and she would have said it too, for she wouldn't
hold her tongue with her mistress after all this time out of
fear for her position. But she would, she sighed again, and
did, out of fear for her lady's feelings.

But sometimes a current of thought runs so true between
two minds that it needn't be said, for her lovely lady
looked deep into the glass and said softly, "It's very nice,
to be sure. But gold's a color for the cool and blond, Katie.
Are you sure it suits a gypsy like me?"

"A gypsy?" Katie gasped, honestly horrified. "A queen
of the Egypts, more like, my lady, not of the gypsies."

For so she looked, Katie thought proudly, with her dark
tresses swept up high and cascading down in one great
curl. And with the gold-colored gown that fit just as it did in
the latest fashion plates, as though it had been carved on a
statue rather than buttoned onto a living body. Only no
fashion plate illustration Katie had ever seen had possessed
such a lavish bosom or curving hip as did her lady. It was
almost too much for a gentlewoman to display and still
look a complete lady. It would have been too much, Katie
decided, for any other. But not for her mistress, and the
way she carried her head high and walked so regally.

Katie was about to enlarge upon her theory when a faint

scratching was heard at the door. "I know, I know," the maidservant grimaced, "it's Miss Greyling," and without further word she trudged to the door to admit the visitor. Katie's affection for Annabelle, Leonora thought as she watched the reluctant maid approach the door, had undergone a rapid deterioration even as Severne's had increased. But then, she mused a little sadly, that had nothing to do with Annabelle herself, for Katie's loyalty was such that she would have despised an angel if she thought its glow cast her mistress into the shadow.

Leonora sighed and looked at herself again in the glass and tried to share Katie's enthusiasm for her appearance. It was important to her that she look very well tonight, if only to show Severne that his conduct hadn't affected her in the least. She doubted that she appeared as magnificent as Katie would have it, but was about to settle for "attractive" when her cousin's reflection came into view beside her own.

Seeing herself, bold and gold and dark and voluptuous, at the side of Annabelle, who was tonight all milk and butter, flower-stem slim and graceful in a flowing gown the color of peaches, with her fine light hair a drift of light caught up in a simple ribband, she felt like a two-penny tart beside a princess. As the glass threw back their contrasting reflections, she mused that it was no wonder Severne thought her fit only for furtive embraces, while he reserved his loftier emotions for her gentle cousin.

"How very nice," Annabelle said. "In that gown, cousin, you will be sure to be seen immediately by everyone at the concert."

"Ah yes," Leonora breathed, as Katie reminded herself of years of Sunday church going in order to prevent herself from using the curling iron she held in a decidedly creative fashion.

Annabelle's attitude had subtly changed since Severne had taken up with her, Leonora thought. Then she decided that it was likely only that the poor girl had more confidence now, and that combined with a lack of social experience could produce an effect which might be misinterpreted. Annabelle did not actually smirk at herself in the glass now, rather it could be said to be merely a little smile and nod of approval at herself. And it was not precisely gloating, Leonora thought, when her cousin said,

"Oh cousin, the marquess gave me a book today, when he visited with me. I searched for you all afternoon to show it to you, but Katie said you were suffering from the headache. I'm glad to see you recovered so that you may accompany us to the concert. Joscelin said you might not, you know."

Joscelin! thought Leonora, it is Joscelin now? But it was Joss for me once. Is it that he knows that even in that he must take no liberties with a true lady? And finds her a lady bred, and me a lady born, but only that? She was so taken with the thought that she did not make an immediate reply after her cousin went on to describe some virtues of the book and urge its perusal.

"No," she said distractedly when she could, "no, Belle, I don't wish to read with you now, even if it is a lovely book by Mr. Blake."

"Tomorrow then," Annabelle said comfortably, "for I know you'll like it. Joscelin said he purchased it years ago when Mr. Blake had a showing of his pictures here in Town on Broad Street. And that he was so pleased that someone took an interest in his works, for very few had come to view them, you see, that after Joscelin had purchased a few, he offered him a volume he had just done with composing. It hadn't even been published as yet, and still has not been. And it is mine now."

Leonora repressed an urge to scream, Am I to keep count? Is that it? To see how many "Joscelins" you will utter in an hour? As Annabelle went on, "Joscelin said that he felt very guilty about buying an uncirculated book, but Mr. Blake insisted, and practically pressed it upon him. But that he didn't feel badly about it now, knowing it would be mine. I think you'd like it, cousin, there are two very nice pictures in particular; two angels, one is dark, and one is light and has a face that looks very like mine, Joscelin said."

Three "mines," five "Joscelins." I understand, please stop, thought Leonora.

"What are we to hear tonight, cousin?" Annabelle asked, changing the subject abruptly.

"Some of Mr. Purcell, some of Corelli, some Bach, of

course, among others I think," Leonora said immediately, relieved to be on a less painful subject. "It's to be a baroque recital, and we'll hear several compositions for the brass."

"I've had no opportunity to ever hear such before, as you know," Annabelle said softly. "Do you think I'll enjoy it?"

"Oh yes," Leonora said. "I know that I do, enormously."

"But cousin," Annabelle said quietly, plaintively, "I don't know half so much about music as you. I shall feel quite out of place knowing nothing about it, and having nothing to say."

"Don't worry," Leonora smiled in a more kindly fashion, for her cousin did look like an abashed little girl as she sat down with her eyes downcast. "No one will expect you to give a critique. With music, it is always enough to merely listen and take pleasure in it and say as much."

"Oh," Annabelle cried, "but I should never presume to comment on music in such learned company. You mistake me, cousin. I only wondered if you would explain it a little to me, only so that I don't feel so altogether out of place and out of my place tonight, you see."

Leonora did see, and though she was not a supernaturally forgiving soul, she could step back enough from her unhappiness to know that with Annabelle, at least, there was nothing to forgive. If Annabelle had won Severne, she could dislike it, she could envy it, but she could not hate her cousin for it. She might as well be angry with a blossom for attracting a honeybee. And so, to take her mind from the coming ordeal of the evening, and in some small way as expiation for the intense, though just as intensely resisted and denied dislike she felt for her former protegée, Leonora passed the time before they had to leave by explaining the intricacies of baroque music, and expounding upon music in general.

"And so," Leonora concluded, her eyes shining with enjoyment, for as so often happened, she had been carried away by her own enthusiasm and her attentive audience, "I think that when anything becomes too great to express in words, then one must turn to music. For music is to emotion as poetry is to prose. It is what happens when a soul, or when a thought must sing . . . or so I have always imagined," Leonora ended in embarrassment, realizing that she had become overemotional from the way her audience, Katie and Annabelle, sat watching with wide-eyed wonder.

"You ought to write that all down, my lady, yes, you ought," Katie said, nodding her head vigorously, "for I never felt that way about a tune before, and now I know I always shall."

"Ah well," Leonora laughed, "from what I've just said, I suppose it would be far better if I sang it instead."

They laughed and sported with this theme, oddly in charity with each other, until word came that the marquess had arrived, and the viscount and his wife awaited them. Then Leonora fell silent, and gathered up her wrap and went to the door like the late French queen to the block.

She let Annabelle go down the stairs first, so that Severne could see her at once. And so never knew that his lip curled in disdain as he saw her later entry upon the long staircase, for, his breath taken away by her splendor, he thought only that she *would* know how to make an entrance so as to take the attention away from her poor cousin.

The marquess was so splendid in his stark white and black evening array that Leonora kept her eyes averted from him after one brief glance at his grandeur. It was only after he'd been greeted by acquaintances in the lobby of the concert hall, when Lord Benjamin and Sybil had joined their group, that Leonora dared to follow that tall lean figure with her gaze.

It was Annabelle that he took in on his arm, after she had hung back in confusion and so was discovered to have been left behind as their party began to mount the stairs to their seats. Leonora walked beside her sister in their wake.

"You," Sybil breathed in annoyance, "are a fool, my dear. Or at least, you are allowing that creature to make you into one."

"Nonsense," Leonora replied in such a hushed whisper that her sister had to bend her imperially dressed head to hear her. "She's an innocent. She cannot help it if he prefers her." Leonora no longer thought to dissemble about her feelings for the marquess, knowing that once Sybil got hold of an idea, she could never hope to shake it loose,

and knowing, moreover, that she was not so good a liar as
to dispatch a notion that was, unhappily, quite true.

"I repeat," Sybil said, "you are a fool. A great ninny,
sister. And I only hope that you do not learn it too
late to change things. For although that is a very flattering
gown, I cannot say that I like to see you in that cap and
bells."

Sybil timed her statements better than the London-to-
York stagecoach schedule, Leonora thought. There was no
retort she could make. The thing had been said as a killing
exit line, and so it remained, since the last syllable was
uttered just as they reached their box. There was little time
for thinking about a possible rejoinder either. For soon
Leonora forgot Sybil and even the marquess and Annabelle for a space. The flickering lights dimmed, and the
music soared, and Leonora allowed herself to fly with it
and in it.

It was a fine performance. The musicians played as
though inspired. Leonora heard her favorite pieces, and for
all her previous unrest she found a certain peace in the
night. The harpsichord beat out a fine silver skein while the
horns trumpeted like great golden beasts calling to each
other across the ornate hall, and she was, for that little
while, truly happy.

During the intermission, of course, Sybil and Lord Benjamin were out of their seats at once, since they must
promenade to see and be seen by anyone of any importance. The viscount excused himself to visit with a certain
baron of his acquaintance, and the viscountess, looking
about the box blearily, like a sleeper awakened (which she
just had been), demanded her remaining daughter's escort
to the lady's withdrawing room.

The viscountess met up with a dowager as big with news
as she was with importance, and Leonora was relieved
when her mama waved her off so that she could hear a
particularly good red bit of gossip unfit for an unwed
daughter's ears. They were on the balcony level, not so far
from the family box that Leonora would be remiss in
walking back to her seat alone. But still, she could not like
being seen loitering in the corridors alone at intermission,
as she knew that only Cyprians seeking patrons would
behave so. Though very few would mistake the viscount's

daughter for such, hers was not so marvelous a reputation that she could afford the slightest error. Thus, she wanted to go to her seat, and knew that she ought to as well. It was only a pity that she could not.

For as she stood just outside the curtained entry to the box, she remembered that Severne and Annabelle were there together, and so far as she knew, alone. There could be no question of her interrupting an embrace. It was quite proper for them to be alone there, the box, after all, could be seen from every angle of the hall, and thus they had no more visual privacy than they would if they were upon the stage itself. But perhaps they were discussing something important together, such as a proposal, Leonora thought. She should not like to walk in on such. When it came to that, she didn't wish to be the only other person in the box with them, either. So she stood by the velvet drape, and dithered. Until she heard him call her name.

He said it with warmth, with love. "Oh, Nell," she heard him say, as one says the name of one's beloved. "Oh, Nell," he said it with a sweet pretense of exasperation. "Oh, Nell," he said on half a laugh. There was such a wealth of tender, amused welcome in those two simple words that Leonora drew back the curtain and looked upon him with gladness and relief at this unexpected chance for homecoming. And as she entered, she saw him smiling down at Annabelle with such tenderness in that stern face as she had never hoped to see there, even for herself. It had been, of course, she realized, "Oh Belle," that she had heard.

She had only just enough wit left to rock back the one pace she stepped forward. And she let the curtain slowly, soundlessly, drop back. But she did not take her hand from it, and she did not move another step. Instead, because she could not resist it any more than she could if they had been the fates discussing the actual date and place of her death, she stayed to listen to their murmurous conversation, even though it might cost her all her future joy in life.

But as it turned out, they weren't speaking of love, or at least not the sort of love she'd feared they might be discussing.

"Yes," Annabelle continued in a clear, confident little voice that was almost unrecognizable to her cousin, "for music is to the emotions as poetry is to prose. It is what happens when a soul or, indeed, a thought must sing. Or," she concluded, in the more hesitant tones that Leonora knew so well, "at least so I have always felt."

"But that's quite a charming notion, don't hang your head for saying it, little one," the marquess commented in the same warm, tender tones. "In fact, you ought to write it down."

"Ah well," Leonora could hear Annabelle say, in eerie reprise, "after what I've just said, I suppose it would be better if I sang it, don't you think?"

The Lady Benjamin found herself accosted in a dim stretch of hallway as she was making her way back to her box. A hand snaked out from a dark niche and clamped onto her arm in a sensitive place, above an emerald bracelet. Before she could call for Lord Benjamin's help, since he never looked her way as they promenaded, she heard her sister hiss, "Sybil, here, at once."

The lady bade her husband continue to their box without her and stayed to talk with her agitated sister. She eyed her sibling askance, for Leonora was as flushed and fervent as though she ran a fever.

"Since I doubt you've been bitten by a mad dog since we've left you, I assume you are in some other sort of dire distress?" Sybil asked coolly.

"Sybil," Leonora said wildly, "I want to be rid of my cap and bells."

"Ah," said Lady Benjamin.

"At once, do you hear?" Leonora cried. "You must help me. I want to stop being a fool, and oh lord, Sybil, for the first time in my life I think I actually want to kill someone."

"Oh splendid," said her sister.

THIRTEEN

The slender volume lay unopened upon the table. Though ordinarily Leonora would very much wish to know what treasures awaited between the soft covers, they lay limp and closed. And not the promise of the vision of a dozen angels with the likenesses of her cousin, or a score more with her own dark face, would have tempted her to turn one page of Mr. Blake's book right now. For her cousin's angelic countenance was before her in reality, and she had far more curiosity about the answers that would fall from those actual lips, than she had for any wisdom contained in any volume, from any author who had ever lived or written.

"Why yes, of course," Annabelle said calmly, although with some evident surprise, as though she were amazed that such a question need be asked at all. "Of course I intend to marry him. I have from the first."

"But you said . . . or at least I thought you seemed to think he was reprehensible, you seemed to think I ought not encourage him. . . ," Leonora faltered.

"Why, of course," Annabelle replied with a little smile that was not remotely angelic upon her pale lips, "because I wanted him, and I thought it wouldn't do for you to get in my way. Actually, as it turned out, cousin, you made it that much easier for me, and I thank you for it."

Leonora did not reply at once. She could not. She only stood and gripped hard upon the edge of her dressing table so that the pain in her hands reinforced the reality of the encounter. For, she thought, if it were not for the fact that her fingers certainly ached, she might believe that she had fallen asleep waiting for Annabelle to come to her

172

room as she had bidden her to do, and was merely dreaming this entire bizarre conversation.

She'd known from the moment she'd opened her eyes this morning that she must speak with Annabelle. Instead, she'd gone to visit Sybil, as they had hurriedly arranged to do the previous night. And nothing that her sister had said at their early morning council of war in Sybil's ornate dressing room had changed her mind. All the schemes that Sybil had concocted in the night were unworkable, or at least, she'd known they were so for her. For she'd listened to plots that were far too Machiavellian, too complex, and too full of subversion for her to seriously attempt to follow for any longer than it took for her sister to lovingly detail them.

Sybil might well have been able to carry off the exquisitely convoluted deceptions that had to do with forged notes and double-edged comments, feigned disclosures and servants paid to spy, but Leonora knew she could not. It was, as she had finally sighed, turning down one last scheme that involved a great deal of skulking and lurking, admittedly her own fault. Obviously, she wasn't feminine enough to be up to such rigs, exactly as Sybil, who was very irate at her refusal, snapped at her so crossly. But, as she'd replied as she arose and prepared to take her leave, if it was indeed masculine for her to approach Annabelle and plainly ask for explanation, then she'd just have to be fitted out for trousers, for that was precisely what she intended to do as soon as she returned home.

And that was precisely what she'd done, not ten minutes before. She'd postponed luncheon and summoned Annabelle. Then her cousin had entered the room with her usual meek grace. Katie had been sent away, though Leonora didn't doubt that her maid wasn't somewhere in the vicinity with a tumbler up against an inner wall and her own wondering ear attached to that glass, for without doubt Katie was as feminine a creature as Sybil might wish her sister to be.

But then Leonora had never equated stealth and deceit with femininity, nor did she for one moment consider that her gender had any special proclivity or talent for such, either. She reasoned that oppressed creatures of any sort might well develop such tendencies, but she'd never considered herself particularly oppressed. Then, too, all her life she'd known that the gentlemen she knew the best and admired the most were likely her nation's most superior spies. And none of them were remotely ladylike.

No, whether she'd been born male or female, Leonora knew she lacked the qualities necessary for effective espionage. She was a poor liar, an uncomfortable conspirator, and an abysmally bad actress. She regretted, but accepted these deficiencies in her character. They were, after all, the very reasons her life had been shaped as it had been. She became estranged from her father when she'd been unable to face him knowing what she did of his mistresses, and she'd given up the thought of marriage after learning of the hypocrisy evidently necessary to keep up the semblance of wedded bliss. From such painful experience, Leonora knew she was bad at semblances and worse at hypocrisy.

And so she didn't count it as either brave or honorable to refuse to resort to deceit. She simply realized that she had no other course but to face Annabelle squarely, and have the matter out in the open.

But she'd never expected Annabelle to be as candid with her. Nor had she expected Annabelle to be such an adept at the family trade as to make her own father appear to be merely an amateur.

Though it took a while for Leonora to frame her question, and longer still for her to actually nerve herself to ask it aloud, when she at last did, it didn't seem to discompose Annabelle in the least.

For, "Oh," Annabelle said softly, laying the book she carried down upon the table when she was told there was something more pressing upon her relative's mind. And then, "Yes," she had said without a blink when she was asked if it were true that she had literally quoted everything her cousin had said about music to the marquess, without ever crediting the originator of the commentary.

"Of course," Annabelle had then said, smiling, completely undismayed at answering a question whose creation had turned her inquisitor's cheek to flame, "for it was a clever thing to say, and I know nothing of music, I told you so, cousin. And I needed to impress him. He's almost at the point of offering for me, and needs a bit of encouragement, you know."

Leonora was so staggered at this calm admission that she didn't even take affront when Annabelle then proceeded to thank her, with more evident amusement than she had ever shown on her bland, pale face, for making her task easier by encouraging the marquess's company. Leonora only clutched at the dressing table to convince herself of her wakeful state and then, despite her amazement, managed to pluck the chiefest, most salient point from her cousin's answer to ask, "But then, Belle . . . that means . . . has he asked?"

"Not yet, I told you," Annabelle said with some perturbance before she smiled again and sweetly said, "but he will. Soon too, I expect. Shall we read now, cousin?"

She placed her hands over the book, and it was that sight, the vision of those two delicate white hands closing over the tan volume, just as two other strong tanned hands had doubtless closed over hers when he had given her the book, that spurred Leonora to action.

"Belle," she said, shaking her head, not angry yet, but confused by the traces of evident amusement mixed in with the other girl's calm demeanor, "I don't understand you, I do not. All the while you were cautioning me against encouraging Severne, you were angling for his attentions? I can scarcely believe it of you."

It might have been that Leonora only wanted her relative to lower her lashes over the brilliant gleam in her usually mild eyes. And had she done so and whispered, "Ah, cousin, but I cannot help it, it was my heart involved, and I never thought he'd have a thought for me," Leonora would have taken it, and then left it. Forever.

Of course, she would doubtless have wept in private, and perhaps railed against fate. Perhaps too she would have been disappointed at her cousin's parroting her favorite opinions for the purpose of fascinating her favorite gentleman. But she likely would never have said or done another thing about the forthcoming betrothal, except to offer felicitations and purchase a suitable bridal gift. She was used, after all, to self-denial and self-denigration. And defeat was such a frequent visitor that she commonly set a place for it each day at her table, and left a pillow for it on her bed each night.

"Ah cousin," Annabelle sighed at last, just as she ought, "can I help it that he prefers me to you?"

But she said it with a smile, and she ended it with a comfortable little chuckle.

And during the statement her expression subtly altered. In that moment it held such a look of repletion and fond memory that it was almost embarrassing for Leonora to see. For it was more like the smile on the face of a confirmed voluptuary after a feast or an orgy than it was ever like that of a shy young girl's memory of her lover.

And she continued to smile at Leonora, as though the joke were too rich to swallow up all at once. It was that which made Leonora realize that a theft had been committed.

Some little fragment of pride had been pricked by that smug and knowing smile. It was as though some crumb of self-worth refused to be swept away with all the debris of her hopes. It was then that she remembered that however much Severne might prefer Belle's person, there was no question, she had heard it with her own ears, that it was *her* own words he had admired as they left her cousin's lips. Whatever else was true, then, it was undeniable that her cousin had stolen her own thoughts in order to more easily steal away her own choice of gentleman. And though Leonora did not believe in herself, she did believe in justice, and where fate might go unchallenged, crime could not.

She did not ask if Annabelle loved Severne; with all of her inexperience in such matters, Leonora was never a fool, and that query would provide her cousin with far too facile and unanswerable an answer to give. She only asked calmly, with no trace of embarrassment now, since she decided it was a matter of ethics and not of the heart which she broached,

"Why do you want him, Belle? You did not at first, I'll swear it. Is it because I did?"

Annabelle's eyes widened and her brows went up in her characteristic response to surprise. But it wasn't the propriety of the question that shocked her, it was the question itself.

"But he's a marquess, cousin. He has a great deal of money and when his papa dies, he'll have more and be a duke besides. Of course I showed no interest at first, for I didn't know I had a hope then. But where in the world would someone like me ever get a chance at a marquess?" Annabelle answered in amazement. "You can wed anywhere you wish, and if you don't care to wed, you'll still have a great deal of money."

"But I introduced you to a great many young men with comfortable fortunes, Belle," Leonora said reasonably, although she felt a chill wind blow across her soul at her cousin's omission of the one word she had dreaded, but nonetheless expected to hear used in defense.

"Yes, you did," the fair young woman admitted with a more honest, open smile, "but it will be better for me with Severne. He doesn't expect much, you see. Once he has his heir, he'll be content. And even if he's not—" and here the young woman grinned as she picked up the volume of poetry— "he is, you see, the last man in all of England to do anything about it. Well," she giggled, her pale face animated with her delight at her own jest, "he's *had* one divorce, hasn't he? He's not likely to ask for another. No one gets two, you know. And I don't think he'd murder for his freedom. No, he'd be the most complacent husband on earth, I think, don't you? For he'd have to put up with whatever he got, wouldn't he? And he's got a title, and a fortune. I can't see how I could do better. Really."

Annabelle shook her head for emphasis, and after one last little encouraging smile toward her cousin, she asked, "Now, can we read this book together, Leonora? I think it will be most interesting. Joscelin said you'd like it."

Leonora took a tiny involuntary step backward. She gazed into her cousin's wide, mild blue eyes and understood at last that there was and had always been something very odd about her cousin.

It was never a thing that was there for a person to see or comment upon. Even such voluble, verbal creatures as Katie and Sybil had been unable to precisely define more than their unease or dislike of something in the girl. But it would be the most difficult thing in the world to express, for there never had been any one thing in Annabelle to find fault with. It was not anything she possessed or did that caused the feeling of wrongness. The problem was the reverse. It was nothing that was in Belle. Rather, Leonora suddenly discovered, it was the lack of something that should have been there.

For here she had just calmly announced her larceny. She did not bother to deny her outright theft of the attentions of a gentleman she knew her cousin cared for. And there had been no word of love, or even of physical desire without love, which Leonora, remembering Severne's reaction to herself, could now unhappily, well understand. It hadn't been that lean, striking face, nor those piercing eyes, nor even that strong graceful frame that Belle had rhapsodized over. Nor had there been a word about his keen intellect, wry humor, or evident compassion. It was his purse she lusted for, his title she admired, and his sad history which brought her thoughts of future joy.

And now, having divulged all this, she smiled and asked Leonora to read the poetry of William Blake with her. Forgetting she was speaking with a rival, and still not willing to believe that she was dealing with a sort of monster, a human with one important piece left out, and that piece, for want of a better word, a heart, Leonora cried in confusion,

"Belle! How can you? How can you say what you've said, and then expect me to sit and chat with you as though there was not a thing upon our minds?"

Annabelle looked up from the book, from an illustration of the face of one particular dark angel that Severne had said, somewhat wistfully, reminded him of someone, and looked directly into an almost uncannily identical pair of deep and sorrowful eyes before her.

"But we needn't be enemies," she said benignly. "I like you very well, cousin, and you have been very kind to me. After I am wed, I hope that we may still be friends, for indeed, I have no reason to dislike you at all. In fact, after I'm wed, I'd like you to visit with me often. And if it transpires that Severne should like you as well by then, I shouldn't mind at all. Do you understand, cousin?"

As Leonora gaped at the slender girl, trying very hard not to understand, Annabelle went on softly,

"For you two are very much alike, you know. You both admire Master Shakespeare and poetry and music. Once I am safely wed, I vow it, cousin, I would not mind whatever you and Joscelin did together. You would find me, I promise, understanding, and willing always to look the other way. And I do not mean just when you two were having discussions," she smiled, "for I am not blind, and have seen the way he sometimes looks at you. And as I don't care for that sort of thing at all myself, I should not mind. Now, can we read?" she asked politely, holding out the book to Leonora.

"You are a monster," Leonora gasped, knocking the proffered book aside.

Annabelle sighed. She bent to pick up the book, and looked so very weary, very young, and very unhappy that Leonora, like a great many others who had dealt with Annabelle in the past, doubted all that she had just heard.

"I'll be back later," Annabelle breathed softly, "when you're in a better mood, cousin."

"How can you say such things?" Leonora almost wept with frustration as she saw her cousin's placid expression.

"Why should I not?" Annabelle asked.

When Leonora remained mute, Annabelle nodded, as though she'd gotten her answer, and, sighing, she left her cousin staring wildly after her.

Silly cow, thought Annabelle bemusedly as she made her way slowly back to her rooms. But then she wasn't disturbed, for she had spoken only the truth, after all. She didn't dislike Leonora in the slightest. She didn't like her either. For neither emotion ever had occurred to Annabelle. People had always fallen neatly into one of two categories. They had either been in her way, or they had been in a position to gratify her. And if that was what they meant by love and hate, why then she felt those emotions right enough, same as everyone else.

But she could never understand why everyone else thought she didn't, nor why they found such simple attitudes toward each other so important. Papa had cuffed her and left home early on, after hotly denying that she could be his daughter. Then in time Mama had cast her out from her own home, telling her never to return and crying that it was because of her lack of human feelings. Other relatives had eventually sent her away as well, with kicks and curses or with curses accompanied by certain sullen payments, while expressing the same thoughts. Really, Annabelle thought, it never ceased to puzzle her.

She wanted what Severne had to offer her, and now it

seemed likely that she would have it. It would be about time. She'd tried for security before, in many ways. She'd even often lain with the gentlemen, although that was a very nasty, uncomfortable chore, acceptable only because it sometimes brought favors, and moderately bearable because of how foolish the gentlemen looked at such times.

In fact, she'd done a great many unpleasant things, and had to work a great deal harder in the past to far less benefit, and with far less success. She'd been extremely fortunate this time, and she knew it. There was something between the marquess and Leonora, it had been palpably there from the start. But it was something fragile and complicated. It was, however, happily nothing she had to understand. It was enough that she'd been clever enough to notice and use it.

She sighed again, she had so wanted to read with Leonora this afternoon. But then, she thought, brightening, Leonora would get over it. Really, there was nothing else she could do, after all.

Leonora stalked her room and wrung her hands, and dreamed of revenges that made her shudder. But then, after a long despairing hour, she realized that there was nothing she could do. Annabelle had been quite right, there was no reason why she shouldn't have told the truth. For there was not a thing that Leonora could do with it.

If she dared to tell Severne of the conversation, he would never believe her. Indeed, she could scarcely credit it herself. Katie and Sybil would doubtless be appalled but true believers, but anything they might say to Severne would be construed as spite, or worse, as jealous malice. If Leonora were to drive Annabelle from her house, as every instinct shouted for her to do, it would be quite the same as driving her straight into Severne's arms. Any decent gentleman would be protective of a homeless, seemingly abused waif; a fellow who was weighing a rejected ring in his hand would doubtless immediately do far more.

Leonora then spared some extra time to berate herself for all the trust she'd put in Annabelle, and all the improving lessons she'd been so pleased to give, which had all doubtless been fed back to Severne as though they'd sprung from Belle's own fertile imagination. The idea of Annabelle's calmly lecturing Severne on a poem or play she'd just been taught that morning, as though for all the world she'd always held such opinions, caused Leonora's stomach to grow cold and flutter as though it were some giant, newly shucked oyster.

But then she took some care to remind herself that it was not as if she'd lost Severne, since she'd clearly never had him, or at least never had more than his passing lust. Even that, she took a few moments to reflect, might have only been provoked by her own ridiculous physical form, shocking reputation, or provocative behavior. After all, a gentleman could hardly consider a female he had once escorted home from a bawdy house as a viable potential bride. Then (for once she began to flail herself, she was as thorough a penitent as a medieval monk of the strictest orders), she forced herself to recall that it was Annabelle that she'd used for her own purposes, after all. Hadn't the entire idea of coming to London originally been ostensibly to find poor Belle a mate?

Still, with all her conflicting emotions, one idea stood firm and fast. It simply was not fair that Severne should take himself such a bride. It was all very well to pace the length of the room declaiming loudly in one's head that he deserved no better. It was another thing, as one paced back the breadth of the chamber, to picture that lonely outcast gentleman holding Annabelle to his breast, thinking he had at last found a devoted and decent bride. For when she thought of just what sort of a creature her cousin must be, she knew that whatever his sins, it was never fair that after all his travails he should be trapped into wedlock with such.

Leonora realized that Sybil would truly be disgusted with her reaction. Surely her sister would deem it the height of betrayal of her sex that she felt no elation at his deception or triumph at the thought of his certain downfall, no matter how he had misused and misjudged her. Nor did she think any the less of him, or judge him a fool to be so misled. If he were a fool, what could she say of herself, who had known Belle better, longer, and more intimately? But at the thought of just how intimately Severne actually knew Belle, or would know her in the unforgivably onrushing future, Leonora's head began to pound.

Belle had sounded so certain, so confident and content, that Leonora was sure that Severne's offer would not be long in coming. Indeed, he might have meant to ask for Annabelle yesterday after he'd been freed from the proposal he'd felt honor-bound to make to herself. But she expected that perhaps he'd decided it a bit much to make two such offers in one day. Perhaps he'd even felt it would be unwise to put his luck to the touch so soon after such a resounding set-down. But that would mean that so soon as tomorrow she might have to endure Belle's smug pronouncement of her engagement. Knowing what she did made the thought of tomorrow almost unendurable.

The Lady Leonora, much to her mother's and sister's eternal disgust, had never suffered from one vapor, or taken to her couch from an attack of nerves in the whole of her unnaturally unfeminine and hardy young life. But now in her confusion and inability to hit upon a solution, or indeed a suitable place to lay all the blame for her sorrows, she made up for this deficiency in a manner that would have gratified those two ladies enormously. She sank back upon her bed and decided that she would not arise from it until death or tomorrow came. And on the whole, she thought, as Katie put a cool compress upon her brow, she preferred the former, but it would be just her luck if she were only to wake to the latter.

FOURTEEN

Usually a traveler hastens the few remaining steps of a long journey, but the lone horseman rode more slowly when he at last approached the entry to the great house. Even then he seemed reluctant to dismount, and only sat and gazed about himself at the vibrant green lawns to either side of the gravel drive as though he could not bear to surrender the day and mount the stairs to enter human habitation. The wet, warm spring had been kind to the countryside, and it was as if he could not take in enough of the verdant color or breathe in enough of the sharp sweet scents of the day. But then he saw the waiting groom and, grinning at the frankly curious look upon the youth's face, he swung down from his horse and with an amused shrug, relinquished it to his care.

"Good afternoon, my lord," the butler said, as the boy had done, and with the same warm sincerity in his voice.

"Hello, Afton, how have you been keeping?" the marquess said, smiling, as casually as if he had last spoken with the fellow the week before rather than the season before, as he actually had done.

"Oh very well, my lord," the butler replied just as calmly as he took the traveler's riding coat. But that usually serene fellow gave a hint of his surprise and pleasure at seeing the marquess by saying all at once, "And I know that his grace will be delighted to see you, as well. Shall I announce you, or would you rather go straight in? He's in the library, but then, if you'd prefer to wash and change your clothing first? I don't see your valet, so if you require Gibson's services I can call him immediately, he's only tending to his grace's boots at present . . . how I do run on, my lord," he paused to say regretfully, shaking his head. "Do forgive me, but it's only that we are all that pleased at seeing you again so unexpectedly."

"Never apologize, Afton, for giving a fellow a warm welcome. It's a rare enough gift," the marquess said, putting his hand upon the older man's shoulder. "And I've never grown to be such a Town beau that I'd primp and powder before saying hello to my father. He'll have to take his son with a liberal dose of horse, but if I know my man, I think he'd prefer that to taking him a few hours later, even if he were all neatly dusted off and sprinkled with rose water by then.

"Don't announce me, I'd like to surprise him. And don't fuss, Afton, it was a spur-of-the-moment decision to visit, and I left my valet and half my kit in London. So if there's to be a gala ball tonight, I'll have to hide out in the barn, the way I did after I broke the pantry window that time, remember?"

And smiling at the memory, and at the prospect of seeing his father again, Joscelin gave the butler a grin so similar to the one he'd worn decades before that the old fellow smiled back with a most unprofessional mistiness before he caught himself at it. But before the butler could regain his more habitual expression, the marquess was across the hall and at the door to the library. He waited only a second, trying to frame some amusing jest to account for his presence. Then, smiling even more widely as he gave up all plans at feigning impassivity for the sake of that jest, he opened the door and stepped into the room. And then he ceased smiling at once.

"Joss!" his father said immediately, leaving off his conversation with his guest in the middle of a sentence with a cry of happy surprise that was almost a yelp of gladness. "Ah Joss, how good to see you, my boy."

As the gentlemen met in the center of the room, the older of the two caught the younger in his embrace, and hugged him as frankly and warmly as if he were a farmer or a woodsman greeting his son after a long absence, and not a nobleman from a line almost as old as the kingdom itself. He was a bit shorter and trifle leaner than his son, and his coloring was more subdued. Although age had muted its tint, his brown hair had never been so stark black as his son's, and if his lean face had ever been as hard as the younger man's, then age, and perhaps experience, had softened it as well. But there was a clear likeness to be seen in their matching smiles. And when the marquess turned from his father and looked about the room, and his smile faded away again, then it was their watchful indigo eyes that gave testimony to their relationship.

"How do you do, your grace," Joscelin said coolly, bowing to the other gentleman who sat deep within a deep chair near the window.

"Joss, I know I'm the last fellow on earth you expected to find here, but not so formal, please. I'd rise and thump you as soundly as your papa did, more so I think, for I outweigh him by several stone, but it's the gout, you see, and it's all I can do to be allowed to sit down here and not molder up in my rooms. How are you, my boy?" the stout gentleman asked breathlessly as he attempted to lean forward to take the younger man's hand, despite the handicap of his outstretched, bandaged leg which lay propped on a chair before him.

As he released the older gentleman's hand and watched him sink back in his chair with a relieved grunt, Joscelin noted that the fellow was red-faced with more than that simple exertion, and that his person reeked not only from several pungent medicaments, such as turpentine, camomille, and spirits of camphor, but of the more telling and recognizable scent of gin and cloves.

The older man had grown obese, and was clearly steeped in more than medicinal spirits, but the eyes that watched Joscelin narrowly were still keen, as the rumbling voice went on in an attempt at jocularity,

"Afraid I can't step out so that you two can have a chat. Indeed, I believe I couldn't easily do so at all anymore even if the devil hadn't sunk his damned teeth into this cursed limb, since I've enjoyed a feast or two too many since we last met, my boy. But, as you can just as clearly see, your father has forgiven me. Well, then," he coughed to cover the silence that followed this statement, "we were friends forever, weren't we?

"Ah well," he went on quickly, as though he were anxious not to be interrupted, "you see as we grew old, we decided we still needed that friendship no matter what ill

turns we'd served each other in our day. I don't suppose
that a young chap can see that at all. But, Joss, here's my
hand again, and I'll say it loud and clear: I bear you no ill
will, and hope you bear me none. And I hope that you can
tolerate me here in your house, for I don't see how I can
clear out too fast if you won't. Forget, if you must, that I
was once your father-in-law. But please remember that I
was once your father's friend."

Both father and son fell at once to attempting to put the
stout gentleman at his ease, the older man because of the
distress he heard so clearly in his old friend's voice, and the
younger because of the illness he read so clearly in the
other man's weak grip and unhealthy color.

It was only an hour later, after the Duke of Burlington's
attendant had struggled to transfer his charge to his invalid
chair and, with the aid of a few footmen, had gotten his
master to his rooms in order to wash and change for
dinner, that the duke at last could speak privately with his
newly returned son.

"I'm sorry for the surprise," he said at once when the
door closed behind his friend. "And if you dislike it, Joss,
I'll tell him to leave. He's right in what he says. I suppose
that since his wife's gone, and his daughter as well, he's
lonely. But I discovered that although I am not, just the
same, old friends are a comfort in old age. No, don't deny
it, Joss, for I can count, you know," he said before his son
could dispute his mathematics.

"Still, if you dislike it, he goes, and at once. You are, at
any age, my preferential visitor. Although," he chided gently
even as his son shook his head in the negative, "never a
frequent one, alas. We ought never to have made Deaver
House so comfortable for heirs to the dukedom. I remember I was loath to leave it when I came into the title
myself. Adam may have worked himself to a shadow here
in Basset Hall, but Deaver House is beautifully situated
there in the midlands. But what am I speaking of? It's
London that you've been cavorting in when you haven't
been abroad slipping about on Talwin's behalf, isn't it?"

"I don't know what possible good I can have done the
viscount," the marquess said with a wry expression, "when
it appears that every chap in England knew of it."

"I do hope that isn't so," his father replied, matching his

tone, "for I shouldn't like to think that every chap in England believes himself to be your papa. You see, Talwin felt that certain persons required certain explanations when certain chaps refused to explain where they were sneaking off to every so often whenever certain of their paternal relations inquired.

"I see," Joscelin said with a grin, and when they were done laughing, he said more seriously, "And as for Burlington, sir, never fear, I don't harbor a grudge. Actually, in a way it seems that the fellow who divorced his daughter is as dead and gone, with all his disappointments and anger, as that poor girl of his is now. So don't worry. I'm glad you two have patched it up, and hope that he holds out long enough to continue as your friend for a few years more."

"You've changed, Joss," his father said, looking at him sharply. "Is it possible that you've returned with glad news? If so, your mother will never forgive herself for being absent just now. But she's off to help little Willie celebrate his third birthday and await your sister's presenting him with a new sister or brother for the occasion. Shall you wait for her return, or have you something to tell me now?" he asked eagerly, as a frown of incomprehension came over his son's brow. "Can it be that you plan to add to the family too, Joss?" he asked anxiously. "It's what we've all been waiting for, these many years."

The marquess paused, and hesitated as he put down his glass of sherry. Then he said very softly, "You amaze me, sir, and always have done. You remember years ago when I hid that stray beneath my bed and when I came down to dinner you asked if I wanted a puppy? Then, I believe it may have been the bits of fur upon my nankeens and the breath of kennel about my person that tipped you a hint. But now, do I reek of orange blossoms as Burlington does of spirits, or is there rice on my lapels? For I confess, as I did not even to myself until just now, that such thoughts aren't far from my mind. But no, I haven't such an announcement to make as yet," he said with a rueful grin as he saw his father's expression of disappointment.

He grimaced and then went on, "Yes, I came here to think the thing out. But it isn't just one lovely lady, sir, as you might expect. Rather there are two that revolve, as on a little turning stage, in my admittedly strange mind. Clearly,

I cannot commit bigamy. And I do not think I can have the one I want, without wanting the other I do not, so the question is whether I ought to have either. No," he laughed ruefully, "if it confuses even myself, I certainly won't burden you with the tale. And no, I'm sorry, but I can't wait for Mama to be done with playing ministering angel. I'm only here for a brief visit, for a hasty repairing lease."

Even as he changed the subject by asking for news of the family and the district, he realized that every word he'd uttered was true. He could never lie to his father as easily as he did to himself. Every excuse he'd given himself for leaving Town so suddenly, whether it was the need for a change of scenery, or a desire to look in on his parents, had been a subterfuge. He'd come home to his past, to think on his future. To try to envision in his mind's eye the female he ought to bring home to stay with him as his wife.

For suddenly he knew, as though he'd always known it, that he wanted a wife. It was time and past time for him to settle down, he thought. It might have been because he had lately seen Torquay's domestic happiness, or it might have been his bitter experience with the lovely, faithless Lady Lambert that had made him resolve to be done with all relationships that he had to pay for in coin or in flattery. Or it just might have been that he had at last met a female that he could not erase from his mind, for to do so would be to leave a terrible void there.

But there were two females to reckon with, and they were linked in his mind as they were in his life, for good and real reason. He knew that in all honesty, he could not offer for the one until he was finally prepared to turn his back forever upon the other. To do otherwise would not be fair to himself, and would never be fair to her.

And he saw that he could not remain here long, even if it were not for the fact that he could have no real resting place while he was undecided. Certainly, he must leave here soon, since his former father-in-law was in residence. No matter how lightly he'd dismissed it, he was aware that grim memories were like a miasma surrounding the old gentleman even as the scents of his physical illness clung to his huge person.

As he dressed for dinner that night, he thought of the

two females who haunted him. They had followed him from London, and would, he knew, follow him everywhere until he cast one entirely out, and took the other unquestioningly to his heart. He thought of the one, all seriousness and quaint wisdom, and the other, all laughter and sharp wit. He thought of the one who would bask in the full sunlight of his love, and the one who would glow in the midnight realms of his passion. Then he thought of the one whose face would not leave his mind, and the one whose voice never let his conscience rest.

And he began to know, even then, as he stood within the familiar walls of his childhood, where his heart lay, where his mind lay, and at the last, how narrow the gap between them really was.

That night, after dinner, after the obligatory port and tobacco and incidental chatter, the gouty duke caught at his sleeve as he prepared to go to his room for the night. His father was at the far end of the room, pouring more port for himself and his friend, but even so, the old man lowered his voice.

"I want you to know I don't bear you a grudge, Joss," he said, with tears in his eyes, and perhaps real tears at that, and not only ones induced by alcohol, or the chemical fumes that arose from his bandaged leg, "for you did the right thing by our girl, after all. We wed her to Alsop a year after the divorce, y'know. Alsop, that cur, that scrambler, that bastard. Aye, Joss, he was that. For he didn't mind getting her with child, not he, and right away, too. She hated it, Joss," the old man said, his white lips trembling.

Though the marquess didn't want to hear more, he had to wait until the old man recovered enough to go on to say, "We never could make her understand why she was getting so stout, nor why she felt so ill. And when she was dying, having the babe, she wept and asked me why it had to hurt so much, this illness she had. And I lost her and the babe, and she never knew why. So you did right, Joss," he said fiercely, "and I curse the day I didn't see that right often looks dead wrong. And that the best thing a man can be is honest with himself, no matter how it hurts to be so."

The old duke was amazed, when he had done with wiping his streaming eyes, to see how his one-time son-in-law gazed at him. For there was a look of purest relief and gladness upon that usually stern face. It might have been the gin, or the opium or the port that he constantly took that made him imagine that arrested look the marquess wore, the duke was to think later, or it might truly have been that the lad was glad he'd been forgiven. He was never to know that it wasn't absolution for the past the marquess was wondering at, but rather the glimpse of insight he'd been given to his future.

As he bade the two elderly gentlemen a good night, the marquess thought he actually would enjoy the first good night he'd had in weeks. He had his answer, even though it had come from a completely unexpected source. And he knew that it was the correct one, because it felt entirely right.

He would leave for London on the morrow. He had learned from the past, and knew his future. He couldn't forget her for the simple reason that he really didn't want to. And he would wed her, or never wed at all. For this time he would wed where honesty was, he would marry where truth lay, for in so doing, surely, he could never step wrong again.

Leonora took a deep breath in, and expelled it slowly through her slightly parted lips. Then she frowned, and inhaled again, but this time through her mouth, and then let all the pent-up air out slowly through her nostrils. She kept one hand upon her abdomen as she did so, and looked perplexed again. So much as she tried to recall the article she'd read, she couldn't remember precisely whether she was supposed to breathe in deeply through her mouth so that her stomach filled with air and then resumed its shape as she breathed out through her nose, or whether she was supposed to breathe in through her nose so her stomach became flat as her chest swelled, letting her abdomen relax only as she exhaled through her lips. Whichever method had been detailed was the one that was a sure cure for nervousness.

Now as she stood outside the door to her father's study, she only felt giddy. She'd been breathing in and out for several moments, attempting to follow the directions from that long vanished article from a lady's journal, and not only had she forgotten the method, but the results had made her even more anxious, for now she was faint as well as apprehensive.

But whatever she was, she realized as the hallway around her began to stabilize again, she was certainly not going to spend the rest of her life in a hallway for fear of facing her father. He had summoned her, and now she had to summon up the courage to face him. So she took a deep breath again, this time not caring what part of her anatomy expanded, and before she let it out, she tapped upon the door. And then, when she was bade to enter, she opened the door and marched in, remembering to breathe out only because she needed to do so in order to say, "Good morning, Father. You sent for me?"

He stood behind his desk and smiled at her, and said only, "Yes, Leonora, I did. Won't you sit down?"

She sat at once, eagerly, if a bit inelegantly, plopping down in a chair opposite him, glad to have something under her, glad to have something solid behind her back to straighten it as well.

He gave her one shrewd look, noting the shadows beneath her great dark eyes, noticing how her cheeks seemed leaner and her frock a bit looser here and there.

"You're probably wondering why I called you here," he said then, turning his attention to some papers upon the desk, thinking that his Nell would have giggled at how ponderous he sounded, but that this stranger, Lady Leonora, would only nod and answer seriously.

"Why, yes," she said, for she didn't know what else to say, for her papa, the one she'd known so well, would have never been able to utter such a pompous phrase without some laughter creeping into his voice.

Suddenly, he was tired of this, he was weary unto death with it. He looked up at her, with his face naked of artifice, totally devoid of the many several deceptions he was capable of, and, as she stared at him as though he'd appeared in a vision, he said, as strongly as he felt,

"You've not been happy. Not for some time since you've come to London, certainly not at all in the past week. I don't have to be a genius to have noticed that. I'm your father, Leonora. I might have been more of a friend once, and have never understood why that had to end, but you needn't say anything upon that head if you don't wish.

That's not why I called you here today. You haven't confided in your mama, and if you have in Sybil, I don't know
of it, and honestly don't know if she could help if you did.

"But I can, Nell," he said in a rush. "I know that if it is
humanly possible for another being to help you with this
problem you have, I can. And I merely wanted you to know
. . ." He faltered, his voice tapering off, for now that he'd
come to the end of his statement, he realized how ineffec-
tual it sounded, and how useless it all likely was.

"I wanted you to know that I care, and would like to
help," he ended at last, a bit gruffly, for he was embarrassed now at how she continued to gape at him, and was
a little angry at himself and how he had left himself open to
insult from this stranger who reminded him so much of his
long-lost beloved Nell.

But she sat and stared at him in silence until he looked
hard at her, and saw that her face was very white and her
eyes very wide and filled with tears. And then she cried, in
a voice that he remembered very well, "Oh Papa, I have
been so very unhappy."

For he had called her "Nell." That surely was what had
done it, she thought a few moments later, when she had
enough self-awareness to be a little ashamed at how hard
she was caterwauling into his lapels. And when she at last
accepted his handkerchief and resoundingly blew her nose,
and they both laughed at how loudly she did so, as they
always used to do, she discovered that she didn't know
quite what to say to him as she left his comforting embrace.

"What was it?" he asked simply, as she drew away. "It
likely took a great deal of pain to bring my daughter back
to me, and I think I know what's causing it, but it occurs to
me now that it took something similar to drive you away
from me so long ago. Can you tell me what it was then,
Nell?" he asked quickly, before either of them had time to
put back the barriers they had let down.

And before she could think to suppress it, as irresistibly
as a hiccup or a sneeze, the word that had lingered in the
forefront of her brain throughout the last moments popped
out of her lips. "Phoebe," she said, and then "Phoebe,"
she said again, as he stared at her in puzzlement, and she
thought she sounded rather like a demented cuckoo clock.

So she said slowly, looking down at his handkerchief

twisting in her hands, "It was at Vauxhall Gardens, one night five years ago. You didn't see me there, Papa, I was with Miss Thicke and some beaux and friends. They didn't see you either, but I did, with Phoebe. Or so you called her."

"Oh," said the viscount, sitting back on the edge of his desk, lost in thought. "Oh yes. Phoebe. I'd forgotten her. Actually," he said with a ghost of a laugh, "I forgot her the next day, and I'd not remembered her again until you spoke her name just now. Why didn't you say something to me?"

"What could I say?" Leonora asked in a muffled voice.

"You could have asked for an explanation," he replied reasonably.

"So that was it!" Leonora cried, sudden color and animation coming into her face. "Only think, all those years wasted for nothing! For I told Sybil, I did Papa, I told her even then that there was some good reason we were not to know of. Though she denied it, I thought it might be that, I did!" She laughed gaily. "The girl was some agent, or some spy you had to lull, it was something such as that, I swore it . . ."

"Nell," he said on a sigh. "Nell," he said seriously, taking her hands in his and stopping her happy spate of conjecture. "No. No. You saw what you saw. I could lie, of course. I could tell you a tale, I'm very good at that, you know. But I like you too well for that. Phoebe was only a common tart, just as you imagined. I was unfaithful for the sake of my own needs, and not my country's."

He released her hands, and stood and began to walk about the room, his pacing and not his words showing his agitation. "We have a great joke," he sighed, "all of us who work at my trade. It has to do with a philandering nobleman, I'll spare you the details. In any event, the ending line, which occasions much laughter (Torquay tells it very slyly, and very well), has the gentleman, caught in a very damning position, crying out to his outraged wife, 'All in the line of duty, m'dear, all in the line of duty.' So I won't say as much to you, for your sake as well as mine, since neither of us belong in a smutty jest.

"Your mother and I, and our marriage . . .," he began,

frowning, before she cut in rapidly and said, "Oh, no, Papa, you don't owe me an explanation."

He stopped and stared at her. "Oh, yes," he said solemnly, "but I do, Nell. Whatever arrangement your mama and I decided upon is only our own business so long as it does not affect other people. When it does, then it becomes their business as well. Your mama and I are friends, but only that, and have been only that to each other for years.

"She does not, however, feel the need for any other companionship, nor does she mind that I," the viscount said very softly, "as I confess, often do, and often have, but I swear, I've always attempted to be discreet. It's ironic, and just as the sermons warn, that the one time I failed, of course, I failed in your eyes. I'm sorrier than you can know for that."

"It's just as Sybil said, then, isn't it?" Leonora mused aloud after a time. "Marriage in our set is only for the purposes of producing offspring."

"Definitely," her father said, smiling. "Why only look at Torquay and his duchess. No, Nell. It's only so for those of us who discover that our unions no longer work, whether they were entered into for political or social reasons, or even in the expectation of love. And then, too, for some of us, once we are wed we discover that our lives may be committed to each other, but that does not mean that we are. But it doesn't have to be that way, indeed, it oughtn't to be that way, and need never be that way for you."

"Ah well," Leonora said, with a great deal of false vivacity, "and so it won't be, for I shall never wed."

"I was thinking," her father went on, unruffled, "rather more along the lines that Joss was no more the sort to be faithless than you are."

"I don't doubt," Leonora said stiffly, "that Annabelle is very fortunate then."

"Ah," said her father. "He has offered for her?"

"No," Leonora answered in an unsteady voice, "but she says he shall, and I believe it."

"Then he is a most unlucky gentleman," the viscount said sadly, "and I'm sorry for him, for I like him very well."

"It's very good of you to say so," Leonora murmured from beneath the handkerchief which she was now using

again for her eyes. "But after all, you are my father. And of
course, you'd prefer that he preferred me, if only for my
sake."

Leonora was so busy with the handkerchief, now attending to her nose by giving it a determined blow as if to dare
it to snivel again, that she didn't see her father smile a brief
passing smile, as though he'd just had something important
verified. When he spoke again, his face was impassive.

"Not just that, Nell, but only have a look at this," he said
as he passed the sheaf of papers on his desk to his daughter.

Leonora frowned in incomprehension when she took the
papers, but then she began to read, and then to flip through
the pages avidly, and then put them down and stared,
wide-eyed and mute, at her father. But, he noted, color
had returned to her cheeks, and light to her eyes. Oh yes,
he thought on an interior grin, my Nell and no doubt about
it.

But, "Torquay suggested I compile such a report," was
all he said laconically, before he added, "The fellow has
the devil's own nose for wickedness, it never eludes him.
I'll swear he can sniff it out. He claims it's a case of like
calling to like. But, however he does it, I'll confess with all
my experience I never thought to discover half of it."

"I can scarcely believe it," Leonora breathed. "No, I can,"
she amended, "for I had some intimation of it recently,
when she told me why she wanted him and I learned how
she deceived me. That's why I've been so wretched. But I
never would have credited . . . Papa, this says that she has
been cast out of a dozen homes for blackmail, cheating,
and unchasteness. We cannot let Joss offer for her," she
said fiercely. "Not simply for my sake, I promise you, but
surely he's suffered enough. You must show him this!" she
cried, rising and brandishing the papers.

But her father's next calm words made her sit again.

"Ah, yes," he said softly. "And do you imagine he will
thank me for it if he truly loves her? Would you, if I
produced such a dossier about one you loved? Ancient
kings killed messengers for delivering bad news, though I
doubt Joss would go quite so far. But he wouldn't love
someone for it, and I would like his continued friendship.
And so, I think, should you. That is, if you still have it? Do
you? I think, daughter," the viscount said with a knowing

look to Leonora, "that we ought to have a discussion. And
that," he suddenly announced in great booming, pear-
shaped, and portentous tones, "is why I called you here
this afternoon." And then, they both laughed for a very
long time before they began to talk in earnest.

It was nearly teatime when they were done. And when
Leonora went to the door of the study with the viscount,
she knew that she had regained a father. Though this
made her very happy, still she couldn't help but be aware
that long years had passed. For good as it was, it was no
longer enough for her, not as it had been.

No matter how pleasant it was to have his friendship and
love again, there was no denying that she was grown
sufficiently now to realize that she needed a different kind
of love and friendship as well, of a sort that he could never
give her. And it seemed that all their planning and plotting
could bring that love no closer to her. Though he swore
that he knew Joss well enough to know that he was made
for her, and though she at last admitted she wished it were
so, neither of them could think of a way to communicate
that salient fact to the marquess.

They agreed to speak of it again, and they didn't have to
make an appointment to do so, for they were friends, and
of a mind again. She mightn't approve of his habit of
seeking light females, but she could, at least, at last, understand his need for it, and perhaps even see, as he said, that
a divorce would have made a great many people unhappy,
whereas his double life only made himself unhappy. As
well as herself, of course, she thought, when she had been
so very young.

And as they stood in the doorway, reluctant to go in to
tea, since they were not so eager to stretch this newly
reforged tie between them, they stopped talking, indeed,
Leonora almost stopped breathing. For they saw Annabelle
emerging from the library at the exact moment that she
spied them. How much of the newly repaired relationship
she registered, and how much of it she perceived as a
personal threat as she paused and stared at them with her
wide light eyes, they could not say. But after a moment,
she smiled and said, as though there were nothing out of
the ordinary in finding them so much in charity with each
other,

"Good afternoon, my lord, Leonora. Oh cousin, I have been searching everywhere for you. I thought we might read together. But now it is time for tea."

Leonora felt a guilty shame, as if the one she had just been speaking of could guess each word that had been said, but her father, a practiced spymaster, only said cheerily,

"Why cousin, would you have us trade scones for poems? We are not such demons for self-improvement as you, I fear. What's that you have there, my dear? A book by Mr. Blake? Ah, that's a new title to me, *Book of Midnights* is it? He's done with Paradise and Jerusalem and taken on the darker angels and the father of lies now, I see."

"Yes," Annabelle replied smugly, taking the book from beneath her arm and leafing through it. She looked up at them, and added, with more levity than was usual for her, perhaps because she felt that the viscount appreciated it, or perhaps because she felt challenged by the unified front they presented,

"And I think you should know that I've been trying to get Leonora to read it with me for days now. It's the only copy, for it's never been properly published. Joscelin gave it to me, you know. And I've just gotten word that he's coming to see me tomorrow."

She waited and watched Leonora's face grow pale before she said again, "And I so wanted to go over it with my cousin before he came. For it may be that he wants it back now." But this last was said with a titter, and such a note of patent disbelief that it was almost as if she sang it out.

"Now, now," said the viscount in happy, avuncular fashion, though his daughter stood as silent as if she'd been struck in the face rather than merely struck by a horrific thought, "I doubt that's the case, my dear. But perhaps Leonora will find a space to look at it with you. I shouldn't mind having a go at it myself, had I only time to do so. *Book of Midnights*—Brrr, it sounds quite a diabolic book of verse. Are you sure you like it, my dear?"

"Oh, very much," Annabelle said sweetly, "but now I shall put it back in my room, for I don't think it's quite the thing to bring it in to tea with me."

"Oh, no," the viscount agreed. "Well, we'll see you in salon as soon as may be then, won't we?"

It was not until Annabelle had gone up the stairs that the

viscount turned to his daughter. She looked at him in dismay and yet with a certain wild surmise.

"You've read Shakespeare and Blake with her, have you?" He chuckled. "Well, there's a thing that wasn't in the report. And there's one thing we *can* use. Tomorrow, I think, my dear."

"But the book," Leonora gasped, "the one she's been waving in my face all week. It was titled *Book of Moonlight*, I saw it printed plain, Father."

"Yes." He smiled joyously. "But happily, oh luckily, I did not see it so at first. But you're quite right. For so it was printed, plain as pie. For all those who can read."

FIFTEEN

Spring seemed to have danced off from London to some more northern clime, for this morning the sun was egg-yolk yellow and a hot, breathy breeze stirred thoughts of tropical matters. All along the fashionable avenues coaches were being polished and readied for their owners' annual treks to country homes, knockers were being removed from the doors of the privileged, farewell notes and future directions were being distributed by harried running footmen, and it was in all as if the monied classes were preparing for some siege, rather than just another English summer.

The fair-haired young woman checked her appearance one last time in the looking glass over her dressing table. She wore a thin white frock with little puffed sleeves that had a tiny print of yellow flowers strewn overall. A yellow sash circled her tiny waist and she wore her fine, long light hair brushed back with a thin yellow ribband to keep it from drifting into her large light blue eyes. She looked very young and innocent. She looked, she thought, precisely as he would want to see her. And as Annabelle had no preference or any strong opinion as to her appearance, how he wished to find her was the only way she cared to look.

If he'd shown any sensual interest, she would have worn clinging, silken, shining materials that emphasized her shape and showed up her small sharp breasts. She would have moved more sinuously, and spoken both more boldly and more softly. Even her face would have taken on the foxlike, fervid expression it was capable of. But he had moved away from her when she'd pressed close the first time they'd danced, and no matter how often she'd silently offered more, he'd never sought to hold her so again. It made no matter, since Annabelle Greyling could and would be anything that profited her. So if he wanted a child to take to wife, she would be that child.

And she was a very pretty child this morning, she decided, and this morning it was most important to be so. This morning he would come, and he would offer for her, and she would blush and breathe "yes" with as much shy happiness as she could put into that one word. That wouldn't be difficult at all, for then he'd wed her and then she would have money and power and all the things she'd ever wanted. If she wasn't too sure of what those things were, at least she'd be able to discover them once she had the means.

If it pleased him to have her remain his pretty little girl, why then she would do so, at least for so long as it pleased her to be, for she wasn't angry at him, he hadn't done anything to anger her as yet. She wouldn't like it if he took her to his bed, of course, but she accepted that he probably would do so when they were first married. But she wasn't a fool and knew that he wouldn't do that for long. He wasn't the sort to enjoy such things with a girl who would constantly shudder and cringe and weep as she planned to do. She didn't want to bear any babies, but didn't worry about that at all. She knew from experience that if she wrenched away from him often enough at the right moments those first times, it wouldn't be a problem either.

No, she decided, the world and her future looked just as pristine and lovely as she did this late spring morning. Yet nothing is ever perfect, she knew that very well. She would have preferred to have gotten her riches without a husband, but that was clearly impossible. Murder, she giggled to herself, had more penalties attached than wedlock did, and anyway, there wasn't anyone to do away with that would have left her a cent.

No, marriage was inevitable, although she would have preferred a different sort of husband. Indeed, she'd expected an entirely different one. Someone old, someone doddering, in fact, would not only have been more suitable, but more manageable. The marquess sometimes made her a little nervous, he was so young and vital and intense.

Actually, she'd never imagined she'd have a chance at him, and she'd been staggered when she realized she did, but was never slow to seize an opportunity for advancement. She'd have him.

Because just as she'd told Leonora, there was actually very little he could do once they were wed. She didn't mind a bit of pain, threats could not move her. When he discovered that, they'd deal very well together. Then too, she remembered, there was the fact that cousin Leonora wanted him so very much. That made it all even better, just as when she'd been a child, a sweet had tasted that much better when another child didn't have one.

So she would marry wealthily and well, and he would eventually leave her alone, and the world looked very bright this bright morning. But even as Annabelle whirled away from the looking glass and caught up the volume Severne had given her that she carried with her almost as a talisman, she knew that there were a few things left for her to do in order to preserve that bright vision. Too often things had slipped away from her at the last moment, too often she'd had a taste of victory only to choke on it later. It took a great deal of self-control, but this time she intended to make certain of it before she rejoiced.

After all, she thought, as her little slippered feet skimmed swiftly and silently down the stairs, although she had tried very hard not to anger Leonora too much, she knew her cousin was very vexed with her. That didn't disturb her unduly, for it wouldn't affect Severne, with all the tales she'd told him she doubted he'd believe Leonora now if she said it was a sunny morning. Lady Benjamin was a right bitch, and a shrewd one too, but she'd look it all right if she spoke up against the match, if she spoke one harsh word against poor, unhappy little Annabelle.

Annabelle paused at the foot of the long circular stair, and looked about herself quickly, her body still, her head lifted to catch any sound, even her nostrils quivering, as though she were some secret creature creeping through a dangerous night rather than a slip of a girl on a sun-drenched spring morning. Or so a passing footman thought, even though he realized it was a ridiculous fancy after she spied him and gave him a shy smile before she slipped soundlessly away and down the long hall.

No, Annabelle thought as she came to the door of the drawing room, those two females didn't dismay her at all. Neither did the viscountess, who could be relied upon not to bother about anything that did not come to bother her tea parties or her naps. But her host, the viscount, troubled her very much. In him, Annabelle recognized a worthy foe, if he should care to be her foe.

She could not attract him, she knew this intuitively, but neither could she appeal to his chivalry as she had done with the marquess, for he knew his daughter too well to believe her. To this date, he had not bothered with her any more than she had with him. But now that Leonora obviously had reconciled her differences with him, things might change. So although Annabelle earnestly thought that matters had already gone too far and it was far too late for anyone to alter the course of her fate, it never hurt to take extra care. There would be marriage swiftly on the heels of an offer, and there would be nothing to impede that offer. She would see to that.

She could count very well, and the chimes of the mantel clock in her room had told her that the marquess was expected quite soon. She'd sent a message in reply to his note, and had cautioned the footman to be very clear: she would be pleased to see him at once, just as he'd requested; she expected him at eleven; she would await him in the library. That was a good time. The viscountess would still be abed, and Lady Benjamin never visited before noon. And best of all, Annabelle thought with pleasure, Leonora and her father would be in the drawing room at that exact same time, safely away from the hall and the library. For she'd sent a message asking them to be there.

Now she stepped into the drawing room and looked about with satisfaction. As she expected, they hadn't arrived as yet. It wasn't quite time. Still, if they'd been early, it would have been no great problem. She'd simply have been vague, asked them to pray wait a moment until she'd gotten something from her room, and then they would have sat and chatted until enough time had passed for her to reenter with her new fiancé to make the announcement of her forthcoming marriage.

She gazed about the room. It was a cool and elegant

chamber, done in tones of blue and sea green and gold. They would be quite comfortable there, she thought on a hastily suppressed titter, as they waited for her. There was a bit of paper propped up on the green malachite mantelpiece. She went in quickly to examine it, but her name wasn't upon it, so she, lightly, blithely, sweetly smiling, stepped away so that she might be on time to greet the marquess in the library.

As she closed the door softly behind her, she wondered what they thought she had called them to say. That she was leaving? That she regretted any inconvenience she had caused and thanked them for their hospitality? Well, she thought generously, she would say that too, then, and more. After she and Severne gave them the happy news.

Annabelle opened the door to the library moments before the huge hall clock was due to strike the hour. She had a moment of unease, as she always did when she entered that vast room, and in those fleeting seconds she wished that her arrangements had been reversed. The sun did not dominate here, sheer curtains filtered it to a constant, glowing, golden light. But it seemed, as it always did to Annabelle, a dim, daunting chamber. She would have been more comfortable in the drawing room, and doubtless, the viscount and Leonora would have been better occupied in this great, book-lined, confusing room. But then, she remembered, it was a place Severne would be at ease in as well, and that, after all, was of prime importance.

She came into the room, scarcely noting the familiar long polished table, the floor-to-ceiling walls of books, the rows of bookcases to the right, and the two side bow window recesses, with their pairs of high-backed chairs that faced the windows. She thought of sitting in one of those tall chairs, with Severne invited to take an adjacent one. But then, that was never an intimate setting, the streets could be seen from one, the garden from the other. Too diverting. No, far better if she leaned back against the long table—yes, just so, so that the sunlight was behind her hair, encrusting her with a gilded outline so that she looked fragile and vulnerable posed against the heavy oak table with its background of dark leather tomes.

She heard a sound, like that of a throat being cleared, and her heart raced, for it was, she realized with joyful excitement, a very thrilling moment. But it was her nerves playing up or the sound of the butler approaching, for it was another second that seemed an hour before the tap came upon the door. And then she whispered "Come in," as though in a dream where you cannot raise your voice, before she took hold of herself and invited in her future by saying, clearly, "Enter!"

He appeared in the doorway even as the clock was striking eleven, just as a gentleman ought, just as she'd known he would. She said nothing further as the butler backed away, but only leaned back against the table, enjoying each second of the unfolding drama. He wore a dark blue jacket and a richer blue vest, and tight cream-colored inexpressibles with high shining hessians. His dark face was serious, and his voice and hand were cool as he greeted her and took her hand in his.

"I'm so glad that you could see me this morning, Belle," he said at once. "I had far more to tell you than I could ever have put in a note, and I thought it could not wait much longer."

Better and better, she thought, but only lowered her eyes and said at once, "Yes, I have wanted to see you, too." Then, "Oh Joscelin!" she cried, breaking from her immobility and drawing nearer to him. "You can have no idea of how difficult it's been for me this past week that you've been gone. If my life was unhappy before . . . I know I should not say it," she blurted, turning her face from his astonished regard, "but I do not know how much more of this I can be expected to endure. It was difficult when my cousin believed you to have an interest in me, but in a way it's become even worse now that she thinks you no longer care about my welfare.

"And," she went on in a husky, broken whisper, for there really wasn't all that much time to spare, and elements of speed and surprise might move things along, "I myself have wondered if I had offended or somehow angered you, as well. You were gone a week," she said, shaking her head, "with never a word, or a message until yesterday." And since no man likes to be berated, she added, "I understand, of course, you owe me nothing, but it is so good to see you again. Now I know I am not alone."

But when she peeked up from under her light lashes, she saw that his face was rigid, and he seemed to be experiencing some difficulty in framing his next words to her. He ought to have clasped her to his breast by now, he ought already to have begun to make some declaration, and she grew a little alarmed. So the face that she turned to him was quite naturally ashen.

"Belle," he said, taking her hand, and that eased her mind somewhat, "I did go away for a while, to think. And that time served me, and you too, very well, I believe. Because I came to see some home truths about myself."

He loosed her hand, and instead, placed his hand lightly beside her face and smiled down at her. "Belle," he said, "you needn't worry. I won't let you remain in an unhappy situation. You are far too nice a child."

She breathed out a sigh of relief and a smile grew upon her lips that was so genuine and triumphant that only at the last did she remember that she ought to dampen it, and let her lips tremble a bit. But by then, it had frozen in place.

For he reached into his vest pocket and instead of withdrawing the ring box she expected to see, he drew out an envelope and held it out to her. And then he went on to say, just as tenderly, "I've made a provision for you, you need not stay on here if you don't wish. And you needn't feel uncomfortable about accepting it, for I promise, I have no designs upon you. There are no obligations. Just look, Belle, it's a bankcheck for a sum that you can invest. And you can live quite nicely on the proceeds for some time."

"But I thought," Annabelle said, too amazed to feel more than the first faint stirrings of rage, "I thought you had a care for me."

"Why, so I do child," he replied, "have I not just shown it?"

"I thought," she said, looking directly into his eyes, her own blazing, and her voice rising, for she was quick to recuperate from any shocks, "that you had a different sort of care for me."

But then she saw something spark in those dark blue depths that sobered her, and she went on, in a smaller, quavering tone, "You led me on, Joscelin, you did. Money," she said, brushing away the hand that still proffered the envelope, "is not what I expected from you.

Indeed," she said, trying for the highest stakes, for as any
true gambler, she'd accept nothing less, "you insult me
and what I thought we had for each other by offering
such."

"Ah, Belle," he sighed, playing for time, for he had been
afraid that she might think this, but hadn't really expected
her to voice it. Instead, he'd thought any objection she'd
make would have to do with her finding some impropriety
in taking money from him, and had only prepared argu-
ments to convince her of the rightness of it. But honesty,
he told himself, you promised yourself honesty this time, so
he then said, as gently as he could,

"Belle, it's true that I may have given you some expectations. And I apologize if that's so. You were not entirely
wrong, for I'll confess there was a time when I didn't know
my own mind. But I do now." He looked down into her
drawn face and continued as sadly as though he were
telling her of the death of a loved one, which in a sense, he
realized with a certain pang, perhaps he was. "I like you
very much, Annabelle. You are wise and your mind is a
good, inquiring one, and I have delighted in communing
with you. Yet, with all I feel for you, my dear, I do not love
you. At least, not as one must love a wife. And you
deserve more. I know you will someday find it," he said
quickly, aghast himself at the clichés he found himself
taking refuge in uttering. "This check will help you to do
so," he concluded with relief.

She stood still, her head thrown back so she could meet
his eyes, as motionless as an alabaster figurine. Then, as he
began to wonder why she did not reply, she spoke. "You
do not have to love me," she said through tightly held lips.

He gave a small start. The conversation was taking on a
nightmarish quality. It was true that he had shown her
some attentions. He'd given her a book, seen to it that she
was invited to a house party, and often kept her company.
But a gentleman could send cartloads of flowers, invite a
young lady to a dozen house parties as well as balls and
fetes, sit with her through everything from dinner to the
Opera, and make no offer without bringing shame upon
himself or her. He might arouse expectations, but not
disgrace, since society conceded that expectations were not
promises.

He had not, after all, held her in anything but conversation, and had never met with her in secret, or ever intimately embraced her. He'd never even kissed her, as he'd been both embarrassed and oddly repelled at the mere idea of it.

It was Leonora he had compromised, and he'd already attempted to make proper reparation for it. But he scarcely knew what to say to this poor child, who was trembling with insult. It was true that he once entertained a notion to take her to wife, but only for the briefest time before he recognized the truth behind the impulse. He never guessed she might be enamored of him, and he was not insensitive to such matters. He thought her only eager for the sanctuary he could provide her; she'd never shown a hint of any warmer emotion, and he couldn't believe it was only shyness which prevented her. There'd never been any of the evidences of love that could usually be detected, indeed, which could not be hidden, in her voice, or expression, or eyes. Even now, he doubted the validity of her emotions, and put it down to her inexperience with men.

"Belle," he said, as he struggled with a sudden, sick sense of shame, for he felt as though he'd enticed a child, "please, understand. I'm in a position to know that love is most important in these matters."

"It's someone else you love then?" she demanded, still frozen in affront, still, he believed, wounded and stiff with rejection. He knew that feeling very well, and so said, as he had not thought he would, "Yes."

And then, because he felt it might be less hurtful if she understood it was none of it her fault or brought about by any failing in herself, he said with a shrug,

"But much good it will do me, for she'll have none of me, and she may well have the right of it. For we've never been able to remain at peace with each other beyond the turning of the tide. So I shall take myself off this summer and repair my estates, and then perhaps when autumn comes, if the world and the little Emperor permit, I'll travel abroad for a time.

"I'm a shocking sort of fellow, really. I can't seem to either stay in, or get into a marriage very successfully. Clearly, wedding cake is not my dish," he commented wryly. "But come, Belle, accept the check," he said more seriously, "for whether or not you can believe right now that it's equally as much proof of my esteem for you as a wedding ring might be, and likely a much better bargain as well, I think when you reflect upon it, you'll agree that there's no real reason not to take it."

But Annabelle had been standing arrested, thinking furiously, and when he'd done speaking, she opened her eyes very wide indeed, and cried out, as though she'd had some dazzling revelation, "Leonora! It's been Leonora you've wanted all along, hasn't it?"

And when he only smiled and shrugged again, since this was not a subject he wished to discuss with her, she accused, "But how could you? After all that I told you about her?"

"Well, there you are," he sighed, stepping back a pace, leaving the envelope upon the table and spreading his hands in a gesture of defeat. "Now you see how narrowly you escaped. I've come to see that most of the polite world was right in their judgment of me. I must not be a very good fellow. For with all you've told me, I cannot dislike her, even though I know I ought. I cannot dismiss her from my thoughts, even though I suppose I'd rather.

"You tell me she's cruel," he said regretfully, "and I excuse it by thinking it only thoughtlessness. You say she berates you constantly, and I absolve it, thinking you are too sensitive. And though you tell me you're abused, I see the pretty gowns you wear and am only relieved to see no bruises. There's no help for it, Belle.

"It's not just temptation and desire," he explained, "they're old companions, and I know their faces very well. No. I am entranced by her entirely. And I think, shall always be. Whatever else I am, unfortunately, I'm not quick to love, nor, believe me, despite my sordid marital history, am I swift to fall out of that love. I'm depressingly constant, whether the object of my affections deserves it or not. So you see, it's to my worse credit that I still want her, and for the best that she refused me, and far better still that you'll be free of us both."

He gave Annabelle a self-mocking smile and was relieved to see her move at last and smile back at him. She shook her head as though in amused acceptance of an

incredible fact. But when she spoke at last, his own smile
faded.

"No," she said softly, still shaking her head in denial,
"no," she said again, as though to herself, "it won't do.
No. I'm sorry, Joscelin," she said, gazing up at him steadily, "but it's far too late. You will marry me, you know. It
would have been better had you offered, but it makes no
difference, not really."

She raised a hand to stop him from speaking, and as he
watched, at first in incomprehension and then in appalled
disbelief, she, still smiling, put her hand upon the top of her
bodice and then, with one quick motion, tore it downward.
The sound of the thin material being rent was as a small
shriek in the quiet room. She quickly pulled the pins from
her hair and sent the bright ribband tumbling with the
shower of her light hair, which she shook around her face.
And then, as one pale, pointed little breast rose clear from
the ruins of her frock and he saw the thin red marks of her
fingernails begin to appear on its milky white surface, she
smiled, and said a little breathlessly,

"You see, Joscelin? Not even a great marquess can win
free of this coil. No, the viscount won't be able to ignore
this attack even though I'm only his poor, distant, neglected relative. He's just across the hall with Leonora, you
see. And you just have time enough to think of how you'll
tell them I misunderstood when you became carried away
with your lovemaking while making your offer. Or else,
you'll have to make that offer entirely in front of them—oh
yes," she urged him, as she saw his eyes, "attempt to still
me, do. That will look even better. No? Then," she went
on in a sort of glad fury, "I shall scream now, I think."

The marquess paled as Annabelle, giving him one last
bright look, drew in her breath.

"Oh save your breath, my dear, and our ears, as well,"
the viscount said lazily, rising from one of the tall wing
chairs in the window niche. "And Leonora, you can take
your hands from your ears now, it's all over."

"My poor lady there," he continued, as he walked to the
astonished couple by the long table, "she was in agonies of
embarrassment when you walked in and began to speak,
Joss. She was all for either announcing our presence or
crawling out of the room on all fours, but I silenced her. I

simply had to stay to listen. Occupational hazard, I fear,"
he mused. "Cover yourself, child," he said in a kindly
aside to a dazed Annabelle as he shook the marquess's
hand. "You'll take a chill with half your person falling out
of your dress."

"You were supposed to wait in the drawing room,"
Annabelle breathed as she pulled the edges of her gown
together. "You said you'd be there. You deceived me,"
she wailed.

"Yes and no, my dear," the viscount replied calmly. "I
angled for a little fish and caught a whale. We left you a
note telling you our direction, child, propped up on the
mantelpiece in the drawing room. But we didn't label it
with your actual name," he said gently, "we addressed it to
'Our Dear Little Cousin.' Yes," he went on, seeing the
dawning comprehension in her eyes, "it was a test. For if
you saw 'Annabelle' or even 'Greyling' upon it, you'd
know enough to have the butler or the housekeeper read it
to you, as I've discovered you'd always done with all other
such notes."

The marquess closed his eyes, as though he'd received a
blow. "Ah!" he said before he opened them to reveal the
dark dismay reflected there. "Well, sir, have you any further revelations as to my idiocy?"

"No, I think I'll allow Leonora that pleasure," the older
gentleman said simply, "although she was the one who
passed hours reading Shakespeare and Blake to her cousin,
without ever an inkling of anything amiss, not even when
her cousin always had some different and creative excuse
for not reciprocating. So I daresay she'll not gloat too much
at your obliviousness. Her credulity persisted to the point
that she believed me mistaken when Annabelle stepped in
here, and was about to apologize for the trick, when you
came in.

"But then, I might never have twigged to Annabelle's
deficiency myself," he said expansively, "if I hadn't mis-
read the title of that volume you gave her, and then was
amazed to find her agreeing with my mistake. It seemed
more than a polite gesture when she completely changed
the name of a book to spare my feelings."

"Actually," he went on, "I've quite a dossier on my
desk, ten closely written pages that I was prepared to show

you if you'd been caught in her net. Our little Annabelle has been a very busy, very naughty little girl."

Annabelle smiled as he shook his finger at her, for she was sensible enough to accept defeat, and just inhuman enough to be immediately prepared to see what she could salvage from the wreckage of her plans.

"In fact," the viscount admitted, "I find myself rather grateful that she never considered politics amusing, for she's got quite a flair for it, I think. There's blackmail and extortion among other things in her interesting past. Come, my dear," he said, turning his attention to Annabelle, "we'll have the housekeeper fetch you a shawl, and then we've a great many things to discuss, you and I."

"All right," Annabelle said simply. "I'm sorry," she said, looking back at the marquess with every evidence of deep regret, "that it didn't work."

After a moment in which everyone in the room paused, except for Annabelle, who was occupied with rubbing at the scratch marks on her breast, the marquess said quickly, "Well, then, I expect I'll be going as well if you have no further need of me, sir."

"I should think not," the viscount said over his shoulder as he steered Annabelle into the hallway. "I should think you've some explaining to do yourself. For I believe I just heard you make an offer for my daughter, even though admittedly, you did make it to another female. It's most irregular, and I'm not enough of a social arbiter to decide how it should be handled. But I'll leave you to work it out with her."

When the viscount left and closed the door behind him, Leonora at last stepped from the window enclosure and said immediately, and in very grieved accents as she twisted her hands together in her skirts, "Pray don't listen to my papa, he has an odd sense of humor. You needn't stay. I understand completely, I assure you. You said what you did to Belle to be free of her attentions. I quite understand."

She wore a simple blue afternoon frock, and her hair had not been dressed, rather it had arranged itself like a dark corolla about her expressive face. She looked, he thought, not only every bit as lovely as he'd remembered her in all his thoughts this past week, but also extraordinarily fresh and vivid, perhaps even more so in contrast to the cold, wan child who had just attempted to ruin his life.

"It's nothing to do with your father," he said. "I was leaving because I didn't think you'd want to look at me, much less speak with me, after our last encounter. But I think it only fair for you to know," he put in quickly before she could speak, "that I'd planned to begin to insinuate myself into your life in these next weeks.

"If you were going to stay in Town, I'd have found so many excuses to visit your father every day that the poor gentleman would have thought I'd run mad. Either that, or he'd have to believe that there was such a sudden influx of suspicious foreign nationals I wanted his advice about that they were thronging the streets and piling up outside my door. And I'd have run you to earth so often in Hatchard's and at the library that you would have had to become as illiterate as Annabelle to escape me."

But she winced when he said "Annabelle," so he went on rapidly, "If you went home to the country, I'd have employed more drastic measures. It's as well your father spoke up, since I'd have disliked laming a horse just to get entry to your house. Leonora," he said, "Nell. I came back to Town to say good-bye to your cousin and all her hopes. I had hopes of my own, you see. But I remember, indeed, I can scarcely forget, that I am a divorced gentleman. If that is what distressed you when I last offered, and still does, I shall leave right now, and understand."

"I'd never refuse you for that!" Leonora blurted, "not when that was what attracted me to you in the first place. That is to say," she said, miserably aware that her reaction to him was causing her to misspeak herself again, "I admired you for it. I did," she insisted, seeing one dark eyebrow shoot up. "It occurred to me then that you were the least hypocritical man in society. For you refused to live a double life as so many gentlemen do, and chose the harder, yet more honorable path, in spite of all the hardships it caused for you."

"Ah Nell," he sighed, understanding a great deal not only from the conviction in her ringing words, but from her flushed face and shining eyes. Though the Marquess of Severne might have been duped by a pale little female, he had often served his country admirably as an excellent spy.

He'd survived by his wits before when his life had been at stake, and now there was something at risk which he valued above that. So he paused to frame an answer for Leonora with as much care as if he faced an assassin with a primed pistol, for he knew her to be armed with a few words that could annihilate his future.

He remembered that the Viscount Talwin was famous among his gentlemen friends as a fellow with a roving eye. And though the viscount was sometimes affectionately mocked by those same gentlemen for his notoriously absurd taste in female companionship, he was no less admired for all that. But that was the gentlemen, and that was their way. Watching the viscount's daughter make her impassioned speech on hypocrisy and a double life, Joscelin thought it no great feat to venture a guess as to the reason for it.

He answered her at last in soft, sad tones. "Nell, believe me, there was nothing particularly brave or noble in what I did. Were it only a matter of not getting on with my wife, I would doubtless have stayed in the union anyway and suffered it, as so many others do. I'd like your admiration, but I'd like to earn it. In this, there was no merit. I'm only a man who couldn't live an impossible lie."

"Father told me of your circumstances," she said, "and it's only a matter of degree, isn't it? After all." she said, smiling, "what would be a possible lie?"

"Any one that I did not have to tell you," he answered.

The room grew still, and he looked at her so intently, and her dreams seemed so suddenly possible after all her recent fears, that perversely, she doubted the truth of her perceptions.

"Nell," he asked softly then, "this is very important. If you wish me to leave, I shall. And I'll not be back, I promise, for I'd never plague you. But I've been remembering you all this past week. I cannot believe I only imagined what I saw in your eyes, and felt upon your lips. Nell, for the last time, shall I stay?"

"Please," she asked anxiously, "don't feel that you must say these things because you admire my papa, or because you still think you compromised me. You really scarcely know me, you know," she added nervously.

"Oh do I not?" he demanded, relaxing, and dropping

his air of tense watchfulness. He crossed his arms and asked challengingly, "Mercutio is your favorite character in *Romeo and Juliet*, is he not?"

"Why, yes," Leonora admitted, "but please believe that my papa will understand if you leave now as—"

"And," he asked, stepping closer to her, "William Blake is one of your favorite poets? And baroque music is one of your chiefest delights even as *Richard Third* is your favorite play?"

"Why, yes," Leonora breathed, amazed. But the look in the marquess's eye was so startling that she stepped back the pace he'd come forward. It hardly mattered. For he scooped her up into his arms and, looking down into her dark troubled eyes, gently smoothed the hair back from her brow.

"I'm so glad," he sighed when she did not attempt to break free. "I couldn't believe that I was such a fool as to fall completely in love with a woman who only excited my every sense and who merely made me yearn to make love to her each time that I saw her. Although," he breathed, as he brought his lips closer to hers, "that is not so terrible a thing, I think."

When he at last had regained enough poise and control to look into her eyes again, they were unfocused and smoky with desire. "You turned me down once," he whispered as he held her tightly, as if to dare her to attempt to leave him now, "but then I deserved it, because I lied to myself and to you. And my only excuse is that Belle's lies made me feel an idiot for continuing to want you. Then too, I think I tried to pretend I was forced into what I really desired, to quiet my own fears and trick myself into happiness."

He paused, and then said, all at once, with no trace of laughter, "I want you, Nell, don't make me plead for you."

He was so serious, his face so suddenly still, and he wore such a look of anxious entreaty that Leonora was appalled that she might cause him pain.

"What do you want me for?" she replied softly.

"Don't be coy," he said on a note of despair, "although doubtless I deserve it. I want you for your wit, and your beauty, and your—"

"No, no," she said at once, horrified, putting her finger

across his lips to silence the flattery. "I meant, be plain with me, please. Do you want me for your mistress? For your lover? Perhaps only for—"

"Nell!," he growled, shaking her none too gently, "I want you for my wife."

"Oh good," she sighed as he felt her relax in his arms, "I had to be sure, you see. I was so afraid I'd have to tear this dress. And it's a particular favorite of mine."

"Wretch," he laughed as he saw where she lay her hand, on the top of the low bodice of her frock. "But don't bother," he whispered as his hand covered hers and her eyes widened, "for I shall be delighted to do it for you."

SIXTEEN

The young woman sat alone in the luxuriously appointed carriage. She kept one hand on the strap by the window to prevent her swaying as they rode over the narrow, bumpy country road. She watched the sheep and hedgerows that they passed with a slight smile upon her lips, but when the carriage halted and the door swung open and the gentleman came in, her smile grew wider still.

After planting a tiny kiss upon the tip of her nose as a greeting, he sat beside her, and as the coach started up again, he took her hand in his and said,

"I've your father's full permission to accompany you, alone, for the remainder of the journey. But as that's only an hour or so more, it's hardly a boon. Still," he said consideringly, "remembering what you were capable of achieving in a deserted library in far less time, I'm hoping you'll look upon these moments in a swaying carriage as a challenge."

She said nothing, but smiled at him so warmly that this time he took far more than her hand in his. Yet, when he raised his lips from hers, he muttered a most unloverlike, "Damnation."

He sighed and then asked, "Are you as sorry as I am that we aren't wed, Nell? I haven't heard you railing against fate, and now and again I get the uneasy notion that you don't mind, that perhaps you've changed your mind."

When her lips were free again, Leonora drew back from the kiss she'd instantly given him. She looked into the softened, bemused face of the marquess and said simply, "No, I don't mind in the least. For, as I calculate, we shall be wed in precisely five days, six nights, and four and a quarter more hours."

"Thank you," he murmured, brushing his lips against the back of her hand. "A chap needs a bit of reassurance sometimes, you know. Confound your sister Sybil," he breathed without heat, as he studied the great sapphire on the finger of the hand he held, turning it to the light.

"No, there was truth in what she said, Joss. If we wed precipitously from St. George's in the heart of Town, then everyone would suspect our haste. Better that we marry from home, among our friends, and when word gets back to Town, it will only be that it was a summer wedding," she said, losing her calm assured tone at the last as she watched those well-shaped lips linger at her fingertips.

"Ah well," he sighed, "if she believes that a marriage contracted by the infamous Marquess of Severne, attended by all his fell companions, with the Duke of Torquay as his best man, will go unremarked, I shall not argue with her. Though I can't shake the unnerving idea that the news may eclipse that of Bonaparte's recent rout in certain circles. He's only a Frenchman, after all, and can't be expected to know better, while we're home-grown villains. Still, I suppose she's the right of it," he added with a bitter wrench to his lips. "Since you're marrying a fellow with such a shocking reputation, we must, of course, avoid all extraneous talk."

"Don't forget, you're marrying a lady with a shocking reputation too," she interrupted, for she could scarcely bear it when his face assumed that cold, troubled look. "What was it Papa said when you asked if he objected to his daughter's marrying a divorced gentleman? Ah yes. 'And you met her in a brothel once, I've been told,' " she mimicked in uncanny replication of her father's laconic tones. " 'Clearly, my lad, you two deserve each other.' "

He laughed, just as she'd wished, but then said with the merest trace of uneasiness, "I worried about that, too, you know. No really, Nell, until I discovered that your anxiety to be quit of London those years ago was because of your opinion of modern marriage, I'd sometimes wondered if those few moments at Mother Carey's mightn't have alarmed or influenced you unduly."

"Well!" she huffed with every evidence of annoyance,

as she sat bolt upright. "We haven't attempted anything that athletic, not to mention comprehensive, but I'd like to know if I've given you any cause for complaint as yet. Are you changing your mind, Joss? Getting cold feet? No," she said, suddenly serious, staving him off with two hands against his chest. "Truly, Joss, have you any worries about it, is there a deficiency in me? No, tell me first, before you show me."

"I'll tell you," he said with more than a hint of threat in his eyes, "that the only deficiency is in your reason if you can't see that I should have to be dead for a week before my feet grew that cold. And my only worry is that you'll come to your senses before I manage to securely wed you. And that you'll damage your arms if you don't employ them more intelligently. Yes, like that."

After a long while, Leonora raised her head a fraction from his shoulder. The sky was just beginning to take on the paler, thinner look of twilight.

"Joss?" she said softly.

"Yes?" he replied, smiling, called back from some happy thought of the future.

"I really thought you were going to marry her," she murmured, and he didn't ask who, for they neither of them could yet easily speak her name, but she could feel his muscles tighten beneath her cheek.

"If I had to go to the Indies for the rest of my life, I would not have," he said grimly.

"Oh, I know that now," she said, "but, you see, I thought she was so beautiful, so delicate, so lovely. I don't know if you can understand it, but she looked so ethereal, and I felt, have always felt, so earthbound. She was light, and fair and slim, and I, so dark and . . . Ah, how can I explain it? Poets sing about her sort of looks, Joss."

"Do they?" he asked casually, although he knew this was important to her, and was thinking on it deeply. "Well," he said carefully, "I wouldn't know about that. Consider Shakespeare."

"Oh Joss," she laughed, "if you quote that sonnet about his dark mistress, the one about her hair being nothing like the sun, but being like dark wires or some such, I'll shout for my papa to come and drag you away. It's a nice bit of verse, but although it's the opposite of what he intended, I've always considered it lowering to a dark lady's spirits."

"I wasn't thinking of it at all," he smiled, for he'd been doing his homework, "rather I was remembering what he had a certain favorite of yours named Mercutio say. Don't you recall?" He laughed. "Why, when he talks about what ails his friend Romeo, he says of his infatuation with Juliet, '. . . He's already dead: stabbed with a white wench's black eye.' I know precisely how he felt," he added, delighted with the soft, wondering look that came over her face.

"Well!" he eventually paused to breathe, after she had done showing him how much she appreciated his taste in literature and lovers. "I shall have to tell Sybil at once. The gossip was all true. What a depraved, passionate creature you are," and then he added fervently, while he was still able, "thank heavens."

The carriage was jolting so very badly that the fair-haired young woman had to hold on to the strap in order to keep herself upright. A summer shower had rattled overhead for the past hour, and now the narrow North Country roads were so pocked by other passing traffic that the wheels constantly caught in holes and splashed through ruts.

Annabelle held on tightly, for she knew that she would soon arrive at her destination, and wished to present as clean and neat an appearance as possible. This time, she would be a lady. She had the fine clothes Leonora had given her and a little money put by, enough to hire this private carriage and some left over, for she was very careful with it. The maid and the landlord at the inn last night might have scowled at their meager gratuities, but Annabelle was tight-fisted and never gave money when she didn't absolutely have to. It was a wonder that the viscount had given her any at all, but Leonora had asked him to, and they had all been so relieved to see her go that it was done and she was gone before anyone had second thoughts.

There was, after all, no one who would dare bring charges against her from her past, and she knew, in the unconsciously clever way that she knew so much, that so long as she left quickly, she would be able to leave quickly. Silly asses, she thought, remembering those she had just left behind, and then, because she had left them behind, she forgot them, as she did all things that did not immediately concern her comforts.

She would go to the Baron McAllister, whose name and address was in the family bible, for she'd remembered it exactly from the moment the butler had read it to her last week before she'd left London. Perhaps because it was so uncluttered with symbols, her memory was faultless. There was no need to read, just as she'd always known, just as she'd told her parents when the village schoolmistress cast her out in anger, and after the tutor they engaged cast her out in tears. Not when one could remember so much and so easily. As it had been simplicity itself to repeat a page immediately after Leonora read it to her, it was nothing at all to remember the direction of the McAllisters.

She would announce that her maid had gotten ill, and she would tell them a tale about London relatives who had attempted to marry her off, for her expected legacy, to an evil, avaricious old marquess. Yes. Then she would tell them of her sadly orphaned state, and show them the family bible so that they could see that they were very distant relations of her mother's. Yes. Then she'd tell them of the dear old lady she'd companioned, who'd died and left her all the money that would come to her on her thirtieth birthday, or her wedding day, whichever came first. Yes, that would do, she was tired of being a poor relation. And as it hadn't been successful again, it might now be unlucky besides.

She looked down at her neat and elegant blue walking dress, and her fine little ice blue satin slippers, and then she paused with a frown. For she'd splashed through mud this morning when she'd entered the carriage and some had dried in a clot on her left slipper. A fine young lady would not countenance this, and since whenever Annabelle became something or someone, she became it completely, she rummaged in her portmanteau on the seat beside her, searching for something to wipe the mud off with.

She found a lace handkerchief and hesitated, for lace was dear, and she was frugal. She put it back and fished out an old shawl a moment later, but it was good wool, and had no holes and might last a while longer. Finally her fingers closed upon something familiar and she smiled. She'd used this before, a few times before, on this long journey to Scotland, and with any luck, there was enough left of it to use now, for it was worthless.

Annabelle pried off her slipper, and frowning with concentration, scrubbed away at the caked-on dirt with one of the last pliable leaves she'd torn from the soft-covered volume. It was of such a high cloth content that it was easy to work into a flexible rag. When she had done, she sighed with satisfaction and put her slipper back on. She lowered the coach window and just before she let the bit of crumpled paper blow away on the wet wind, she looked down at it. A familiar, sad, and great-eyed dark face gazed back at her.

Annabelle considered it and then, as spray from the window blew back in her face, she smiled. Silly cow, she thought, and let the paper go, to journey down the wind.

It blew away from the onrushing coach, and a rainy gust carried it down the road for a fair way. Then it settled in a gully left by the lead horse's right hoof, and lay trembling half in the brown water. The dark angel wept ink tears for a moment, and then slipped slowly down into the mud. At the last, only the title that Annabelle could never read and that had found her out, remained above the ooze. And then the proud signature of Mr. Blake, and then the words "Book of Moonlight," sank to become one with the road that the hired carriage hurried away from.

Author's Note

In 1809, William Blake had an unsuccessful exhibition of his pictures at 28 Broad Street, in London. Between 1808 and 1809, he is also believed to have written two works, "BARRY: A POEM," and "BOOK OF MOONLIGHT." Both are now lost.

About the Author

Edith Layton has been writing since she was ten years old. She has worked as a freelance writer for newspapers and magazines, but has always been fascinated by English history, most particularly by the Regency period. She lives on Long Island with her physician husband and those of her three children who are not involved with intimidating institutions of higher learning. She collects antiques and large dogs.

SIGNET Regency Romances You'll Enjoy